THE EMPEROR'S CLUB

THE EMPEROR'S CLUB

a novel

By

Anthony Gagliano

New York, New York

Praise for The Emperor's Club

"A welcome addition to Florida noir. *The Emperor's Club* is fast, fresh, and compulsively readable."
—Dennis Lehane, author of *Live by Night.*

"Do yourself a favor and spend a few fast hours with *The Emperor's Club.* Tony is a remarkable storyteller whose voice is at once as familiar as those of the great hardboiled and noir novelists of the past, yet his work has its own unique flavor. Quippy, full-throated and emotionally real. With razor-sharp clarity and originality Tony evokes the weird and wonderful world of South Florida and introduces us to a cast of characters as exotic, engaging and ultimately heart-rending as any you'll ever meet."
—James W. Hall, *Going Dark*

"The Emperor's Club is pure hard-boiled, hard-bitten fun. Gagliano revels in the glittering sleaze and menace of South Florida, as will his readers."
—Carl Hiaasen, *Bad Monkey*

"Make yourself comfortable, friend, you're in for the evening. *The Emperor's Club* is a book you won't be able to put down till you're finished. It'll leave you breathless. Best to read it with the lights on and the doors locked. Yes, the bad guys are that terrifying. Tony Gagliano writes like Charles Willeford on speed. What a book! What an exhilarating voice!"
—John Dufresne, *No Regrets, Coyote*

"Hop on the Gagliano bus for a midnight tour of South Florida's underbelly. It's a scary, dangerous place where the men leering at a stripper on stage are 'a pack of cannibals watching dinner turning slowly on a spit.' *The Emperor's Club* will earn a lofty position on the shelf of modern Florida noir."
—Paul Levine, *State vs. Lassiter*

"Anthony Gagliano's *The Emperor's Club* is written in an electric rat-a-tat style that grabs the reader from the first page. It belongs in that Florida *noir* genre popularized by Charles Willeford and Elmore Leonard — but the novel has it's own virtues that set it apart. Great characters, a page-turning plot and a wry way of looking at the often bizarre and always entertaining world inhabited by the odd and unusual that is Florida at it's strongest and best. Gagliano was a unique and engaging prose stylist, and a voice that will be sorely missed in the realm of mystery-thrillers. *The Emperor's Club* is a great read, leavened only by the sense of loss that accompanies it's final pages."
—John Katzenbach, *Hart's War*

In accordance with the wishes of Anthony Gagliano's widow, Lana Callen, the author's share of proceeds from the sale of this book will be donated to the FIU Creative Writing Program.

Dedication

This book is dedicated to the memory of Tony Gagliano, great student, great friend, great guy. His spirit lives on.

Acknowledgments

We would like to thank Lana Callen for her generosity and help in making this book possible. Kudos as well are due John Dufresne and MidTown Publishing Inc. for their confidence in Tony's work.

Les Standiford and Dan Wakefield

FOREWORD

There are times when a student whom you've never heard from before reads something in your class that takes your breath away. That happened when Tony Gagliano read a piece about a fight he'd had with a drunk when he was working as a house detective at a New York Hotel. I knew I had heard an authentic voice, "the real thing."

Tony was "the real thing" across the board—as a writer, a teacher, and one of the best friends I ever had. I was his mentor and he was mine. He worked and worked and did all the tedious revising and honing of his words and his story to make his first novel, *The Straits of Fortune*, an unusual critical success for a first-time author. He did the same with his second novel, pushing himself beyond his physical bounds, as it turned out, but leaving with us *The Emperor's Club,* another rich, riveting, tale that has the smell and feel and look of South Florida in all its glitz and corruption and excitement, with a narrator whose wit cracks through the narrative. I am proud to have known Tony Gagliano, and proud to recommend his work.

—Dan Wakefield, author of *New York in the Fifties* and *Going All The Way*

I will echo much of what Dan has to say about Tony Gagliano, who represents just about everything you might ask for in a writing student and, ultimately, a colleague. When Tony came into the MFA program at FIU, he might have been unsure of himself as a writer, but he was certainly sure of who he was in this world, obviously in command of a vast store of material and dead set on learning the craft that would allow him to share his generous, witty, incisive view of our folly-filled, love-hungry existence. He reveled in every class he took, accepted criticism with grace and humility and dished out his own advice with plenty of reserve and compassion. In time, he came to write the way a teacher hopes and prays that every promising student will—truly, simply, powerfully, with wit and precision.

Straits of Fortune is a wonderfully drawn debut novel, one which promised many more fine books to come. Tony was hard at work on the follow-up, *The Emperor's Club*, when he died. Dan Wakefield and I wept and lamented our loss and the damnable misfortune that robbed Tony and the world of seeing a second splendid book come into being . . . and then one day the idea struck us. What if we were to try and do what Robert Parker did when he completed the unfinished novel—*Poodle Springs*—that Raymond Chandler was working on at the time of his death. Just as in Parker's case, we could not pretend that anything we could do could ever be the equal of what the original author might have brought to bear on the material, but at least there would be an opportunity for Tony's fans and friends to get a glimpse of what he had intended.

So that is what we have tried to do. Following Tony's lead in revising the first two thirds or so of his own book, Dan and I went to work shaping the remainder, trying to be true to the original creator's intention, doing our damnedest to capture the unique, irresistible voice that was his. It has been our pleasure and our honor to work together in Tony's shadow and it is our hope that we have managed to craft a version of a book that gives a hint of what its original creator might have intended.

Professor Wakefield and I are hoping for a passing grade, Tony. Meantime, you have done us proud.

—Les Standiford, Florida International University, May 2014

THE EMPEROR'S CLUB

By

Anthony Gagliano

1

When the phone rings at three o'clock in the morning, it is seldom good news. Chances are good that it will not be Ed McMahon calling to tell you that you have just won the Publisher's Clearing House Sweepstakes, and that you will no longer have to work as a personal trainer. There is also a very high probability that the person on the other end of the line will not be a fashion model fresh from the pages of *Ocean Drive Magazine,* calling to tell you that she is on her way over to your place on a motorcycle, wearing nothing under her poncho but perfume and a little sweat.

And because you know both by instinct and by experience that it isn't Ed or the fashion model on the other end of the line, you hesitate. You swing your legs over the side of the bed and sit there staring at the phone like it was a barking dog, hoping that it will soon stop, hoping that the person on the other end of the line will suddenly realize that it's useless, or that he's got the wrong number, or that whatever it is he's calling about can wait until morning.

Your first thought is to hide inside the darkness and the silence like a child hiding under a blanket. You tell yourself that it's too late for bad news and that you have to get up in three hours in order to train a certain dentist who has begun to drop hints that he is once again thinking of suicide. You have to be strong to listen to crap like that, especially at seven in the morning when you're not feeling all that swift yourself.

It's going to be a long day and you need your rest. You need to be fresh for your clients. You can't afford to show up at the gym looking worse than they do. You have to look healthy, bright-eyed and optimistic, thrilled to be alive. You are a professional and Fitness is your life—at least during the day. But the person on the other end of the line doesn't seem to understand this. He doesn't seem to want to understand that you are trying to run a business here. True, it's a small business with only a single employee, no 401K, no health insurance, no vacation, and no dental plan, but this is not the point. The point is you are trying to run a business.

You stare at the clock and you stare at the phone, which hasn't stopped ringing. Whoever it is must be psychic. He knows you're there all right, Vaughn. He knows you're sitting there in the dark like a rat, trying to avoid whatever it is he has to say, or at least trying to delay it for a few more hours. But by now you know the ringing won't stop. He's a persistent bastard. You have to give him that much, and you also know that this isn't the first time he's called somebody at this hour. He's experienced. That's why he doesn't give up.

I stared at the phone for another ten seconds then picked up the receiver. A woman's voice asked if I was Jack Vaughn and identified herself as Sergeant Amelia Davenport from the Florida Highway Patrol. She asked me if I knew a Cal Belkin. When I told her he was a friend of mine and that he owned the gym where I used to train some of my clients, she got quiet for a moment, and my heart beat faster in anticipation of bad news.

"Well," Mr. Vaughn," the sergeant said. "We just pulled Mr. Belkin's car out of a canal up near Tamarac."

For some reason my heart slowed when she said that. There's something about the sound of the other shoe dropping that calms the nerves. The cargo plane full of bad news has now landed safely on your chest, and the only thing left to do is to unload it at a slow, reasonable pace, one question at a time.

"Is he dead?" I asked.

"We don't know. There's no body in the car, sir."

"Do you think he got out?" I asked.

"We won't know until the divers get here," she said. "The DMV has you down as someone to call in case of emergency that's why I called. I'm sorry, but we thought you would want to know."

Ten minutes later, I was on the road heading north on the interstate with a cup of cold stale coffee in one hand and the Chariot's steering wheel in the other. The Chariot was actually a '68 Camaro I had bought from a client of mine when he found it necessary to leave the country. Apparently, the police had found an unusually large amount of marijuana in his home and wanted to ask him about it. My client, always a private person, decided to move to a place where people are less curious about these things. The Camaro, or the Chariot as he called it, was one of dozen or so cars my client managed to get rid of before the government seized the rest. He let me have it for a thousand bucks. It had a rebuilt engine a new transmission and four hidden compartments that so far I've yet to find good use for. I still call it the Chariot however. It's my way of honoring my former friend and client, a genius in the lucrative field of indoor agriculture.

The traffic on the way up to Tamarac was mercifully light. At that hour of the morning the only drivers on the road are the drunks and the cops who are out looking for them. Once I hit the turnpike, I made good time, doing an easy eighty miles an hour while keeping an eye out for the highway patrol. But it didn't matter. At least a dozen cars passed me by like I was an old lady doing forty in the fast lane.

I saw the bright blue and red incandescent glow of the

police flares and pulled up about ten yards behind the last of five patrol cars parked along the shoulder of the road. I put on the emergency lights as a last line of defense against any sleep deprived drivers careless enough to miss the flares and plow into me from behind. A black tow truck was just pulling out as I was pulling in. There were a half dozen officers poking around in the tall grass with their flashlights when I walked up and introduced myself to the only female officer of the bunch. The stripes and the name tag told me her name was Sergeant Davenport.

"You got up here pretty quick," she said. "I hope you didn't do any speeding, Mr. Vaughn,"

"None to speak of."

The sergeant then led me over to where the tow truck had hauled Cal's '68 beet red Cadillac up onto the bank and set it down on the side of the road. Water was still draining from the car's interior and there was already an inch of water on the ground. All the doors, windows and trunk were wide open. A patrolman had crawled halfway inside the passenger side door and was poking around under the front seats with his flashlight. He straightened up just as his superior and I reached the Cadillac. Just for the hell of it, I peeked into the trunk but there was nothing in there but the spare, the jack, and an orange toolbox.

"Nothing special inside," The officer said. "Just the usual inside the glove compartment."

"How about the backseat?" Davenport asked. "Anything there?"

"Nada."

"This Mr. Belkin," Sergeant Davenport said to me. "You say you work for him."

"Not lately," I said. "He owns a gym in Miami Shores. I used to be a personal trainer there."

"Well, so far what we got is this: Some guy gets a flat, fixes it, then goes to wash his hands off in the canal when he sees something shiny in the water. Wasn't for the full moon and him being in the right place he might not have seen anything. He calls us and we call you and so here we are."

Sergeant Davenport unclipped her flashlight from her utility belt and sprayed the sand colored saw grass with a wide beam of white light.

"Judging by where we found the car," she said. "It must have gone into the canal somewhere around here. But take a look at the grass. It's not bent down or broken or slashed apart like it would be if the car went into the water tonight or even last night. Saw grass is bouncy all right and it grows back pretty fast, but not that fast. You see what I'm saying, Mr. Vaughn?"

"You're saying you don't really know for certain when the car went into the water."

"That's right," Davenport said. "And look here at the road. There's no skid marks like he tried to fight it or anything. You know, fell asleep driving and woke up but not soon enough to stop. Judging by the smell coming out of the caddy, I would be pretty sure in saying that it's probably been in the drink for a couple of days at the very least."

I looked around. There wasn't much to see. Even during the day there was hardly any traffic on this section of the turnpike, especially the north bound side. The reason for that was pretty simple. Besides the far-flung town of Tamarac, there wasn't much of anything out here except saw grass and a few scattered herds of sun-dazed cows and an occasional solitary horse in the open fields on the other side of the canal. On this part of the turnpike, they hadn't even gotten around to putting up lights yet. On a dark night you were on your own. Even so, if Cal had managed to get himself out of his car and had somehow made it to the road, he would have eventually managed to flag somebody down. Then again, his body might be lying out there in the tall grass somewhere, slowly rotting in the heat, or the gators had dragged it into the water.

"When do the divers get here?" I asked.

"First light, or thereabouts."

I used my phone to call first Cal's house then his mobile

number. To my surprise, the home number had been disconnected. My call to his cell went directly into voice mail, which meant his inbox was filled. The former struck me as odd because Cal had had the same number for the past thirty years or so. As for his cell phone, few people had the number, and he seldom used except in emergencies. I found it hard to believe he could have received that many calls in any reasonable amount of time.

"Has the car been reported stolen?" I asked.

"Not so far," the deputy said. "This being Florida and all, people do sometimes ditch their cars in order to collect the insurance money, but considering the car is so old I wouldn't bet on that being the case here."

"No," I said. "It wouldn't be anything like that. Cal's got plenty of money, not that you'd ever know it. He's got the first dollar he ever earned."

"Let's say he was driving up this way. Any idea where he might have been going?" Davenport asked. "Not much along here until you get up near Orlando."

"No, but then I haven't spoken to him in a while," I said.

"When was the last time you heard from him?" Sergeant Davenport asked.

"Right before I went down to the Keys. About a month ago."

"He know anybody this far west?"

"Closest relative he's got is a granddaughter up in New York."

"Does Mr. Belkin have any memory problems?" she asked. "You know anything like that?"

"No," I said. "He's old, but he's sharp."

"Well, then, you got me."

"Can you do me a favor, Sergeant?" I handed her a business card. "Can you give me a call when the divers get here? I'd really appreciate it."

I got back into the Chariot, but instead of pulling out, I just sat there with my hands on the steering wheel, staring at Cal's water soaked Cadillac for a long time while the weight of the bad news settled down into my bowels like a huge stone. I was the closet thing Cal had to family in Miami, but I wasn't quite sure where to start. About his granddaughter, all I knew was where she lived. Beyond that, I knew little. I couldn't even remember her name.

I headed on north, got off the turnpike and drove east for a bit until I hit a line of cheap motels along the main drag leading into Pompano. I spotted the neon sign of a place next to a trailer park called the Dixie Peach Motel that promised free cable and air conditioning, all for the suspiciously low price of thirty-nine dollars a night. The roaches, of course, would be free, but the sign didn't mention wildlife.

The front desk clerk was a middle-aged Chinese with sagging skin, suspicious eyes and no trace of welcome in his expression. When he looked up from his desk and saw me standing by the locked front door, his brain went to work figuring out if he should take the chance of letting me in or not. While he was checking me out, his body leaned slightly toward his right as though he was reaching for something. He buzzed me in. As I walked through the dimly lit vestibule, the smell of bug spray hit me in the face like a burst of mace. I waded through it. Then the clerk raised the barrel of the pistol just enough so that it could peak at me over the counter. He wanted to make it clear that he wasn't alone back there. I didn't take it personally, and I stopped a few feet short of the counter, so he could see that I understood the situation correctly.

"Which hospitality school taught you that?" I asked.

"You want joke or you want room?"

"I want room."

"For how long?" The gun disappeared behind the desk like a snake sliding back into its burrow after getting a little sun.

"A couple of hours," I said. "I missed my plane."

"Why you not look for room closer to airport?"

"I wanted some place nice."

He didn't get the joke and his eyes narrowed. "You alone?" he asked.

I smiled. A door slammed. The clerk's question spoke very highly of his usual clientele, as did the woman who at that moment appeared in the darkened hallway to my left. I told the clerk I was alone. He glanced at the woman as she walked into the light of the vestibule where I stood.

"You want company?" the clerk asked.

I looked at the woman. She was standing at the entrance to the hallway like a cab waiting for a passenger. When I looked at her she smiled. I didn't smile back. Maybe it was the gold teeth; maybe it was the jaunty angle at which her black nylon wig sat perched on her head like a derby; maybe it was the silver hot pants and halter; maybe it was a face that looked like ten miles of bad road; maybe it was a combination of all these things. I turned back to the clerk. He looked at me with the hopeful expression of a man working on commission.

"Not tonight," I said.

The Chinaman looked disappointed. The woman reached up with her hand and straightened the wig on her head and wandered over to the front desk and leaned on it for support. For one brief moment as she passed in front of me, the smell of whiskey overtook the odor of bug spray. She looked up at me and showed me her grill of gold teeth. According to the jewelry in her mouth, the ass business was booming.

"You too cute to be alone," she said.

"I know; that's what everybody says."

I paid the clerk in cash and headed down the dimly lit hallway to my room. The whore followed behind me babbling away until I closed the door in her face. She spent a few minutes out in the hallway screaming at me, but eventually it sank in that our love was not to be and she went away. I didn't bother undressing. It wasn't the kind of hotel room where being naked seemed like a good idea. I didn't even draw back the bedspread. The bedbugs might have called the manager. Instead, I lay down fully clothed, closed my eyes and tried to sleep with the image of Cal's car for company.

By the time I made it back to the crash site the next morning, the sun had already risen, and the divers from the Broward County Police Department were already slowly wading into the murky waters of the canal while the officers from the Florida Highway Patrol stood about, keeping an eye out for the alligators. I leaned against my car and waited with them, sipping coffee and pacing back and forth or sometimes sitting in my car and listening to the radio.

I kept thinking of Cal and how it had been him who had first given me a job at his gym at a time when I was down on my luck, drinking too much and getting soft. Cal had fed me clients and had kept me going during that first very difficult, disoriented year in Miami when I had no friends and fewer prospects, when I was nothing but an ex-cop with a lot of bad memories I wanted badly to erase. Now I was out here at seven o'clock in the morning, standing in the middle of nowhere not knowing whether to think of him in the past or present tense.

I was relieved that they hadn't found Cal's body in the canal or anywhere else for that matter, but that didn't tell me where he was or what had happened to him, or how his beloved, faithfully restored Cadillac with its rebuilt V-8 engine had ended up at the bottom of a canal. One by one, the divers hauled themselves out of the muck and quickly slipped off their oxygen tanks and their protective gear. Sergeant Davenport was long gone, so I spoke to her replacement on the day shift, a young officer by the name of Pike.

"The Caddy hasn't been reported stolen," he said. "But that doesn't mean it wasn't. Could be your boss, this Cal fellow, is still fast asleep and doesn't even know his car is missing. Could be a couple of kids stole it and ditched it when they got tired of riding around.

The idea that a couple of teenagers had taken the Cal's car as a prank then dumped it off into the water once they had their thrills had occurred to me, but the thought felt more like wishful thinking on my part than a theory I really believed in. It just didn't have the feel of truth to it. It was something you wanted badly to believe but couldn't. Still, I didn't want to shoot down Pike's reasonable explanation out of hand.

"I guess you've tried to contact him," I said. "I tried a few times myself. No one answered.

"Sure we called him," Pike said. "No soap on that one though."

I tried dialing Cal's cell phone number again. I tried the number twice and both times my call went into voice mail.

"That Caddy didn't drive itself into the canal," I said. "If Cal didn't do it, then somebody else rolled it in there for some other reason."

"He owe anybody any money?"

"Are you kidding? Cal's a rich man. People owe *him* money."

Pike was silent for a moment. He took of his aviator shades and wiped at his pale blue eyes with his handkerchief then put them on again. He put his hands on his hips and stared at the asphalt road for a moment before looking back up at me.

"Well," he said. "That might be something worth looking into."

I thanked Sgt. Pike and took the turnpike south back to Miami. I needed to get down to Cal's Gym as quickly as possible. There was always a chance that he would be there, sitting in his office, chewing on a cigar and keeping an eye on things floor through the one-way glass partition. I had been away for a while and he would be glad to see me. Maybe we'd go across the street, drink come Cuban coffee together and watch the pretty ladies on their way to work.

We'd sit at the counter and Marta would flirt with Cal and bring us our daily dose of jet fuel. Cal would complain about how dumb his employees were and once again offer me the job of night manager, which I would, as usual, turn down. Everything would be back to normal again. It was a pretty good movie. By the time I was halfway to Miami, I had all the scenes blocked out. It was going to be a comedy and it would have an unexpectedly happy ending. Too bad I didn't believe any of it.

2

Cal Belkin got his start in the bodybuilding business after his discharge from the army back in nineteen fifty-five after serving in Korea. He' been wounded, sent back to the front, and nearly lost a leg due to frostbite. He spent three months in the hospital before making it back to his home in Spring Lake, New Jersey. More often than not when Cal spoke about those times, he didn't speak of the war itself, but rather of those first few months when it had ended and of his return to civilian life.

When Cal finally made it home, he found everything very much as he had left it— that is except for the young wife he had married just before heading off for basic training. She had taken a job behind the counter at a of burger joint called White Castle in Trenton and had gotten a taste of an independent life she had no plans of giving up for a young army corporal with a bad limp and a chip on his shoulder. They divorced six weeks after his homecoming. Cal used to tell me that it had been like coming home to a stranger. She didn't even look the same, he had told me. She wasn't the girl he had remembered. It was as though he had made her up in his head like a kid with an imaginary friend.

So when Cal got a letter from a friend of his out in California telling him all about how great Venice Beach was and how many pretty girls there were walking around and how the guys lifted weights on the beach and how after a workout they would go for a swim in the Pacific Ocean, Cal didn't hesitate. Why should he have? His parents were both dead; his wife had turned out to be a mirage, and Spring Lake was way too serene for his jazzed up, post war tastes, so he bought a car for two hundred and fifty bucks and drove out to find the American version of the Promised Land.

Driving back to Miami from Tamarac that morning, I remembered some of the stories he had told me about his years on Venice Beach. He took a part time job tending bar and spent his days on the beach, lifting weights, girl watching and learning how to surf. Nobody worked at much of anything besides their tans. It was so different from the life he had once expected to lead that he sometimes felt like a castaway who had fallen overboard only to be washed up on the shores of a paradise populated by pretty women and the sun lit potential for pleasures he had never dreamed existed.

Cal saved every dime he made and opened his own gym in a small building he bought for a laughably small sum. He did most of the work himself, including the drywall, the carpentry, the plumbing and the electrical. He even built some of his own equipment. Many of his designs were so far ahead of their time that had he bothered to patent them, he would have been a lot richer a lot sooner than would eventually be the case. Cal built the gym and the people came, slowly at first, then by the dozens. He began to train people, many of them famous people, and that was how Cal became a personal trainer long before anyone ever thought to marry those two words together.

Cal made money and spent very little of it, bought real estate and resold it for a profit when the time was right, and in California that time always seemed to come sooner rather than later. He drove old cars that he repaired himself and cooked his own meals in the tiny apartment he had built for himself above the gym. He got married again, had a son, but that didn't work either, and one day he found a note from his wife that she was moving to Long Island with a fisherman who had his own boat and a much better personality than Cal's.

The western paradise didn't last. Venice Beach got too crowded. Bodybuilding had gone mainstream and Arnold, whom Cal had met when he was fresh off the plane from Austria, was on his way to becoming famous. People were flocking to California and there was no way too stop them. By then Cal was a wealthy man with a string of gyms and a slew of women who circled around him like satellites. I was quite the swordsman in those days, he would tell me with a grin.

But things were changing and so was bodybuilding. By the early seventies, if you were good, you could make decent money at it, though it wasn't easy. Then there were the drugs. Steroids were everywhere and Cal didn't like what he saw. In the old days, all you had was brewer's yeast, protein powder, a few vitamin pills, and, if you were really exotic, a few tablets of desiccated liver. But steroids were different. They actually worked, and once you got on the drug bus, it was very hard to get off.

When the drugs came, everything shifted in their direction. It was as though a goliath with a giant syringe in one hand and a bottle of Dianabol in the other had plopped his massive ass down on one end of a seesaw and changed forever the rules of the game. Soon it was clear you couldn't win a contest without steroids, and gradually the rapidly expanding audiences became addicted to the freak show the sport had become. Even the women builders were starting to look scary. The first time I ever saw a dame with bigger biceps than me, Cal had once said with a laugh, I knew it was time for me to get the hell out of Dodge.

So Cal Belkin sold all of his gyms and all his property and went searching for a paradise no one had spoiled yet, and when he rolled into Miami in his red Cadillac, he knew he had found it.

He bought a building at the edge of a strip mall and opened Cal's Gym and again the people came. By the time I met him thirty years later Cal was still limping around the gym with no intention of ever retiring. Let them carry me out he used to say. What the hell else am I going to do, play golf? That was Cal for you.

The first thing I thought when I pulled into the parking lot outside Cal's gym was that I had turned into the wrong strip mall. When I took a second look, I realized that the only thing that had actually changed was the front of what had once been the health club. The façade had been changed and there was brand new neon sign that said *Suncoast Gym* on the marquee. Beneath the new sign someone had strung a red white and blue grand opening banner and a well-built young woman I had never seen before was standing under it, handing out flyers and sex appeal. I got out of my car and walked slowly toward the mirage.

The woman with the flyers wasn't having much trouble getting rid of them, especially when it came to the day laborers on their way into the Cuban place for breakfast. They would have happily taken a handful of scorpions from her, and I didn't blame them. I couldn't decide whether the black, tiny two-piece outfit she was wearing was a bathing suit or not, but it sure wasn't trying very hard whatever it was. The little black shorts she wore were under a lot of internal pressure and seemed about to explode from within. Her abs were well defined but not hungry looking. She had medium-sized, recently implanted breasts that looked alert and happy to see me. The woman smiled and handed me a flyer. Her eyes were unexpectedly green, her hair an explosion of dark brown curls.

I smiled back and read the flyer while she went about her work. Some of the laborers whistled and made catcalls as they stood around outside the hardware store waiting for contractors to show up with offers of day jobs. Her ass dominated the busy street like a dictator. Cars and trucks slowed down to a solemn, funereal pace as they passed her. She ignored them all, yet never stopped smiling. The flyer offered a thirty day grand opening half-off sale to anybody who joined and three months to any current member who signed up for another year along with a free massage and a session with a personal trainer.

When I glanced up again, I saw something else to think about. Cal had a reserved parking spot directly in front of the gym. No one else was allowed to park there, and Cal was quick to have cars towed away if anyone trespassed. Now there was a brand new red Ferrari parked squarely in no man's land, in clear violation of the Cal's cardinal rule. It was another bad omen.

"Would you like to come in?" the woman said. "I'll give you a free tour if you want one.

"I used to work here," I said, looking up at the sign again. "Or at least I thought I did."

"Oh, I know who you are," the woman said with a big smile. "You must be Jack! We were waiting for you to show up. Vincent wants to talk to you."

I pointed at the Ferrari.

"Whose car is that?" I asked.

"That's Vincent's car."

"And who is Vincent?"

"The new owner. He just bought the place."

She stuck out her hand. "My name is Candy," she said.

"Cal sold the place?"

"Who's Cal?" she asked.

"The old guy who owns the place."

"I don't know. Maybe you should ask Vince."

"Cal didn't mention anything to me about selling the gym."

"Well, he must have. Anyway, Vince wants to talk to you. He says you two used to be cops together back in New York."

"You're not talking about Vince Fernandez are you?" I asked.

"Sure," Candy said brightly. "He said you and him were friends." She pushed opened the glass door for me. "Vince really wants to talk to you. Go on in. He's in his office."

I shook my head and walked past her. The mirage I was in was expanding, coming into focus and becoming more real with a cast that was also getting larger. First Candy and her magnificent bubble butt, and now, of all people, Vince Fernandez, my old friend from New York. Hearing his name again after so long, made me feel as though I were moving backwards in time.

Candy introduced me to the black man sitting behind the front counter. He wore a bright yellow tank top with spaghetti thin straps looped around a pair of deltoids the size of honeydew melons. His shoulder length dreadlocks were held in place by the black satin do rag tied behind his head. The tank top's neckline plunged past his puffed out pectoral muscles and stopped just south of his the nipples. The man was a testament to modern chemistry, and he didn't care who knew it. He nodded at Candy, blew on his fingertips and went back to filing his fingernails with an emery board.

"This is Jack Vaughn, Z," Candy said. "You know, Vince's friend from New York."

"Z" and I shook hands. He gave me the classic I-can-kick-your-ass, jailhouse stare and smiled. Nothing about me bothered him at all. Hell, I wouldn't even be a good warm-up for him. He folded his bulbous arms across his chest and leaned back on his stool as though I was so inconsequential that he might need reading glasses in order to see me.

"So Jack is back," he said. "Oh, happy day."

"What does Z stand for?" I asked.

"Zero," he said. "They call me Mr. Zero. Don't fuck with Mr. Zero. That's my motto."

I scanned the floor of the gym for Raul Ochoa, the trainer who worked the day shift, but he was nowhere to be found. Ochoa was a lady's man famous for sleeping with his female clients then dumping them when he got bored. His specialty was married women with a lot of money and free time to spend on him. Cal tolerated him because he brought in business and was booked solid most of the time. For Raul, the gym was a gold mine, and he would not have walked away from it without good reason. I asked Candy where he was. She didn't answer me right away; her little mouth opened slightly but nothing came out. It was obvious she was either remembering an answer or inventing one.

"He quit," she said finally. "Raul quit."

"Did he say why?"

"You had better ask Vince," Candy said nervously. "I think maybe they had a disagreement or something."

Candy gave me a tour of the new and improved version of Cal's gym. It wasn't the same place, not even close. The walls had been repainted in yellow enamel and the broken mirrors had all been replaced, as had the aged posters and photographs that all of us used to joke with Cal about. There was a row of brand new treadmills along the west wall that looked as though they had been designed by NASA. The ancient Nautilus and Universal machines had been replaced by apparatus-made chrome plated bars and polished steel. It was hard to believe I was in Cal's Gym. The place looked like a showroom. I was looking at a million dollars in new toys at the very least. It was a nice upgrade, and everything was first class, but the more I saw of it the less I liked, and I had no reason to think it was going to get any better.

A gruff, familiar voice from the other side of the door answered Candy's knock. I followed her into the office, but it wasn't Cal I saw sitting behind the desk. It was Vince Fernandez. He was still barking at someone on the phone and didn't notice me standing there. It was obvious that he was back on the juice again. He had gained at least thirty pounds of muscle since the last time I had seen him—none of it natural judging from the web of blue veins covering his deltoids. Sitting there behind Cal's old mahogany desk, he looked not only outsized but out of place as well.

Vince hung up the phone, threw his head back and laughed at the sight of me. He rushed around from behind the desk, and before I knew it, had lifted me off the ground in a bear hug. He put me down and tapped me lightly on the side of my cheek then stepped back, looked me over and shook his head with disbelief.

"Look at you!" Vince said. "Jack Vaughn. I can't fucking believe it. This is crazy, man. Tell me this isn't fucking crazy. Jesus, man, look at you! Candy; look at this son of a bitch. See? I told you it had to be him, didn't I? Come on, man: tell me this isn't crazy."

"So," I said. "How long have you been in Miami?"

"Hey, man. You don't seem very glad to see your old bud."

"It's like a dream or something."

"You meant to say a nightmare, you big, ugly bastard. I heard you were up in New York last year. How come you didn't call me?"

"I didn't call a lot of people. I wasn't there that long, just a couple of days."

"That's all right," Vince said. "It didn't bother me. I was just glad you were doing okay that's all. It's good to see you again, Jack. How's Miami been treating you? You making any money? Candy, be a babe, honey, and do me a favor. Come over here and rub these shoulders. They're killing me. Jack, man, take a seat."

Candy walked over and began kneading Vince's shoulders, working her fingers deep into Fernandez's traps. As he leaned his head forward, I noticed the Rolex on his wrist. I had a client who owned a jewelry store up in Surfside, and I had been to his shop enough times to know ten thousand dollars when I saw it. It appeared the gym business had been a lot more profitable for Vince Fernandez than it had been for me.

Something about the way Candy was rubbing Vince's shoulders gave me the idea that she was highly experienced at her craft. She was working her tits into the back of his neck in a manner that usually leads to more than just improved circulation. She began working on his pecs, tweaking his nipples and grinning over the top of his head at me. I grinned back. I was starting to feel like a peeping tom. Vince moved his head from side to side, producing two loud cracks from the cervical vertebrae in his neck.

"So tell me, Jack," he said. "You making any money here?"

"Not lately," I said. "I've been down in the Keys."

I saw no reason to go into details. In my last attempt to play Batman, I was lucky to escape both the Bad Guys' guns and the Good Guys' indictments with only a rip or two in my cape. I was still a free man with all my body parts functioning, but when the D.A. in Miami told me in a roomful of local, state, and federal lawmen, "It would be better for you if none of us ever sees you again," I took the hint. I figured I'd be doing Cal as well as myself a favor to leave the gym and the city for a while and hang in the Keys. Down there, nobody cares who you are or where you've been as long as you can pay the rent and buy the occasional round at the tiki bar.

I found a cheap apartment in Islamorada, put on my old snorkeling mask to lead pavement-pale vacationers on explorations of the deep (but not too deep) waters, and picked up some gigs teaching water-aerobics at a luxury condo complete with pool. Playing Aqua-Man for fat ladies bobbing up and down on water wings beat being chased by killers on one side and cops on the other. For a while, anyway. Until boredom grew so acute I had trouble drawing a breath. Give me Miami, with its crooked cops and crookeder prosecutors and one-of–a-kind criminals any day, I'd thought. And yet, here I was, feeling like maybe Aqua-Robics might have been the preferable career choice after all.

"I saw your name on some old payroll sheets when I bought the place," Vince said. "I knew it had to be you. I was going to give you a call, but with the grand opening and all, things have been a little hectic. Anyway, I figured you'd show up sooner or later. That's enough, Candy. It's Jack's turn now. Go ahead, babe. Work those magical fingers of yours on Mr. Vaughn there."

"When did you quit the force?" I asked.

"It'll be two years come this June."

Candace walked around behind me and began to massage my neck and shoulders while Vince winked at me from the other side his desk.

"That's enough, babe," Vince said. "Me and Jack have to

talk business. Why don't you go back outside and show your ass to the customers? It's good for business."

"Your friend has nice muscles," Candy said. One last time, her hands moved over my arms and torso then back to my neck where her fingers worked the muscles on either side of my spine. The soft press of her breasts against my neck vanished, and I swiveled around in my chair to watch her leave the room. Vince flashed his teeth at me and laughed.

"Where'd you find her?" I asked.

"She's a stripper at my friend's place up in Hallandale. What do you think?"

"I think she's good for business."

"Come on," Vince said. "I want to introduce you to some friends of mine."

Vince led me over to the far end of the gym where two of the largest men I had ever seen this side of a football field were applying chalk to the palms of their hands. They were not bodybuilders. Their muscles were massive but lacked definition, but what caught my attention were the crudely drawn tattoos that swarmed over their torsos like a disease. The tattoos looked as though they had been made with the blue ink from a fountain pen. They hadn't been bought in a parlor either. That was for sure. They were homemade and right out of maximum security. Jailhouse art. Human graffiti. A way of telling your fellow inmates who you were and what you had done; story board for murderers, thieves, rapists and kidnappers.

The bald one had a hammer and sickle stenciled on his chest. You could just barely make it out under the dark swirls of his fur. The thick creases in his forehead looked as though they had been walked through with a plow. He was wearing a well-worn leather lifting belt around his waist, half of his gut hanging over it like a bib. On the floor in front of him was a barbell with four forty-five pound plates on either end. With the weight of the bar added to the total, and I was looking at four hundred and five pounds of heavy metal.

The other man was a bit trimmer and a bit taller and not quite so thick about the chest but, nevertheless, still weighed a solid two-fifty. He looked more like a track and field man than a weightlifter but was still very powerfully built. He had thick curly hair and a beard and mustache that were flecked with gray. There was a picture of a naked red head on his left arm, her body a serpentine wave of curves and extremely x-rated when it came to vaginal detail. She was surrounded what at first looked to be a bed of nails, but which, as I got closer, turned out to be tiny, blue Cyrillic letters. The bearded man clapped his hands together, releasing a white cloud of chalk into the air.

"Watch this," Vince said.

The bald man squatted down and grabbed the shiny Olympic steel bar around the knurling a foot from either end. The sweat was already pouring down his face as he puffed his cheeks out like a trumpet player. He gave the bar a few tugs that rattled the plates then lifted his chin toward the ceiling and began chanting quietly in a language that sounded something like Russian. His companion slapped his chalk-covered hands together again. The bald man gritted his teeth then straightened up with a shout. As the barbell passed his knees, he dropped under it, flicking his wrists backwards and catching the bar as it landed with a bounce on his chest. He remained in that precarious position just long enough to get his balance. Then he stood up with no more effort than if he had been holding a small child across his chest; and just like that, he was standing there looking straight ahead with four hundred pounds lying across ledge of his sternum.

The bald man's legs didn't shake and his quadriceps didn't quiver with the effort; neither did his body sway from side to side, as I would have expected considering the weight. In fact, he seemed very relaxed and under no real stress at all. He smiled over at Vince and nodded. Then he bent his knees ever so slightly and shoved the bar way up over his head where he held it for a few seconds as he looked around the gym in triumph. Finally his eyes settled once more on Vince Fernandez.

"Hey, Vincent," the bald man yelled, his voice deep, his Slavic accent thick and foreign sounding. "Where should I put this? How about on top of your nice new car outside?"

His friend, the one with beard, threw back his head and laughed, revealing the scar streaking across his throat in a pinkish storm of ruined flesh. It looked to me as though somebody had once come very close to having cut off his head.

"I don't care where you put it," Vince told him. "Just don't drop it. It makes to much goddamned noise."

The other man spoke—or at least tried to. Whatever had been done to his throat had also damaged his ability to speak. His voice reminded me of the rasping sound the breeze makes blowing through a mass of dried out palm fronds. Even if his English had been perfect, I would have had trouble understanding what he was saying. The bald mad let the bar drop to his chest then lowered it to his knees before dropping it with a thud on the wooden palates. The barbell bounced up and down twice before coming to rest.

Vince introduced me to the two men. The bald man's name was Anton Zhukov. The man with raspy voice was called Stefan the Chechen. They had too much chalk on their hands for a handshake, so the three of us just nodded at each other.

"This is the guy I was telling you about," Vince said. "We were cops together up in New York. He's a personal trainer now."

Anton looked me over with a skeptical frown on his face. "A trainer?" he said. "And who is it that trains you, little man?" he asked me.

His friend Stefan whispered something in his raspy voice that made Anton laugh.

"He says you are too skinny," Anton said.

"He's right," I said. "I am too skinny. I'm too skinny and he's too stupid, so I guess that makes us even."

Vince and Anton laughed. Stefan didn't. We spent a few fun moments staring each other down before he finally smiled and nodded. He turned to Anton who it seemed had become accustomed to serving as both his translator and microphone.

"He says you have nerve," Anton said. "But in jail you would be his bitch."

"All right, you guys," Vince said. "Let's drop the macho shit, all right? Jack's a friend of mine and you guys better treat him nice. He's going to be working with us."

"As what?" Anton asked. "Girlfriend?"

Stefan laughed. It obviously hurt him to do so; his eyes reddened and he grabbed at his throat as though he were about to try and choke himself.

"Come on, Jack," Vince said. "Leave these two clowns alone. Let's go get us some breakfast."

We walked across the street to the Cuban place on the corner and took a table near the back near the kitchen. Vince had already succeeded in charming all the waitresses, especially Rosalinda, a round woman in her late sixties who took our orders and treated him a lot better than she had ever treated me. I understood enough of what they said to realize that he was telling her what great friends we had been back in New York and how great a guy I was. All of it was classic Vince Fernandez exaggerated bullshit. Rosalinda seemed impressed then informed him that I needed to learn more Spanish if I intended to stay in Miami for any length of time. Vince laughed and ordered ten egg whites, a bowl of oatmeal and Cuban coffee. I wasn't hungry but our conversation needed props, so I ordered bacon and eggs and a tall glass of hand squeezed overpriced orange juice just to give myself something to do.

"So," Vince said. "How do you like it down here?"

"I wouldn't go back to New York if you paid me."

"You went back a couple of years ago. You were down at Mickey's. Some of the guys told me about it. I guess you must have heard about my little problem while you were up there," Vince said.

"I heard a few things, nothing major."

"Like what?"

"That you left the one twelve and transferred out to the sixty-one in Brooklyn."

"What else?"

"Look, Vince. If you got something you want to tell me then fine, but quit interrogating me about shit you already know, okay?"

Vince smiled. "Who'd you talk to, O'Neal or that asshole Vesecky?"

"Vesecky's dead. I talked to O'Neal."

"Vesecky's dead?" Vince said. "What'd he die from?"

"Prostate cancer. Advanced."

"Serves him right, the motherfucker," Vince said. "They tell you he won the lottery? Yea, that's right. Son of a bitch won six point five million dollars. But get this: he didn't tell his wife about it. He divorces her and runs of with his girlfriend, some stewardess from Norway or some fucking place. His wife found about it but it was too late. The fucker already had the money socked away in a Swiss bank and there wasn't anything she could do about it. I don't know if she ever saw a penny of it."

"Well he's dead now," I said. "It doesn't matter."

"What did O'Neal say about me?" Fernandez asked.

"He said you beat a kid to death out in Crown Heights, and they transferred you out to the sixty-one in Brighton Beach."

"I didn't *beat* anybody," Fernandez said. "I banged somebody's head against the ground and they died. It was an accident. You of all people should understand that."

"Why'd you quit? Brooklyn couldn't have been that bad."

"It wasn't Brooklyn, Jack. Fucking Brighton Beach was no worse than anywhere else. They took me off the streets and stuck me in the evidence room. They might as well have put me in a cell out on Riker's Island. I stuck it out for four months then quit. O'Neal must have told you about that."

"As I recall, he was more interested in talking about what happened when the towers went down. He lost his twin brother, you know."

"I was at the funeral, which is more than I can say for someone else I know."

"Why do I get the feeling you got some kind of beef with O'Neal?" I asked.

"I heard he retired a few months ago," Fernandez said. "I heard he was down here in Miami tending bar some place. You ever hear from him?"

"He called me when he first got down here, said he was looking for work. I never heard from him again after that. So I can't tell you whether he found a job or not. Anyway, he's got his pension. That should be enough"

"If you knew where he was working," Fernandez said. "You'd tell me wouldn't you?"

"Why wouldn't I? You and he were friends, right"

"That's what I'm saying."

"Besides," I said. "If you're so anxious to talk to O'Neal, there are ways to find him."

"I know. I've been working on it," Fernandez said.

"You guys didn't have a falling out, did you?"

"Who told you that?"

"Nobody. I was just asking."

The cook tapped his ready bell and Rosalinda brought our food over. We ate in silence for a few minutes. After a few bites of toast, Vince looked around and shook his head.

"I never seen so many goddamned Cubans in one place in my whole fucking life," he said. "Don't they have any Puerto-Ricans in this town?"

It was time to drop my hook in the water and see what I could catch. The trick lies in being patient, not jerking the line. If I came on too strong with questions about Cal, Vince would dive for the bottom and stay there.

"So you bought the gym from the old man," I said.

"Yea, and I did him a favor too. The place was a dump," Vince said. "What do you think about the way we fixed it up?"

"First class. You said we. You have partners then?"

"That's right. They're good people. They hired me as a consultant then offered me a piece of the action when they saw what I could do."

"Your partners must have some pretty deep pockets," I said. "They sure put a lot of money into the place."

"That's the only way to do it, Jack. The days of renting a hole in the wall and throwing in some broken down Fred Flintstone-style equipment and hoping to make money are over. That mom and pop shit don't work any more, not in this business. If you want to compete with Bally's and the big franchises like Gold's, you got to do it right. I don't know how the old guy lasted so long. Nowadays, it's upgrade, upgrade and upgrade—that is, once you found a good location."

"How'd you talk him into selling? I always thought he would die in that place."

"It was easy. He was old, and he was sick sick. He wanted to sell. What's the big deal?"

"What was he sick with?"

"How the hell should I know?"

I was getting impatient. There was a part of me that wanted to tell him about the state troopers hauling Cal's car just to see what his reaction to the news would be. But that would have been jerking the line way too soon. I remembered what a boat captain had told me the first time I had gone out deep sea fishing with him. Sometimes the best way to fish, he said, is to pretend you're not fishing at all. His theory was that doing so created a calm in the water that lured the fish into getting careless. You had to sit back and not care about whether you caught anything or not.

I had to wait, bide my time. Besides, maybe everything was kosher after all. Maybe Vince and his partners had showed up with enough cash to convince Cal that hanging on for another year or two didn't make sense. Maybe my phone would ring and it would be Cal calling from Acapulco with a beer in one hand and a sweet young thing in the other. As they say: it was not beyond the realm of possibility, but I didn't think it was going to happen. The key was to act like it didn't matter.

Vince had been eating with his head down, shoveling egg whites into his mouth without interruption. Now he sat up, took a sip of coffee and glared at me across the table. Then he belched so loudly a woman sitting at the counter turned around and threw him a dirty look. Vince laughed and wiped his mouth with a napkin then squeezed it into a ball. I took a sip of coffee and put the cup down in the saucer. Vince tossed his balled up napkin into the busboy's dish tub then began picking at his teeth with a toothpick.

"How much did you make last year, Jack? Thirty-five, forty thousand dollars?

"Why do you ask?"

"Come on. Tell me. How much did you make?"

"The whole thing?"

"Don't worry," Vince said. "The IRS ain't under the table. You can tell me the truth."

"About forty grand."

"I guess that makes you Donald Trump right?"

"That's a pretty nice watch you're wearing, Vincent. They give you that when you left the job?"

I thought he would come out of his chair at that, so I pushed mine back from the table to give myself more room. Instead, Fernandez leaned in close and whispered through gritted teeth. The high-protein diet he was on hadn't done much for his breath.

"I bought this watch with my own money," he said. "Money I earned. Don't get wise with me, you fucking loser."

"What kind of 'roids are you on these days, Vince? You look like the goddamned Hulk."

"Kiss my ass."

I stood up and dropped a ten-dollar bill on the table. Vince grabbed my elbow as I started for the door, though not with as much force as I knew he was capable of exerting.

"Come on," he said. "Sit back down. You know how I get when I'm on the juice."

I sat down. Vince slid the ten spot back over to me, but I didn't pick it up. He smiled at me, but I didn't smile back. Have you ever had a friend you didn't like? That was Vince Fernandez and me. The thought that the two of us might be more alike than I cared to admit was beginning to claw its way up my spine again. It's always uncomfortable being around people too much like ourselves.

"I've got a contest coming up," he said. "The Mr. Miami. This could be my last chance to get my pro card before I get too old. I've been hitting the weights hard five days a week, twice-a-day workouts, each body part twice a week for the last three months. I been cycling on off for the last six months, stacking Deca and Anadrol with a shot of Equipoise once a week for a chaser. That's the stuff they give to racehorses. I didn't mean to call you a loser. You and me are friends. It's just that all this shit I'm taking makes you a little hot headed, so quit looking at me like you're going to kick my ass and let me make you the fucking offer of a lifetime."

Rosalinda came by and refilled my cup. Fernandez grinned at her and said something in Spanish to which she responded by slapping him lightly on the shoulder.

"What kind of offer?" I asked.

"Manager of Suncoast Gym. You get a base salary plus commission plus a cut from whatever the personal trainers bring in. I figure you'll make two hundred grand the first year alone."

"I thought you were the manager"

"Listen to me, Jack. The people I'm working with now aren't bullshitting around, okay? They've got a lot of money and they need to invest it. They like the gym business and best of all, they like me. This time next year we're going to have a dozen gyms in South Florida alone. We already got two in Tampa and another one under construction over in Naples. They're going to make me regional director, but we need a good man here in Miami to keep things running smooth when I'm not around. I want that man to be you. What do you say?"

"Two hundred grand is a lot of money for someone working in a gym. Even most owners don't make that much, at least not from a single location. How much are you planning to sell the memberships for?"

"Listen to this son of a bitch, will you?" Vince said. "You been in the business for what? Twenty minutes? And already you're quoting numbers to me like you know what the fuck you're talking about! But you know something? You're right. That is a lot of money for a gym rat to make, but I'm telling you, Jack, the people I'm with got a whole new business model for the way they run their operations. These are some serious people, Jack. If you want to make a lot of money, they're the way to go. But I tell you what: think about it, but don't take too long, all right? There's a ton of guys out there that would jump at the offer I just made you."

"Tell me something, Vince," I said. "When did you start running around with the Tattoo Brothers?"

"See? That's how much you know. Neither one of them is from Russia. They just speak it. Anton, the bald headed one, he's from Belarus. And don't ask me where it is, because I don't fucking know. Stefan is from Chechnya. That's the problem with this country. Nobody knows shit about world geography anymore."

"We've got a few more problems than geography," I said. "And I pretty sure I just met two of them at the gym."

"All right," Fernandez said. "Go ahead. Get it off your chest. I know what you're going to say, so just go ahead and say it."

"Are those two the partners you were talking about before," I said.

"And what if they are?"

"Nothing. I just like to know who it is I'm going to be working with," I said. "That's all."

"So you're serious about the offer?" Vince asked.

"Why not? Two hundred grand is a lot of money. I would need five years to make that much just training people. This might be just the right time for me to make a move up to management. You know: make money off of other people's work. That's the American way."

"Good," Fernandez said. "That's just what I wanted to hear. Now listen to me. You're right. The two guys you just met, they were gangsters, real hard cases too, and they've both done some hard time—but not here. Not in this country. Anton was a weightlifter. Stefan threw the discus. That's a plate that weighs about four pounds in case you don't know. Neither of them ever worked a day in his life until the Soviet Union crashed down. All they knew how to do was play sports and take steroids and the other shit the government gave them. Then, the next thing you know, they get dumped. They're big, they're stupid and they're unemployed, but they're also strong as shit, so that's what they did. They sold the one thing they had more of than anybody. They sold their muscle. You can't blame them for doing that can you?"

"What is it they sell over here—Tupperware?"

"Go ahead, Jack, be a fucking comedian. But those guys, as dumb as they are, are making beaucoup bucks. A few of my current associates sponsored them. When they got to New York, the people I work with gave them jobs and places to stay. They're actually two very nice guys—once you get to know them."

"Those tattoos would indicate otherwise, but then who am I to judge?"

"That's right," Vince said. "Who the fuck are you to judge anybody? Anyway, you don't have to worry. Stefan and Anton work security for the big bosses. With you it's strictly management I'm looking for. No guns and no rough stuff. Your hands are clean and everything is legit. Every now and then you might get an envelope with a little something extra in it, but other than that, you got nothing to worry about."

Vince took a call on his cell phone and handed my ten-dollar bill back to me. We shook hands, and I left him sitting there with his phone cupped to his ear, his massive shoulders hunched forward over the table like a fullback at the line of scrimmage. Then I got my car and headed back across the MacArthur Causeway toward the mainland.

3

Eighty years before Katrina nearly drowned New Orleans, a hurricane blew through Miami Shores with such force it never recovered. That was in 1926, at a time before they gave hurricanes names. Back then, a lot of people were getting rich in the real estate business and there was plenty of land for the developers to develop and plenty of snowbirds eager to buy a piece of the Sunshine State, and this despite the fact that the invention of air conditioning was still a decade away. Someone even wrote a song to help lure would be buyers to town. It was called "Moon over Miami," and while it now sounds terribly outdated, it was a big hit back in the day

A few years before the big storm hit, a developer began building the city of Miami Shores, most of which, despite its name, is fairly far from the nearest body of water, Biscayne Bay. The company's name, inappropriately enough, was the Shoreland Development Corporation and the people who ran the company had big plans for their new town.

Much of the architecture was to be based on what they called the Mediterranean Revival Style, a style perfect for the warm, sunny climate with plenty of plenty orange roof tiles and pastel colored stucco walls. Part of the construction plans for the city called for a large apartment building on Grand Concourse Boulevard that is still there to this day, as well as a number of private homes, most of which also survived the storm. There were even plans for a big swanky hotel on the order of the Biltmore down in the Gables. But when the storm hit, everything changed. The Shoreland Company went bust, the posh hotel never got built, and three years later the Great Depression put the real estate boom into suspended animation until after the war.

By the time Cal Belkin showed up in 1975, a truncated version of Miami Shores had become a quiet place with a prosperous main street and a small town peacefulness that reminded him of some of the places he had passed through on his long drive across the Midwest, Texas and the Deep South. There was a small movie theatre, a library and an old fashioned diner all within walking distance of one another. Cal liked the town so much he bought a house there, one of those Mediterranean style houses I mentioned before. The house was on Shoreland Boulevard, the only remnant of the real estate developer it had been named for.

There was still a small part of me that was still hoping that when I pulled up to his house, Cal would be sitting on the front porch, smoking a cigar and cursing at the teenagers who had stolen his car the night before. It was not a very big part of me, and it was shrinking pretty fast, and as I drove slowly toward his house down the wide expanse of Grand Concourse Boulevard, I felt like a man who is desperately trying to keep a fire going in the midst of a rainstorm.

I was stopped at the light across from the house when I spotted the for sale sign on Cal's front lawn. I stared at it for a long moment; then somebody blew their horn behind me. I glanced up at my mirror just in time to see the angry face of a young woman as her black Escalade swerved violently around me. I followed her across Shoreland Boulevard, expecting it to disappear into the distance, but instead it braked to a sudden stop then fishtailed into a spot directly across the street from Cal's house. There was a magnetic blue and white sign on the door of her car with the words Kozinski Realty written on it along with a phone number.

I pulled up in front of Cal's house and sat there behind the wheel as the woman jumped out the Ford and jaywalked stiffly across the street toward Cal's house. As I watched, she plucked the red and white for sale sign out of the front yard and tucked it under her arm. I got out of my car and approached her. She saw me coming and pulled a can of mace out of her purse and pointed at my face.

"Nice driving," I said. "You beat me here by nearly a second."

"I don't know what you want," the woman said. "But you had better go away right now."

The woman glared at me from the other side of the Mace canister. Her small blue eyes showed more annoyance than fear and she held the canister with the steady grip of a veteran. She wouldn't be the type who would hesitate to give me a good face full of nasty juice if I blinked at her wrong.

"Are you the agent on this property?" I asked. "I've been looking to buy something in this neighborhood."

She looked at the Camaro then glanced quickly at my watch. It was as quick a credit check as I had ever seen outside of a bar on South Beach, and, as usual, it was quite accurate: Neither my car nor my watch, as dependable as both were, added up to a house in Miami Shores and we both knew it.

"When light is green, you should drive through it."

"My apologies. I was having a flashback."

"This house already sold," the real estate agent said.

"Really? How long was it on the market?

"Not long. This is very popular neighborhood. Houses here sell very quickly."

"You know," I said. "Now that I've got my settlement all straightened out, I was looking to buy something around this neighborhood."

The Realtor still looked a bit wary, but at least she had

lowered the can of mace to half-mast. Not that I didn't understand the need for caution on her part. In Miami, showing empty houses to strangers isn't the safest way to make a living, especially for a woman. She had probably had trouble before, and for all I knew that can of Mace might be very well be half empty.

We stood there looking one another over. She was tall and thin, and like a lot of people who live year round in Miami, she had very pale skin, but what struck me most about her was the way her light blue eyes contrasted with the coal tar blackness of her ultra-straight hair. It had an almost artificial sheen to it that made it look as though it had been simonized. I kept waiting for her to get tired of frowning at me, but it never happened, and I got the feeling that her face would look the same way when she was asleep. I had seen the same look in the faces of gang members back in New York. It's the look of people who have known little kindness in life and who expect even less in the future.

After another moment of silent calculation, she dropped the canister back in her purse and handed me her business card. Her name was Marina Gero. I introduced myself and extended my hand, which she accepted with all the enthusiasm of someone who has been handed a hot dog without the benefit of a bun. Property values in Miami Shores had risen sharply in the last ten years, and it was clear to both of us that I was not part of her usual clientele. The only thing that had gotten me this far with her was my fib about the settlement. It had given me just enough false glitter to keep her from spraying me like I was a bug.

"I know this place is sold," I began. "But I was wondering if you would mind letting me see what it looks like on the inside. There have to be others like it around here, and if I could see this one from the inside, I'd have to something to tell the wife."

"You're not wearing wedding ring."

"I broke my finger playing basketball. I was waiting for it to heal."

"House is 3-2. Five thousand square feet."

"That sounds like exactly what we're looking for."

"Okay," Marina Gero said. "No problem. I show you house."

I hadn't been to Cal's place since his birthday party in June the previous year, but from the outside at least not much had changed. It was a two-story mustard yellow stucco house with Spanish styles roof tiles with plenty of well-kept lawn on either side of it and clematis climbing the walls like crazy in all directions. Shade was provided by the expansive banyan tree that spread its boughs like wings over the house and the adjacent garage with the double-wide wooden doors that Cal had built himself. The real estate agent opened the wooden gate and led me along the narrow paved footpath path past the limestone birdbath where a grackle was pecking away at the brackish water. It lifted its wings and flew away as we passed.

Marina Gero opened the front door and stood aside as I walked into an empty foyer with bare white walls that had been freshly plastered. Here and there I could see where someone had spackled over the tiny holes made by picture frames and mirrors, and the air smelled of wet paint. My guide led me into the living room, where Cal had had his birthday party, and pointed out to me the fully functioning fireplace and the hardwood floors. Then she proceeded to take me on a tour of a house I knew it better than she did.

The Russian's spiel was prefabricated, overly starched, with all the warm appeal of a Spartan's eulogy. Listening to her, I got the impression that she hadn't been in the business very long, but it didn't really matter. I wasn't listening that closely anyway.

What mattered was that the place had been scraped clean of any trace of Cal's presence. No amateur was responsible for this job. It had to be the work one of those professional cleaning services that sweep in to a place armed with heavy duty garbage containers, industrial strength plastic bags and a team of mercenaries with orders to pick a home clean as quickly as possible.

"What is your job? What is it you do for living?" Marina asked.

"You want to know if I can afford the place?"

"With better job. Is easier to get good mortgage."

"I work for an investment firm—I'm in risk analysis."

She nodded solemnly. I'm pretty sure she had no idea what a risk analyst did, and neither did I, but she didn't want to admit to it.

"I like your accent," I said. "Where are you from?"

"Kiev. I can get you good rate. A friend of mine is mortgage broker. Maybe five and a half percent for thirty year."

"Fixed rate or adjustable?"

"Fixed."

"Tell me something," I said. "Who was it used to own this place?"

"An old man."

"What happened? Did he die or something?"

"This I don't know," Ms. Gero said.

Just then her cell phone rang, and she turned her back to me. It may have been impolite, but I didn't take exception, especially since it gave me time to slide back the deadbolt on the back door when she wasn't looking. When the agent was done with her call, I asked her who had bought the place.

"I can't tell you his name. That is against Florida law. You have money, I have other houses. I show them to you. You have my card. Make appointment."

I said goodbye and left her talking on her cell phone in the empty foyer. I closed the front door behind me, went quickly across the street, got in my car and circled the block. I parked the Chariot one block west of Cal's place then walked back through an alley on the other side of the street and waited for her to leave. A few minutes later, Gero exited the front door, still talking on her cell phone.

I waited for a few minutes then crossed the street again and went around the side of the house past the well-trimmed hedges, down a narrow paved path to the back door. It was still unlocked. I stepped inside the empty kitchen and listened as the silence spread out in front of me, expanding until it had filled the entire house. Cal, I thought to myself, where the hell are you? Where's old stink of your eternal cigar? It's not right that a man should vanish so easily, drift away like the smoke from a pyre, with so few questions asked, with not even a few lines or an old picture in obit section of the *Miami Herald.* It's not right but it happens.

I went through each of the rooms, starting with the two bedrooms on the second floor then proceeded to the living room and kitchen on the first. The house had been picked clean. The walls had been scrubbed and the pitted wooden floors sanded down and freshly varnished. The air, in places, smelled faintly of Pine-Sol. There was nothing to indicate how long the house had been vacant; it might have been a week or a year or anything in between.

I searched all the kitchen cabinets as well as the broom closet. I was in the process of checking the cabinets under the kitchen sink without much hope when I spotted the card on the counter near the sink. At first, I thought at first it was an imperfection the tile's surface, but when I looked more closely I realized it was a business card lying face down next to the soap dish. On the flip side was a laminated picture of a naked woman wrapped around a stripper's pole. Printed along the bottom, in slanted neon yellow print, was an invitation to the club itself and an offer for a free drink and lap dance at a place called the Emperor's Club for any senior citizen over the age of sixty-five. But what really got my attention was the name stamped in purple ink in the lower left hand corner: Raul Ochoa, the missing personal trainer I knew from what had once been Cal Belkin's gym.

The surface of the card smelled vaguely of perfume. I sniffed it over for a second then slipped it into my wallet. I made one last sweep of the house but found nothing else, not even dust on a light bulb. As I was on my way downstairs, I heard someone coming through the front gate. At first I thought it might be the Realtor again, but when I was halfway to the backdoor, the doorbell rang in the hollowness of the foyer behind me.

I started to leave then realized that whoever it was must not have a key. That eliminated the real estate agent, so I went back to the living room and listened. The bell rang again. I crossed over to the window near the front door and eased the Venetian blinds away from the sill just enough to get a peek of my unexpected visitor. As I did so, a yellow cab pulled away from the curb.

First impression: Long brown hair with bangs that either needed trimming or had been cut that way intentionally as part of a style that required the chronic gesture of brushing them out of her eyes. She did it twice while ringing Cal's doorbell. Thirty-five, maybe a bit more, medium height, loosely built with a slight stoop to her shoulders that for some reason I found attractive. Tight jeans and a well worn slightly faded black T-shirt without a logo. Some kind of tattoo on her forearm as she rang the bell. Naturally lean, no obvious implants, and, for a white girl, a nice ass.

She rang a third time, brushed her unruly bangs away from her eyes then stepped back from the door and looked up at the second story before trying again, this time with a bit more desperation. I thought about it for a very thin moment then went over and opened the door.

"Who are you?" I asked.

"I'm Cal's granddaughter. Do you know where he is?"

I looked up and down the street. An older woman pushing a baby stroller was walking toward us. The woman waved. I had never seen her before in my life, but I waved back anyway.

"We can't stay here very long," I said. "You had better come inside."

I stepped back and closed the door behind her then watched as she panned around the empty foyer and living room like an undersea cameraman inside a sunken ship. When she had absorbed as much of the emptiness as she could tolerate, she looked back at me like I was the ghost of Christmas past. I answered her question before she had a chance to ask it.

"You know as much as I do," I said. "I just got here myself."

I heard some banging out in the street and stepped quickly back to the window to peek through the Venetian blinds again, but it was only the garbage men or sanitation engineers as we used to call them back in New York. The brown haired woman watched me nervously.

"What's going on?" she asked.

"Nothing; I thought I heard something." I tried to smile but gave it up.

"You're Jack, aren't you?" she asked. You work for Cal."

"I don't remember your name, but we should go now."

She extended her hand. I shook it. A car door slammed somewhere down the block. She also told me her name. Dawn Belkin. It took a moment to register. I was still half tuned to the noises out in the street.

"Dawn," I said. "We need to go some place where we can talk, and this isn't it."

Again, the brushing of the bangs, but something in my tone must have convinced her, because without a word she followed me into the kitchen. I led her out the back door and helped her climb over the fence that led to the alley. Neither of us spoke until we were safely in my car and heading south on Biscayne Boulevard.

"Have you been to the gym yet?" I asked

"No, not yet. I wanted to stop by here first, but last week, I spoke to a man at the gym. He told me Cal had sold the gym to him a few weeks back. I told him I hadn't been able to reach Cal for the last month and asked if he knew how to contact him. He said he had no idea."

"The man you talked to. Was his name Vince Fernandez by any chance?"

"I think so. I was so surprised, I forgot to write it down."

"Did you tell him who you were?"

"Yes, of course. He seemed very concerned. When I told

him I was coming down to Miami, he said he would pick me up at the airport."

"You came in a cab," I said. "What happened? Fernandez didn't show up?"

"It was my fault," Dawn admitted. "I told him I was flying into Miami instead of Fort Lauderdale. By the time I realized my mistake, it was too late. He said he'd send a couple of his people to pick me up, but I told him I would just as soon take a taxi. I told him I'd meet him the gym at eleven o'clock, but I decided to stop here first just in case Cal was home."

"It's a good thing you did," I said.

"What do you mean?"

"When was the last time you talked to your grandfather?"

"Maybe six weeks ago, right before I went to Paris. What about you?"

"A little bit less, but not by much. What were you doing in Paris?"

"I sing. I had a show there."

"Cal say anything about selling the gym to you?" I asked.

"Not a word. He didn't mention selling the house either. Why? What are you thinking?"

"I'm thinking that there's something rotten in Miami. That's what I'm thinking. I'm thinking that if Fernandez and his men had met you at the airport, we wouldn't be having this little conversation right now."

"Why not?"

"Because you'd be dead; that's why," I said. "I'm not sure what happened to your grandfather, but I'm pretty sure my friend Vince Fernandez does. Whatever it was, whoever did it must have been fairly certain they were dealing with an old man with no friends or family to look out for him. They might have grabbed him, thinking that no one would come looking. They could get Cal to sign away his gym, his house and anything else they wanted and not have worry about any family member showing up and making trouble for them. Then you show up."

"Who is this 'they' you keep talking about?" Dawn asked. "Do they have a name?"

"Fernandez introduced me to a couple of hard cases over at your grandfather's gym this morning. Both of them spoke Russian and both of them were gangsters."

"You mean like the Mafia, only Russian?"

"That's right. They're with some kind of syndicate. Probably out of Brooklyn, which is where Vince probably met them. They don't get as much press as the Italians or the Colombians, but pound for pound, they're a lot worse. They got guys who will shoot you just to see if their gun is loaded."

"You really think they would have killed me?" Dawn asked.

"Of course they would have. They would have taken you someplace nice and quiet, and that would be the end of you. They wouldn't give it a second thought. And there's something else too. There was a real estate agent standing on the front lawn when I pulled up. She told me the house had just been sold. She sounded Russian or somewhere in the neighborhood. That's not a good sign. "

"You say it so casually," Dawn said. "As though it's completely normal to pick people up at the airport and then kill them for no reason."

"Oh, they have a reason all right, and the reason is money. Let's say I'm right, and they've got Cal somewhere. He's tough but it wouldn't be long before they'd be able to get him to sign over whatever they wanted: his business, his house. It happens all the time. You show up and make things complicated. Cal becomes a liability and both of you wind up dead. Like I said: it happens all the time."

"Not in my world it doesn't," Dawn said.

"Evil is like Velcro, Dawn. It can only stick something like itself. Most people go their whole lives without running into the kind of guys I'm talking about. When they do, the average person doesn't have a chance."

"And you do?"

"Maybe, but if I do, it's only because they can't surprise me anymore. I've looked into the eyes of people like the ones I told you about, and let me tell you: even when they're cuffed and in shackles and you're the one with the gun, they still scare you. And you know why? Because they're dead. You'd be surprised how many people in a big city like Miami or New York are actually stone cold dead, Dawn. You can actually see it if you know what to look for. If you ask me, it's probably better not to see it."

"Why would it be better not to see it?"

"Because most of the time there's nothing you can do about it. You see them sitting across from you on the subway or in restaurants sometimes, and you know that it's just a matter of time before they hurt somebody, but there's nothing you can do about it."

"You're beginning to scare me."

"That was my intention."

"Should we call the police?"

"And tell them what? That your grandfather sold his house and business? There's nothing unusual about that. They wouldn't know what to do with it."

"We could tell him that he's missing," Dawn said. "We can tell them that neither of has spoken to him in at least six weeks. That would have to mean something to them wouldn't it?"

"Listen, Ms. Belkin, if you want to go to the police, I'll drive you there right now, but if you ask me, you'll just be wasting your time. The fact that we don't know where Cal is doesn't mean he's missing—at least it won't to the cops. I think we need to have a little bit more meat on this thing to get them interested."

"Like what?"

"Well," I said, "as far as the gym's concerned, there would have to be licenses, a certificate of occupancy, insurance.

That kind of thing. All that would have to have been put in Fernandez's name in order for it to be legit. But for now, let's us assume that everything's completely kosher. There's still the question of where the money went."

"What about the house?" Dawn asked.

"The house means another paper trail to follow," I said. "We're talking about two heavy duty deposits into your grandfather's bank account within the last month or so. If there's no record of any such transaction, then where did the money go?"

"Maybe into another account."

"You mean if he moved out of state or something like that? If that's the case, then he'll have closed his accounts here. Your grandfather's been using the same bank for the past thirty years. It's a small, local bank with only one branch. If he's left the state, or even Miami for that matter, he'd have no choice but to transfer his money to another bank. We'll start there."

4

Miami Shores Savings and Loan had been part of the original plans for the city before the storm of 1926 blew to scattered bits the developer's dream of a dynamic new city. Eighty years later, little about it had changed. The bank was a throwback to a simpler time, a small town, brick and mortar institution that had never tried to be anything other than what its founders had intended—the financial nucleus of the neighborhood. The bank's reputation was as solid as the structure that housed it, a two-story; colonial style red brick building with a green gabled roof supported by a pair of sturdy Doric columns and behind those, a porch complete with a pair of wrought iron benches flanking the eight-foot high whitewashed double oaken doors. Dawn Belkin and I signed in at the receptionist's desk and took a seat in a couple of wooden chairs outside the bank president's office.

"This place looks like a movie set from the forties," Dawn said. "Check out the grills in front of the teller's booths. They're solid brass."

"Everything about this place is solid," I said. "And it's not that easy to open an account here either. The first time I tried, they turned me down because I had an out-of-state driver's license. Your grandfather had to come down and vouch for me. After that, they treated me like I was the Prince of Wales."

A receptionist led us across the wide marble floor to Eileen Potsdam's office. Her office had cherry wood paneling and a ceiling high enough for kite flying. The walls were covered with photographs and plaques and commendations from just about everybody from the Knights of Columbus to the local chapter of the Boys Club. A picture of a much younger, quite attractive, Eileen shaking hands with President Kennedy peered down from behind her desk.

The bank president was on the phone when we were escorted into her office. When her call was completed, Ms. Potsdam stood up, buttoned her jacket and offered her hand for shaking. She seemed to remember me and asked me how I was. I introduced her to Dawn. At the mention of Cal's name, the bank president's mood lightened considerably. When I was done telling her about Cal's disappearance and the sudden sale of his property the banker nodded thoughtfully. "Mr. Belkin was fond of you, Mr. Vaughn. Do you suspect foul play in this matter?"

I shrugged. "I'm not sure, Mrs. Potsdam. That's why we came to talk to you."

She turned to Dawn. "I don't suppose you've arranged for power of attorney in your grandfather's absence?"

Dawn shook her head. "I just arrived. We, I mean, Mr. Vaughn…"

Something in Mrs. Potsdam's demeanor suggested she wasn't as stiff as her workaday exterior suggested. And behind the spectacles and the bosom-crushing suit, lurked a handsome woman. Cal Belkin had never seen a good-looking woman he didn't go out of his way to charm. So I took a chance.

"The thing is, Mrs. Potsdam, time's of the essence. I'm not looking for you to divulge any state secrets. But experience tells me that 'foul play' usually has something to do with money." I cast a sidelong glance at Dawn before I continued. "If you know Cal Belkin as well as I think you might, you know he'd want you to help if he were in trouble."

Mrs. Potsdam blinked, as if I'd just blurted out the combination to the bank's vault, then coughed discreetly into her hand. "Let me see what I can find out for you," she said, turning to tap away on her computer's keyboard. A few minutes later she turned back in our direction.

"Your grandfather has quite a bit of business with us," she said to Dawn. "His payroll; his taxes; estate planning; even your trust fund, young lady. All his investments. It'll take me a while to access all of the information on his various accounts, but I can tell you a few things. The first is that on March 1st, Mr. Belkin came into the bank to cash out a CD for a sizable amount."

"What's sizable?" I asked.

"I'm afraid that our regulations prohibit such a disclosure, Mr. Vaughn." She gave me a banker's blank look. "If I were to tell you that Cal Belkin had redeemed a certificate for $200,000, I could find myself in considerable trouble."

"I understand," I said. "I'd never ask you to compromise yourself."

"So long as we understand each other," she said. "Most of the money was deposited directly into his personal checking account. That account, strangely enough, is now nearly depleted."

"Maybe not so strangely," I said. "You're saying Cal came into the bank in person on March 1?" I said. "Were you here at the time? I mean did you see him yourself?"

"I may have been," the banker said. "But I have no recollection of having seen him. Why do you ask?"

"I was just wondering if there was anybody with him, someone who might have been strong-arming him."

"It's hard to imagine Cal Belkin being strong armed by anybody," Mrs. Potsdam said. I thought I saw a bit of color in her cheeks. "But I can check with the manager who handled the transaction. Maybe he'll remember something."

"What about his other accounts?" I asked. "Have they been tapped into?"

"Not so far. He has an IRA and a sizeable stock portfolio that haven't been touched. He also has another CD that matures in a few days."

"How much is that worth?" Dawn asked.

"I can't give you that information. It's against state law. Suffice it to say, it's a very large sum. $500,000 if a penny."

"Suppose," I said, "a third party wanted to get his hands on the rest of Cal's money. Is there any way they could do it without him being present?"

"As far as the checking accounts go," the banker said, "all one would need is access to his personal checks and be capable of a reasonable facsimile of his signature. As far as the CD's are concerned, if the client wants to cash out, he has to do it in person, not over the phone. If a third party is involved, there would have to be at the very least a power of attorney signed over by Cal in the presence of a notary public."

"Suppose the client doesn't show up?" I asked. "What happens to the certificate of deposit?"

"We roll it over for another six months at the same interest rate."

"Cal never told me he had set up a trust fund for me," Dawn said. "I wonder why not."

Mrs. Potsdam smiled. "Perhaps he was afraid you'd squander it, or give it away to some foolish man," the banker said.

"Why do you look at me when you say that?" I asked.

"I remember vividly the first time I met you, Mr. Vaughn. You had two days' worth of stubble on your chin and a breath that smelled like a night of whiskey. Let me be clear with you. Neither of those two attributes is particularly offensive to me. I like a drink myself from time to time and my husband—God rest his soul—was known to miss a day or two of shaving. Still, banking is a conservative business and we are cautious with our customers. But despite your disheveled appearance, you were a gentleman; however, I sensed in you something of the rogue, and I see no reason to change my opinion now. Though I must say, you two do make a handsome couple."

"Thank you," I said. "I've often thought so myself."

"One more thing, Mr. Vaughn," the banker said. "Cal's Social Security checks. Like most people these days, he elected to have his deposited directly by the government into his savings account. As a rule, the money arrives on the third of every month. The last government deposit into Cal's account was made in February. The March money never arrived. I checked to see why and it turns out the check has been rerouted somewhere else. The deposit agreement with this bank has been cancelled."

"Where's the government sending his checks now?" I asked.

"I have no idea."

"Can you find out?" I asked.

"I can put in an inquiry, but it will take a few days to go through. Now let's go back a minute. You said Cal sold both his business and his house recently. Is that correct?"

"That's right," I said.

"I ask because both his checking and savings accounts are nearly empty. In other words, if someone bought your grandfather's house and his gym, then he didn't deposit the money with us."

"Is it possible the he has an account with someone else?" Dawn asked.

"Certainly it's possible," the banker said. "As much as we value Mr. Belkin's business, we always advise our wealthier customers not to keep all their money with us no matter how much they may appreciate the service we offer. Still, I would have expected that at least some of that money would have wound up with our financial people."

Eileen Potsdam walked us to the door, her hand on Dawn's shoulder.

"Let me ask you something," Dawn said. "A trust fund like the one my grandfather set up for me has to have a trustee doesn't it?"

"That's correct."

"Any idea who he is?"

"Cal asked me to act as trustee," the banker said, her voice softening. "Do you find that satisfactory?"

"I'm curious," Dawn said. "I'm thirty-five now. Shouldn't I have gotten the money by now?"

"You have another five years to go, my dear." Mrs. Potsdam said. "Apparently you had some trouble with drugs and such when you were younger. Your grandfather thought it best you have a chance to grow out of such behavior before coming into any sizeable amount of money. Forty seemed a reasonable age. If a woman doesn't have her wits about her by that time, there's not much sense in waiting any longer." The look that Mrs. Potsdam gave me suggested that I had best restrain any ungallant thoughts about Dawn Belkin. I hoped the bow I attempted put her mind at ease.

"We'll be in touch, Mrs. Potsdam," I told her.

"I don't doubt you will," she answered.

At eleven thirty, just as we pulled up in front of the Holiday Inn down on South Beach, Dawn's cell phone rang.

"It's Fernandez," she said. "What should I do?"

"Don't answer him. In fact don't answer anybody except for me or people you already know."

"Won't that make him suspicious?"

"Not right away. By the time he realizes you're ducking him, this whole thing should be over one way or the other."

"What makes you say that?"

There was no sense in waiting any longer, so I told her about Cal's car. When I was done, she sat quietly on the Camaro's hood while I fed quarters to the parking meter. People never react the way you think they will, especially when it comes to bad news. Some break down right away. Others have a filter that slows the news down to a slow, manageable drip. I was glad Dawn Belkin belonged to the second category.

"You look like you're playing the slots out in Vegas," she said.

"They're pretty quick with the tickets around here. You have to be careful. If they get you, it's eighteen dollars a pop."

"Do you think he's still alive?" Dawn asked.

"I don't know."

"What are the odds?"

"That depends," I said.

"On what?"

"On whatever the game is. Once I get a better idea of the scam and who's running it, the better I'll be able to say."

"You're sure it's a scam then?"

"Unfortunately for all involved," I said. "It would seem my old friend Fernandez has thrown in with some very nasty people," I said. "They're masters of extortion, as good as the Italians ever were and much smarter. In the beginning, they specialized in small businessmen out in Brighton Beach then moved up the food chain to professional hockey players and prize fighters. Based on the two gorillas I met this morning at the gym, they seem to have opened up a local chapter. We have to be careful. These guys are the worst of the worst."

"You think we're in danger then?

"Not yet," I said. "But we will be."

"Let's get a drink," Dawn said.

"It's a bit early, but I know what you mean. There's a tiki bar out back by the pool. The prices are too high and the drinks are too weak, so don't say I didn't warn you."

We walked through the hotel's brightly lit lobby and followed a troop of kids free on spring break out to the pool deck where a bored looking bartender was polishing glasses under a thatched roof. Dawn and I ordered beers and sat facing the ocean where a girl in a parachute was being towed into the sky by a guy in a motorboat.

"You must feel like you're always on vacation living down here," Dawn said.

"The postcard fades after a while," I said. "But I still like it just the same."

"Why would they bother keeping him alive?" Dawn asked.

"You heard what Eileen said back at the bank. Cal's got another certificate of deposit coming due and there are other assets they might want to tap into. If that's the case, they'll need to keep him alive until they've gotten everything they think they can get. After that…well, they won't keep him around too long. So we don't have a lot of time."

"Do you really believe he still alive, or are you just saying it for my benefit?"

"Maybe I'm saying it for my benefit. What made you decide to come down to Miami now?"

"I call Cal once a week. About a month ago, he stopped returning my calls. I didn't think much of it. I was busy and singing and trying to break up with this crazy, beautiful Algerian who hated Americans but who wanted to marry me anyway so he could bring his entire family to the United States. Somehow, I managed to get away from him. I called Cal as soon as I got back to New York. No answer, so I called the gym and someone answered and told me the gym had a new owner. The phone at the house had been disconnected. I got worried and took the first flight down here I could get."

"It's funny we never met before," I said. "Your grandfather showed me your picture a few years back, but it was from a long time ago. For some reason, I thought you were still in high school or something."

"So you were expecting a cheerleader. I hope you're not disappointed."

"It's not that; it's just that the way he spoke about you made me think you were still a kid."

"Cal took care of me after my dad died. I was with him till I was fifteen. As far as he's concerned, I stopped aging after I ran away."

"Why'd you run away?"

"Cal was way too strict, and I wanted to be with my mother. God knows why, because she certainly didn't want to be with me. I was just a reminder to her that she wasn't all that young anymore. Plus there was the coke and all her boyfriends to put up with, but she let me do what I wanted, and at that's pretty much what I did."

"I remember now. Cal told me your father died in Iraq, in the first war."

Dawn laughed. "And you believed him?"

"I had no reason not to."

"My dad died from an overdose of smack in a rat-infested shithouse down in Alphabet City up in New York. You know where that is, Vaughn?"

"I know where it is all right. And call me Jack."

"I'm not surprised he changed the story," Dawn said. "His little boy Albert was always a big disappointment to him. Cal wanted the next Arnold for a son. Instead, he gets this dope fiend with a passion for French poetry and drama school. I think he had somebody more like you in mind."

I let that one sail by me like the girl in her parachute and tried to imagine Cal discussing the subtleties of Baudelaire and Voltaire while smoking a Dutch Masters cigar and sipping a Jack and Coke. It was not an easy vision to conjure.

"The last time I was down here," Dawn said, "you were up in New York." Do you still have family up there?"

"No, it's just me now. I may not be the last of the Mohicans, but there's not too many ahead of me. I can tell you that."

"I'm going to play some music," Dawn said. "Anything you want to hear?"

"Anything with words you can actually understand."

I took a sip of beer and studied Dawn Belkin's backsides as she leaned against the jukebox, reading the list of songs, brushing her bangs back, finally sliding a couple of dollars into the machine then punching in her musical selections. You can tell a lot about a person by the songs they buy, and I waited to hear her picks. The first song was Marvin Gaye's "What's Going On." It was a good song and an even better question. When Dawn returned to her seat, I slid the promo card from the strip club across the bar to her. She looked it over then handed it back to me.

"No thanks. "I've already got a job."

"I found that at Cal's house," I said. "It was in the kitchen next to the sink. Whoever cleaned the place out did a hell of a job. I almost missed it."

"You think Cal was a customer there?"

"Cal always did have a bit of a sweet tooth when it came to the ladies. I'm sure you must have heard that before. But there's something else. The name stamped on the card, Raul Ochoa. He's a personal trainer at your grandfather's gym, or at least he was the last time I saw him. The new girl Candy at the gym told me he had quit, but she seemed a bit touchy when I brought it up."

"You think this Raul knows something?"

"Raul was making good money at your grandfather's gym. It's hard for me to believe he would leave it for a job working at a strip club."

I knew where Raul lived but first I wanted to check out the records on the sale of Cal's house and business, so we took a drive downtown to City Hall. We passed through a metal detector and were directed up to the sixth floor to a large office with slowly whirling ceiling fans and a busted AC and took a number and waited our turn with about fifty other disgruntled looking people. There were two clerks on duty behind the desk. One moved like a sleepwalker, disappearing into the back room for such extended periods of time that on several occasions I thought I might be at the post office. The other clerk was very chatty and very friendly and so cheerful and animated that it was hard to get mad at him. It was clear that his job was interfering with his social life, but he was the kind of guy you invite to parties even if you don't like him just because he'd keep things from getting too dull.

Ten minutes after they called our number we had answers to at least two of our questions. The house had been sold a week ago to a man named Jerry Bock of Miami Beach for $596,000, but the clerk, the happy one, pointed out something strange in the purchase.

"Your grandfather's house was sold with what we call a quick claim deed," the clerk said. "That's a bit odd in a situation like this."

"What's strange about it?" I asked.

"Is Mr. Bock a close relative of your family," the clerk asked.

"Never heard of him," Dawn replied. "Why do you ask?"

"Because a quick claim deed is usually used say, between a husband and wife who are getting a divorce. Something like that. Let's say the guy has to turn over the house to his wife. Both parties know the place, and there's no need for an inspection or a waiting period. You see what I'm saying? With a QCD, the husband just signs on the dotted line and the house or whatever goes to the wife, no muss, no fuss. It's a lot cheaper and you don't need a lawyer. But it's not usually used between strangers. Of course, it's perfectly legal. It's just a bit fast for most people to take a chance on is all I'm saying."

"Is there an address for this Jerry Bock fellow?" I asked.

"Why?" the clerk asked. "Is there something wrong?"

"You know how it is when they get older," Dawn said. "Sometimes they rush into things. We just need to check to make sure everything is kosher."

"No problem," the clerk said. "I understand completely. Let me get that for you."

As for Cal's gym: again, according to the records, it had been sold on the first of March to the Phoenix Corporation, an international fitness consulting firm with offices in New York, London, Dubai, Moscow and Miami. The clerk assured me that the purchase was completely legitimate, that all fees, insurance, titles, inspections and requisite licenses had been either been dutifully acquired or applied for by the company. There was even a brand new certificate of occupancy. It had been issued in the name of one Mr. Vincent Fernandez who was listed as the CEO.

It was close to four in the afternoon when we left City Hall and, as usual, the courthouse steps were swarming with pigeons and lawyers, dashing up and down with their overstuffed briefcases. The wind was blowing in from the west, and I thought it might rain. I bought a hot dog with mustard and sauerkraut from a vendor on the corner not far from where the chariot was parked and ate it while we walked. Cal's granddaughter watched me with obvious disapproval.

"I thought you were supposed to be into health and fitness," she said. "Those things are horrible for you."

"That's what you think. This hot dog represents a complete meal. "The frank is my protein source, not the best, a little high in fat and nitrates and mystery meat but not bad in a pinch. The bun? That's my carbohydrate. The sauerkraut's cabbage; it's got a lot of roughage and vitamin C."

"What about the mustard?"

"The mustard I'm not sure about," I said. "I'll have to look it up."

"This man who bought Cal's house," Dawn said. "Jerry Bock. Don't you think we should talk to him?"

"That address the guy gave is up in Hollywood. It's too late to drive up there today. We can do it tomorrow."

"Why not call him first? Get his number from information and give him a call, see what he has to say."

"No," I said. "It's better if we catch him off guard. If we call ahead, it'll give him too much time to get his story straight. Better if we sneak up on him."

"I keep forgetting you used to be a cop," Dawn said. "You still think like one."

"The problem is so does Vince Fernandez. I'll have to be very careful. If he finds out I'm asking too many questions about your grandfather, people will wonder what happened to me."

"How well do you know Fernandez?" Dawn asked.

"I knew him when we both on the job. He always claimed we were friends, but I was never too sure if that was the right word to describe it."

"How would you describe it then?"

"When I was a rookie Vince was the big shot in the precinct everybody hated and looked up to at the same time. An ego the size of Mount Rushmore. Very good athlete too. Every year the cops and firemen have a charity football game. Vince played both ways, offense and defense. They had a bodybuilding contest and he won that too. He was a good cop too. Some people thought he was too reckless, but when Vince kicked in a door, it stayed kicked in. I remember once this apartment house was on fire. The fire trucks were stuck in traffic and the roof was falling down. Flames and smoke everywhere. Guess who runs into the fire and pull this little black girl out? Everybody said it was the steroids that made him do it, but I never thought that was it."

"So what you're saying is that you admired him? Is that it?"

"To a point, yes."

"When he ran into that fire," Dawn asked, "where were you?"

"Right behind him."

"Does that mean you're on steroids too?"

"I am a steroid. I don't have to take them."

"Why did you quit the police force?" Dawn asked.

"Cal never told you?"

"If he did, then I don't remember."

"You would have remembered if he told you."

"Maybe he didn't think it was any of my business. Maybe he thought one day you'd tell me yourself—if you felt like it."

"About five years ago, Fernandez, me and another cop were on a stakeout outside the projects. We got the call to go in. I took one staircase and Vince took the other. We didn't know it at the time, but there was an off-duty cop living in the building. A neighbor had banged on his door that somebody was getting mugged in the staircase. Like I said, nobody knew anything about that. The cop—his name was Ed Henry—didn't know about us either. He comes charging down the staircase, gun drawn. It's completely dark because his lovely neighbors had stolen all of the light bulbs. He sees my gun and I see his. Ed fired first. The bullet grazed my cheek. You see this scar? That's where it came from. Anyway, I dropped to one knee and fired. I hit him right in the center of the forehead."

"So they fired you?" Dawn said. "Is that it?"

"They didn't fire me. I quit."

"But it was an accident."

"That's right, and, as they always say on TV, I was cleared of any wrongdoing, but Ed was black and I was not, and that muddied the whole thing up. You know what everybody was thinking? If Ed had been white, would I have shot him? The fact that he had fired first got buried under all the suspicion. Besides, compared to being dead, this little scar on the side of my face didn't count for much."

"But you said it was dark in the staircase. I don't see what black and white had to do with it."

"It had nothing to with it. In the dark, everybody's the same color. Neither of us could see worth a shit, but it got turned into a black and white thing for reasons that go way back long before either Ed or I joined the force. Me killing Ed brought up a lot of old stuff that had nothing to do with either of us, and I got turned into a symbol of something I was never a part of to begin with. But that's the way it goes sometimes. There's nothing you can do about it."

"So it was your decision. You didn't have to quit the force?" Dawn asked.

"Ed had a wife and kid. I had to do something. I couldn't just go to work, punch in, and act like nothing had happened."

"So you went into exile. What made you pick Miami?"

"Siberia doesn't' have cable, so I came down here."

Neither of us spoke for a while. The girl in the parachute sailed by again, this time exit stage right, and the music on the jukebox changed to a song from a band I had never heard before.

I asked Dawn who it was.

"That's my band," she said. "It's a cut off our first album."

"Is that you singing?"

"Do you like it?"

"You have a nice voice."

"That's like saying I have a nice personality."

"No, it's like saying you can sing. There's no bubblegum in your voice. If I heard it again, I'd know it was you without asking. There's a lot of feeling in it."

"You know, Cal always talked a lot about you," Dawn said. "He even mentioned you in his letters. I think he was trying to get me interested enough to come down here to have a look at you for myself."

"Well," I said. "Here I am. What do you make of me?"

"I don't know. You seem durable enough. It would take a strong wind to blow you away."

"We'll find out soon enough."

"I bet you're a Sagittarius. What's your sign?"

"Neon."

"Cal never really approved of any of my boyfriends. I tended to go for chain smokers with bad posture and artistic personalities."

"What about now?"

"Now?" Dawn said. "Now all I want to do is find my grandfather." She stood up and signaled for the check.

"This one's on me," Dawn said. "I'm going upstairs to take a nap. Give me a call when it gets dark, and we'll go and have ourselves a real drink at a real bar."

I sat my durable self down behind the wheel of the Chariot and thought about how Raul Ochoa's name had been so neatly stamped in pretty purple ink on the Emperor's Club's promo card I had found over at Cal's place. I wanted to have a talk with him, but first I made a pit stop at my apartment over at the Lancaster Arms. The first thing I did was call all my clients to let them know I was back in town. Then I checked my email. Not much to see there, except the usual spam. According to this one guy from Nigeria, it was my lucky day. Circumstances beyond his control were forcing him to deposit three million dollars into my bank account. All I had to do was give him the routing number to my checking account so he could send the money on its way.

After I was done trolling through the mail, I typed the name Kaminski Realty into the browser to see what came up. That was the name on Marina Gero's SUV. There was the usual South Florida broker's website, with plenty of pictures of condos and well groomed homes, most of them with ocean front views and beautiful young couples lounging around, looking luxurious. Kaminski Realty specialized in condos and homes starting at five hundred grand and to hell with you if you couldn't cut it. If you were lucky, your half million would get you a view of a Walmart parking lot and a big green dumpster at the far end, but then, what could you realistically expect for chump change?

I scrolled through the site's list of real estate agents, who were listed according to sale's performance. Sure enough, Marina's name was right there at the top of the list. There was even a sexy looking picture of her that showed some nice cleavage and a smile that looked as natural as a gold Christmas tree in Macy's window. Beneath the picture were Marina's sale's figures for the previous year. They were high enough to make me look twice. Based on her numbers, it appeared that for the second time in my life I had chosen the wrong business, because even with just the three percent standard commission per sale, Ms Gero was pulling in over three hundred grand a year. I shut the computer down and headed out. I still intended to talk to Raul Ochoa, but I had decided I needed to make another stop along the way. I didn't necessarily like asking for help from certain sources, but the smell I'd caught rising off of this mess suggested I might be able to use it.

5

It had been two years since I had last seen Special Agent Miles Hackbart, and now, looking at him across his desk at FBI headquarters, I realized just how little I had missed him. The feeling appeared to be mutual, and I understood why. Once upon a time, I had done a favor for a friend, or at least for someone I had once thought of as a friend. In doing so, though not intentionally on my part, I had come close to almost single-handedly sinking an investigation very dear to Hackbart's heart. Not only that, I had pretty much gotten away with it, and we both knew it. It wasn't hard to understand why Agent Hackbart wasn't too happy to see me. In fact, I'd been surprised when took my call and agreed to see me.

He listened patiently while I told him the story of Cal's disappearance, his Cadillac, the rapid fire sale of the house, and the mysterious takeover of his gym. I told him about Vince Fernandez and about the steroid trafficking in the gym. It took me all of twenty minutes to weave it all together into something the FBI might be inclined to look at, but I had to admit that it didn't look good. Hackbart sat across from me with a face as expressionless as an empty parking lot, and when I finished my spiel, he leaned back in his chair, stretched his arms high above his head and yawned.

"Well, that's quite a story you have there, Vaughn," he said. "Why'd you bring it to me?"

I glanced around the cinderblock office. No pictures on the walls, a hairline crack zigzagging the length of one side of side of the room. The kind of place that would turn Dale Carnegie sullen. "I was under the impression you still worked for the FBI."

"You know, if it was up to me, you would just about now be coming up for your first parole hearing."

"So you're not interested. Is that what you're telling me?"

"I don't know. From the Bureau's point of view, there doesn't seem to be much in it. I mean, come on, where's the beef? Your old cop pal is selling 'roids out of a gym—I'm surprised you're not in on it." When he saw the look on my face, he raised an eyebrow. "So take it to the DEA. Maybe they'll set up a sting operation."

"What about Cal Belkin?" I said. "The Cadillac in the canal. What about that?"

"A geezer cashes in his chips and then has a traffic accident? Show me the connection to the rest of it."

"That's what I just spent the last thirty minutes trying to do."

Hackbart waved his hand. "This is all local stuff. Why not just take it to the local cops?"

"The local cops are in Fernandez's pocket. Not all of them, but enough to make going to them for help a bad idea. Look, the Russian mob is involved, Miles, that's pretty clear. Who knows everything that's going on? This could be a big deal. "

Hackbart looked at his watch, looked down, put his right index finger on his chin and tilted his head to one side in an obvious attempt to make me think he was taking what I had told him seriously. Then he placed both hands flat on his desk and raised himself up.

"All right," he said. "I'll do this. I'll pass it upstairs to my boss, see what he says. Also, I have a friend and at the FDLE. I'll give him a call too. That's the best I can do. In the meantime, stay away from it. Everything you touch turns to shit, so I suggest you leave it alone until I get back to you. Now, if you don't mind, I've got a meeting to get to. Excuse me if I don't shake your hand. To me, you're never been anything but a pain in the ass, so don't take it personally."

"Tell me something, Hackbart. How close are you to retirement?"

"Why?"

"Because twenty years ago you wouldn't have let pettiness get in the way of doing your job. That's why."

"You know, Vaughn," Hackbart said. "I just remembered something. There's still a sealed indictment with your name on it. A couple of phone calls might change that. Isn't that funny?"

"Think about it. You could go out with a bang instead of a whimper."

"Right. Now get out of my office. If I get anything, I'll be in touch, but don't waste your life sitting by the phone. We're pretty busy down here."

I stood up slowly. I was heavy with the deserted feeling of a kid who has gotten himself lost in a crowded amusement park and finds surrounded by thousands of strangers, all of them walking about, holding hands, laughing and having a grand time. To them he's invisible, a character in another story. If you've ever been that kid, you know there's no lonelier feeling of being in the midst of strangers who, while they might not mean you any harm, won't do you any good either.

Maybe he saw something of that in my face as I stood up. I stopped when I got to the door. When I turned around, Hackbart was still watching me with those small, intensely feral gray eyes of his. They were the eyes of a man who had spent the last twenty-five years of his life looking for people, looking for mad men and monsters and serial killers, but also looking for lost children and for those who, like my friend Calvin Belkin, had gone missing. They were not good eyes; they were not bad eyes; they were simply the eyes of a man who, if he decides to set off on your trail, would keep coming and coming, and because of that and other things, I could be sorry that he and I would probably never find a way to be friends.

"Look," Hackbart said. "I didn't mean it about the indictment. You understand me? I may not like you but I wouldn't do something like that."

"I know you wouldn't."

I looked down the hall toward the open bullpen and listened to the rush and hubbub of a workplace filled with people, people with a purpose. It had the fizz and whir of a newsroom, but with cops instead of journalists. I turned back to Hackbart. It seemed to me that some of the steel brush resentment I had sensed in him when I had first arrived had diminished somewhat, though not, of course, completely.

"Enjoy these last few months, Hackbart," I said. "All of this"—I waved my hand around like Merlin weaving a spell—"all of this will be hard to replace, especially the people, even the ones you don't like. Take it from me. I know what I'm talking about."

Hackbart's frown deepened again, but this time for another reason. He looked at me and nodded. It was the first thing we had agreed on since I had walked in on him half-hour ago.

"I know," Hackbart growled. "I know. I miss it already and I'm still here. Now do me a favor get the hell out of my office and don't get yourself killed before you hear from me."

A few minutes later, I was headed up I-95, bound for Raul Ochoa's house in Hialeah. Driving west on Seventy-Ninth Street put me in a somber mood, the kind that leaves you feeling that there' no hope for humanity and that most of life is just a matter of lasting until happy hour. There may be more depressing streets in Miami than Seventy-Ninth Street, other streets more barren of beauty and hope, but if there are, I've yet to drive them.

The light changed and I entered once again the narrow canyon of used car dealerships wrapped in barbed wire and false promises, of pawn shops full of stolen watches and payday desperation. It would be like this for at least another two miles before the street would widen again. As the traffic slowed, I had plenty of time to take in the lack of scenery. When I passed Fourth Avenue, I was reminded once again that a friend of mine had recently gone out of business. There was a big for rent sign on the window and some kind of notice taped against the window.

I had warned Haitian Eddie about naming the place *Casket Depot* in the first place, but he'd insisted. Still, it's never pleasant to see a small business close its doors for good, and Eddie still has a cab to feed to his wife and son with, but let's face it, when it comes to coffins, no one can compete with Costco's prices.

But nothing lasts forever -- not even the concrete misery of Seventy-Ninth Street. Once I was headed north again, the streets grew wider if not more beautiful. As usually happens whenever I drive in Hialeah, I got lost a few times and had to ask for directions, but it wasn't long before I found Ochoa's house. It was in the middle of a block full of single family homes with barred windows and neatly clipped front yards and kids playing in the streets and the smell of good home cooked comidas, savory and inviting in the humid air.

A tall black rooster with a blood red coxcomb was standing in the middle of the street when I pulled up to the curb in front of the Ochoa residence. He didn't seem too impressed when a battered Chevy pickup swung around the corner and headed right for him at a high rate of speed. The truck came to a stop a few feet in front of the rooster. The driver banged on the side of his truck and leaned on his horn until the rooster got the message and ducked between two parked cars. The truck took off down the street, shedding Cuban music and black exhaust fumes as it headed in a hurry for the bright lights of Forty-Seventh Street.

The woman who answered the door was about eighty years old with short white hair brushed straight back over her head without fanfare or attempt at style. She had reached the age when vanity has retreated never to return. She opened first the wooden door, then the screen door but not the door made of shiny black steel bars. The house behind her smelled so good I was tempted to ask what was for dinner and could I get some of it to go, but it would not have mattered. She didn't speak English, though she did nod when I mentioned Raul's name. I told her in my pathetic Spanish that I was his friend and was looking for him. This time she shook her head as though denying my claim. Something moved in the darkness behind her and a man came forward out of the shadows and pointed a small, silver plated gun at the center of my face.

I smiled as smile you must on such occasions when you are caught off guard, unarmed, not expecting any trouble, and someone is pointing a gun at you. I thought about raising my hands but decided that for now, no move was the right move.

"I was looking for Raul," I said.

"What?" the man asked.

The woman said something in Spanish and stepped to one side. She began nervously wiping her hands with the dish towel she was holding. She looked worried. I shared her concern.

"I'm a friend of Raul's," I said.

"Then how come I never saw you before?" he said.

"I didn't know you were looking for me."

"Where do you know Raul from?"

"I used work with him at the gym, the one over in Miami Shores," I said.

He took a step to one side and waved me inside with the barrel of the gun.

"Come inside, and if you move, motherfucker, I'm going to shoot your ass completely off."

He stepped back and let me walk by him into a small living room with the claustrophobic feel of too much furniture, too many knickknacks and too many photographs and pictures on the wall. He pointed at a well-worn recliner and told me to sit down, which I did. My host then sat down on other side of the coffee table in another recliner and leaned back with the gun still pointed at me. Neither of us said anything as we sat watching each other. He told his mother that it was okay and to go back to her cooking.

The old woman mumbled something I didn't catch and gave me a mournful look before returning to the kitchen.

"What do you want with Raul?" he asked.

"You're his brother?"

"Don't worry about who I am. Worry about who you are."

"Listen to me okay? My name is Jack. Jack Vaughn. I work at the gym with Raul. I'm a friend of his. Don't tell me he never mentioned my name"

"Sure he did. He said you were a stupid ass cop from New York who thought he was funny."

"Did he say anything else about? Maybe something a little more positive?"

"Yea, he said you were a motherfucker."

"Look," I said. "This isn't going too well. Maybe I should just come back another time when Raul is here."

The man straightened his arm, extending the gun a little further in my direction. He held the gun sideways like the punks do. Who they learn that crap from, I do not know, but from that range, he could have hit me holding the gun with his feet.

"You ain't going any fucking place, homey. You just sit there till I make this call."

"I hope you have the safety on that gun," I said. "They've been known to go off accidentally."

"Trust me. If this baby goes off, it ain't going to be by no accident."

He flipped open his phone and made the call. His mother carried out two tiny cups of Cuban coffee and a silver rimmed plate of little pastries dusted in white sugar and set them down in front of us. She didn't seem to understand that this was a hostage situation and not a tea party. The man with the gun finished his call and sat back in his recliner."

"Now we wait," he said.

"Who are we waiting for?" I asked.

"We're waiting for Pit."

"Brad Pitt'?"

"You know something? Maybe I should just shoot you right here. What do you think about that?"

"I say we wait."

"Then shut the fuck up and eat your cookies."

I took a sip of the high-octane coffee and nibbled on one of the pastries.

"These are good," I said. "Did the lady make them?"

"Damned straight she did."

"You didn't tell me your name."

"Nestor. You like soccer?"

"Not particularly."

"Fuck you then." He reached for the remote and switched on the television, the most modern appliance in the house and by far the largest—one of those new plasma jobs with colors so bright you are spoiled for life. The giant TV glowed like a gift from the future. Nestor watched me with one eye and the soccer game between Honduras and Colombia with the other.

Five minutes later there was a knock at the door and a short man with glistening black hair and a thick gold chain around his neck walked in with a scowl on his face. He and my captor spoke to one another in rapid fire Spanish for a few moments; then the man with shiny black hair reached under his red silk shirt and produced a small revolver, which he pointed at me by way of introduction. He made me stand up whereupon Nestor secured my hands with some of those plastic ties the cops use instead of handcuffs. I was still operating under the belief that once they spoke to Raul the whole matter would be cleared up, so I wasn't greatly worried, but with my hands tied and another gun to think about, I wasn't as sure as I had been,

"You must be Mr. Pit," I said. "I'm a friend of Raul's. I need to talk to him."

"You're the cop, right?" Mr. Pit said. "From New York?"

"Not anymore. I'm retired."

Mr. Pit shook his head

"No," he said definitively. "Don't give me that shit.

You're working undercover. You're with those fucking Russians, the ones who threatened my brother."

"Then why would I come here? That would be stupid"

"I agree."

Mr. Pit smiled, wiped his hands on his shirt, and slapped me across the mouth. I saw it coming and got my head turned away but not quite enough. I tasted blood pooling along my gum line.

They walked me out the back door where an old white van was waiting. I thought about making a run for it but decided against it when I felt the tip of a gun barrel in my back urging me toward the rear doors. The floor of the van was streaked with blood and guts and there was a crate of chickens up against the front of the cabin. I hesitated for a second out of sheer disgust as the stench of rotten and unrefrigerated meat roared out of the truck the moment the doors were thrown open. Mr. Pit put the gun against my temple and laughed as I stepped up into the van and slipped onto a metal floor made slick and treacherous with blood and entrails. Then they locked the doors behind me.

We drove long enough for me to get used to the smell—perhaps ten or fifteen minutes. Then the doors opened, and I found myself at the back of a giant warehouse with high concrete prison-like walls that were surrounded by an iron gate topped off by whorls of barbed wire. Three pit bulls and a giant Rottweiler came running around the side of the building at full speed then slowed as Mr. Pit barked something that scattered them to either side of us.

The backdoors of the warehouse were wide open, and there was a row of trucks and cars parked to one side and a wide steel ramp that led up to the doors and a set of metal rollers stacked with crates of chickens lined up and ready to be loaded into the trucks. As I was being led up the steps to the side of the ramp, a small white goat came running out through doors and bolted across the lot. He was quickly followed by a skinny, bare-chested black man who chased the goat around the yard like a character in an old Warner Brothers cartoon until he finally recaptured his prize and carried it back inside. It was then that I realized that I had been brought to a slaughterhouse.

They walked me into a warehouse filled with people, most of them men, standing in groups of five and ten. They were huddled around things I could hear but not see. The place smelled like a larger version of the van and the air was filled with the squeals of pigs and the sounds of chickens being badly handled and of sheep and goats bleating at the top of their lungs. We walked through that bedlam until we reached a large fenced-in area covered with straw where five or six pigs were busy sifting through their own waste and whatever else was buried under the straw. No one seemed surprised to see me, though a few did glance down at my bound hands. One of those who did grinned widely then drew his finger across his throat as we passed him.

Mr. Pit asked an old bare-chested man with a cigar jutting out of the corner of his mouth where Raul was. The man pointed across the room to where a crowd of men were standing in a large circle. Some of the men saw us coming, and a murmur passed quickly amongst them as we approached. As they moved aside, I saw Raul Ochoa standing over a long wooden crate, his torso bare and covered with blood. In his right hand he held a large gray hammer with a single spike sticking out of the business end. It was a hammer designed with a single purpose: to bash in the skulls of pigs.

As we got closer to the circle that had formed around him, I could see that there was a big pig in the crate. It must have weighed at least three hundred pounds. There was barely enough room for him to move as he thrashed from side to side with so much force I was sure he would break it apart. The only part of the crate that was open from above was the section at the front where I could see his massive head and snout thrusting up and down and from side to side as it tried to free itself from the rope tied around its neck. The men nodded at Mr. Pit as he and walked up and began speaking to Raul. Raul looked over the heads of the men standing below him and scanned the crowd until found me standing there. He nodded and pointed his finger, first at the crated pig at his feet and then at me.

It occurred to me then that I had been doing some exaggerating when I told Nestor and Mr. Pit that Raul and I were friends. In fact, we rarely spoke to one another except to say hello and so long to one another in one of those vague attempts at camaraderie between coworkers that never grows into anything except a few easy low-maintenance gestures and a sense of familiarity that serves to keep things fairly civil between people who otherwise have absolutely nothing to say to one another.

That had been pretty much the extent of Raul's and my relationship, that and the fact that we both worked at Cal's Gym. Seeing him standing there covered in blood, staring me from across the bedlam of the slaughterhouse over the back of the doomed hog reminded me of that fact in a manner that wasn't comforting. As I watched, Raul closed his eyes and sketched the sign of the cross over his bloody chest, his lips moving in silent prayer. Then he raised the hammer over his head and brought it down with all his might onto the head of the pig trapped in the crate beneath him.

The pig let out a squeal of such terror and pain it was hard to believe it hadn't come from a human being. But it was more than pain. It was fear and knowledge and perhaps something that sounded like self-pity. Raul hit the pig twice more before it dropped. There was no more screaming after the first blow, which I was grateful for. The crowd cheered and chugged their beers as Raul left the circle, still holding the bloody maul in his hand. He didn't seem at all happy to see me.

"What the fuck are you doing here, Vaughn?" Raul said. "This ain't your side of town."

I lifted my wrists so he could see that they were tied. "Believe me," I said. "It wasn't my idea. I stopped by your house to talk to you, and your two friends here grabbed me."

Raul studied me with small, suspicious eyes. "You shouldn't have come here, man," he said. "This is the last place you should have come. Here, it's all about knives and hammers and pistols. Look around, Jack; all these people know me. All these people are my friends. Even your boy Fernandez and his Russian crew wouldn't come here. But here you are looking stupid. Why? What you want? To get sliced up?"

It was time to talk fast. I told him about Cal's car and my trip to the gym and the sidebar visit to his house in Miami Shores. When I was done, Raul fell quiet for a moment then spat on the sawdust covered floor and stuck his hammer into the dirty leather sheath he wore on his belt.

"Why didn't your friend at the gym tell you where the old man is?" Raul said. "He said you and him were practically married up in New York."

"If I could get it from Fernandez why would I be in this shit hole asking you?"

"Fernandez said you and him were friends," Raul said. "You telling me he was lying when he said that? He told everybody you guys were buddy buddy and shit."

"We were friends like you and I are friends, Raul. We were both cops. We used to work together. Don't make it sound like Batman and Robin because that's not the way it was. I had no idea Fernandez was in Miami until this morning. I just want to know what happened to Cal. That's the only reason I'm here."

Raul stared down at the ground as though he was trying to read the swarm of red and white entrails on the floor. After a few moments of deep thinking, he looked up.

"Okay," Raul said. "I hear what you're saying. It's like when you're in a gang or some shit like that. You don't have to like everybody, but you wear the same colors and know all the same girls and people, but you don't got to be necessarily all that tight with each other. Is that what you're saying?"

"That's exactly what I'm saying," I said.

"In other words," Mr. Pit said. "You're saying that being a cop is like being in the Latin Kings or the Crips. Shit, man, maybe I should take the cop test. Get myself a police car with a red light on top; pull me over some bitches up on 441."

"I'd think twice before I said shit like that," Nestor said. "We got much better guns than the police do. Ain't that right, homeboy?"

"He's right," I said. "In New York, we don't even get automatics, just revolvers."

"That's because you guys shoot too many niggers up there," Mr. Pit said. "I saw how the cops in New York shot up this African dude just for reaching for his wallet. Shot the motherfucker something like eighty-five fucking times. I mean, they don't even shoot the fucking Hulk that much."

"That's not true," Raul said, shaking his head. "With the Hulk, they break out the tanks and atom bombs. Bullets don't mean shit to him. Ain't that right, Jack?"

"He's right," I said. "With the Hulk, you can't take too many chances."

"What about Uzis or A-Ks?" Nestor asked. "The cops in NYPD get any of those?"

"No," I said. "Nothing like that. Sometimes they give you a shotgun if there's a riot or something, but that's about it."

"What about flamethrowers?" Raul asked.

For a moment I thought he was kidding, but his face was so deadly serious. I knew better than to laugh.

"Too many people complained," I told him. "We had to give them back."

"Man, that shit is unconstitutional!" Mr. Pit said. "Somebody better write a letter! No wonder you quit."

"Yea," Raul said. "Now you can have all the guns you want. Down here, you can even get yourself a bazooka if you want to. My cousin's girlfriend got him one last year for Christmas."

"I know it's none of my business," I said. "But why would your cousin need a bazooka?"

"I'm not sure," Raul said. "I think he had some problems with one of his neighbors playing loud music or something. Either that or it was family shit.

The guns and gangs comedy hour went on for awhile longer; then Nestor and Mr. Pit excused themselves so they could go and watch the dead pig get turned into pork chops. Raul lit a cigarette, and we walked outside to talk things over. The way he dragged on his Marlboro made me think he was nervous about something that had nothing to do with pig killing.

"I don't know if I should even be talking to you," he said. "You and me ain't exactly Batman and Robin either you know. For all I know, you might head right back to Fernandez with whatever I say."

"Come on, Raul," I said. "What the hell are you doing in this godforsaken place?" You were pulling in close to two grand a week at Cal's place. Now you're over here in Hialeah, bashing pigs over the head with a hammer. What's going on with you, man?"

A tractor-trailer rumbled through the gates of the slaughterhouse and blew its air horn loud enough to make Raul jump. There was a loud rumbling sound as the metal door was lifted, and two men in white coats pulled a rack laded with sides of beef out onto the loading dock. Raul stubbed out his cigarette with a blood soaked boot and immediately lit another. He looked at me like a man on the verge of crossing a very wide and dangerous street, a street without stoplights or speed limit.

"I don't want you talking about this shit to anyone, okay? They know where I live. They know where my family lives. You understand that?"

"Don't worry; I'm not going to say anything. But you know why I'm here though, right?"

"You want to know what happened to the old man."

"That's right, and if you know and you tell me, then no matter what happens, no one will ever know I got it from you. I just want to know where he is, that's all, nothing else."

"Okay. There's a strip club up in Hallandale called the Emperor's Club. I used go to with my homeys sometimes. About six months ago, the place got bought out by some Russians from up your way in New York. Fernandez was with them. Right away,

I could see he was pretty tight with the big boss. They all use to sit around at a big table with their gold chains, drinking vodka like the fucking Godfather and shit. Fernandez seen I was into bodybuilding so we got to talking. He offered me a job promoting the club. All I had to do was hand out cards with my name on them, and I'd get a kickback every time someone turned them in at the door. Then Fernandez tells me that soon he's going to be down here permanent and that he wants to buy some gyms for his boss. So I tell him about Cal. I tell him that Cal's kind of old and maybe he might want to retire soon, so maybe he should check it out. So about a week later, Fernandez and these Russian dudes come walking into the gym like they own the place. They're going around checking out the equipment, looking at the walls and measuring shit with a tape when all of sudden Cal shows up and asks them what the fuck they were doing. They just laughed at him, so Cal goes into his office, and when he comes out, he's got that shotgun of his and they leave real fast. I thought it was kind of funny, but then about a week later I come back from Tampa, and the gym is closed, and there's a chain on the front door. Then I come back a week after that, and Fernandez is there and they're changing everything, bringing in all this new equipment."

"And Cal was gone?"

"Gone and nowhere to be seen," Raul said. "I called his house phone and nobody answered, so that night I drive over to his crib in Miami Shores and sure enough that big red Caddy of his is parked right out front. I see that, and I'm thinking to myself, Cal's at home, right? I'm just to get out of my car, when the front door opens and out comes Cal with a couple of bouncers from he Emperor's Club. One of the guys got into the back seat with Cal while the other guy drove."

"How did Cal look?" I asked.

"He looked old."

"He's eighty-two," I said. "How do you want him to look?"

"I didn't mean that," Raul. "What I'm saying is that Cal

looked confused, like he didn't know where he was going. The two Russians had to help him down the steps. And there was something else that bugged me out. Cal was wearing this old looking sports jacket and a regular shirt with a collar. I mean, come on, Jack. When did you ever see Cal dressed like that before? All he wears is workout clothes. He had regular shoes on too. Funny thing was, nothing matched. It like he just threw the shit on without looking."

"Were his hands free or were they tied."

"No," Raul said. "They weren't tied. But I noticed that he kept his hands in his pockets like he was cold or something."

"What did you do?"

"I followed them. They drove up north. I tried to be careful, but they must have spotted me, because the driver made a turn down a dead end street and I made the dumb ass mistake of following him. When I tried to back out, another car blocked me in from behind. I threw my truck into reverse and went up on the sidewalk between two trees. Then I heard all this shooting. I think they had machine guns because they blew my back window out. I mean, it just popped apart. Man, that was some fucking bad ass driving I did that night. I tell you."

"Are you sure they know it was you?"

"Definitely. Fernandez called me the next day. He said if I opened my mouth, they'd kill me and everybody I knew."

"Let me ask you something. You still seeing that little Honduran girl you were going out with?" I asked. "What was her name?"

"Sonia. Yea, I'm still with her. We're getting married next June. Why?"

"I don't mean to scare you," I said. "But you might want think about moving somewhere else, at least for a while."

"Why? As long as I keep my mouth shut, I got nothing to be afraid of, right?"

"Let me put it to you this way. The only reason they haven't come after you is that Vince Fernandez hasn't pushed for it. But he's not the big boss. That's the one you have to worry about. Whoever he is, I can tell you this much. He didn't get to be king by leaving loose ends, and that's what you are, Raul, a loose end on steroids. Someday, it might get back to the man on top that Fernandez let you walk away with what you know. When that happens, it won't be up to Vince anymore. You've been quiet, so maybe, whoever he is, he decides to forget it. But then again, maybe not. Let's say he's at the club one night, drinking shots and snorting lines of coke through a hundred dollar bill like it's the Alaskan pipeline. Only this time he gets paranoid and your name pops up in his head, and he gets to thinking that it doesn't make sense to take any chances, so he makes a phone call. That's all it will take, Raul—just one little phone call."

Raul looked down at the swirls of blood and guts and shit smeared across the floor like a man searching for his future. The air around us smelled so loudly of shit and blood and death that I could not only smell it, I could taste it and hear it as well. You want to know the real price of meat, spend some time in a slaughterhouse; that's my advice. It's enough to make an atheist say grace.

"You think I should leave Miami then?" he asked.

"You told me you had family up in Tampa," I said. "If I were you, I'd think about paying them a visit."

Raul nodded. "Yea," he said. "That's right. I do. My sister lives up there. Her and her husband, they got a house on the Hillsborough River. I go fishing with them sometimes."

"Maybe you could go and stay with them for a while. Take Sonia with you, at least for a while."

"You're trying to scare me, man."

"That's right. I am."

"What about you?" Raul asked. "What are you going to do?"

"Cal's a friend of mine," I said. "You know how it is."

"You ain't a cop no more, Jack," he said. "And this ain't New York where you had a gun and backup. Down here, you're all by yourself."

"You're saying I should just forget about it then. Let it ride."

"The way I see it, Dawg, you can either deal yourself in and make yourself some big time money with Fernandez and his crew, or you can deal yourself out and go on with your business somewhere else. If there's a third way to play it with those guys, I sure as hell can't see it."

I was about to head back to the Lancaster Arms when I remembered what Dawn Belkin had said about buying her a real drink, so I headed for the Holiday Inn instead. When the desk clerk tried her room and there was no answer, I walked outside past the tiki bar where a bored looking trio of calypso singers with a snare drum was playing for a pair of Japanese businessmen in Hawaiian shirts. Dawn was sitting at a table under an umbrella next to the pool reading a magazine. Her long legs, already bronzed, were stretched out in front of her and crossed at the ankle. She saw me coming and waved. I ordered a beer and told her about my little adventure at the slaughterhouse.

"Well," Dawn said. "At least we know Cal was still alive the night they ditched his car."

"From Raul's description of things," I said. "It sounds as though he might have been drugged. They took a big risk taking him to the bank though. If anyone there had gotten suspicious, the whole thing could have blown up in their faces. The question is: will they try it again? Two days from now, another one of your grandfather's CDs matures. That means they'll have to bring your grandfather to the bank again to cash it out. After that, he'll be expendable."

"All right," Dawn said. "In that case, all we have to do is call the police and tell them the whole story. They can have some waiting at the bank. When the kidnappers show up with Cal, they can grab them."

"That's sounds like a great plan," I said. "And if this were TV or the movies, I'm sure it would work. Unfortunately, however, this is real life, and things don't work that way."

"Then how do they work?"

"A lot more slowly. It's a big shaggy story with a dozen moving parts. The cops won't like that, especially a little department like the one in Miami Shores. Another thing they won't like is the fact that the trail is over a month cold. Be that as it may, they'll assign an overworked detective to work the case. He'll start making phone calls. The first one will be to Fernandez. Once he does that, Cal is dead."

"You don't have a very high opinion of the police, do you?"

"On the contrary, I have a very high opinion of them," I said. "But this thing is a lot bigger than your grandfather. It's big and it's going to get even bigger. Vince Fernandez didn't come down here to Miami just to grab Cal for his house and business. That's just a little sidebar to the main action—whatever the main action is. The local cops will call in the feds. Once they get hold of it—and trust me, they will—they'll want to build a case. They'll want to get a feel for the big picture and that will take time. Cal won't be the main focus of anything they come up with. If your grandfather turns up, he'll just one more piece of miscellaneous evidence."

"Let's say you're right. What do we do?"

"Our best chance is to be waiting at the bank when they show up with Cal on Wednesday. Naturally, I'll have a gun, but that won't really matter, because by the time I whip it out, you'll have already called the police. We'll make a scene. Once the shit hits the fan, whosever got your grandfather will have to back off fast if they want to stay out of jail."

"What happens if they don't show up at the bank on Wednesday?"

"Then we'll have nothing to lose by going to the cops."

"Because Cal will already be dead," Dawn said.

"Tell you what," I said. "Why don't we go have that drink I owe you? Maybe something else will come to me."

6

Mac's Club Deuce was, and still is, located at Fourteenth Street in South Beach, between Collins and Washington Avenue. It's a yellow brick box of a building that sits in the center of busy street with the stubborn authority of a small armory. The old school neon sign on the weathered façade looks like it belongs in a painting by Edward Hopper, and the place has been there so long that no one living on the beach under the age of fifty can remember when it wasn't there. The Deuce is owned, as you could guess, by a man named Mac. Mac is a 150 years old, and no living person has ever seen him smile.

There is no happy hour at Mac's Club Deuce. There are no buybacks either. They do not take credit cards. If you want a happy hour you must either go to another bar or bring your own happiness with you. If you want a buyback, you are in the wrong place. You could drink away the equity in your house and you would still not get a free drink at the Deuce. People who drink at the Deuce, hoping that the next drink will be free, are often found sleeping in the alley out back, financially ruined, alone and insane. The cash register looks to be about five days older than water. As for the men's room, I can only say this: I would not care for my children to know that I had been found dead there. On the plus side, at Club Deuce, you do not need reservations.

Above the window across from where we sat hung a black and white photograph of Humphrey Bogart in fedora and trench coat, standing against the silhouette of a Japanese flag with a cigarette butt pinched between his fingers like it was a joint of really good shit. On the other side of the bar, near the ceiling, the neon outline of a naked woman reclined above the mirror. The place was not yet crowded. Two construction workers in their safety helmets and sagging tool belts were shooting pool under a cone of light while a third struggled with a reluctant cigarette machine over in the corner. A man in a red dress sat drinking alone near the window with his wig lying stretched out on the bar next to him like a faithful pet.

"This place is the perfect dive," Dawn said. "You have good taste."

"A friend of mine works here," I said. "We have a certain mutual acquaintance in common I want to speak with him about."

A few moments later, Dennis O'Neal came out of the storeroom cradling a few cases of beer in his beefy arms and set them down on the counter. When I called his name, Denny stared at me from across the bar as if from the other side of a canyon. Finally, and with much effort, his mouth slid apart and a smile as weak as watered down tea. This was only the second time I had seen him since he had moved down here with his wife six or seven months ago, and he probably thought I had been avoiding him, which I was. Denny was a chronic complainer with a talent for unnecessary worrying that sometimes required medication. He had quit drinking a few years back, but sobriety had not made him a nicer person and had destroyed what little sense of humor he had. The unflattering truth is I had liked him a lot better when he was an alcoholic. As he walked toward me, I saw he still he had that strange little hitch in his step that made him jump every few feet, as though he had been hit by unexpected jolt of electricity. After the introductions, I asked him about his wife Delores, and his face fell like spring with a weight attached to it.

"She went back to Queens," he said. "She couldn't take the summers down here. Said it was too hot, the bitch."

There was a lot more to the story than the summer heat, but I didn't want to hear it, though if Dawn hadn't been with me, I'm sure he would have told me anyway.

"So how do you like it here?" I asked. "Mac treating you all right?"

"Yea, especially when I don't see him. Thanks for putting in a good word for me with him. We get a lot of fags in here for my taste, but the tips are good."

"I stopped by to tell you that Vince Fernandez is in town. I'd thought you'd want to know."

The corner of O'Neal's mouth twitched a bit as he glanced over at the man in the red dress, still sitting alone in the corner, nursing his drink and looking pensively off to the side.

"That's Dan," O'Neal said with a flick of his chin in the man's direction. "He just lost his job. That's why he looks so gloomy."

"What does he do?" Dawn asked.

"During the day, he's a plumber," Denny told us. "A good one too, if you ever need one. At night, it's a different story. Him taking off his wig like that is his way of telling me I need to turn up the AC, but the boss likes to save money, so he's out of luck. You said Fernandez was in town. What's he doing down here, taking a vacation or something?"

"He bought himself a gym," I said. Him and his partners. In fact, he bought the gym I used to work at. I went over there this morning and there he was: big as life and full of steroids."

"Did he ask about me?"

"He wanted to know if I knew where you were working. I guess you're home number is unlisted."

"What did you tell him?" O'Neal asked.

"What do you think I told him?"

"Did he believe you?"

"Probably not, but he didn't push it. He was kind of casual

about it. I guess he thinks he'll run into you eventually."

"I guess you're probably wondering why I asked you to keep it quiet about where I was," O'Neal said.

"I hate to break the news to you, Denny. But not that many people have asked."

"So, Vince bought himself another gym," O'Neal said. "Did he tell you what happened to the ones he owned in Brooklyn?"

"How many did he own?"

"He had three of them. They were doing pretty good too. He didn't tell you what happened?"

"We didn't talk that much about New York," I said.

"The government took them," O'Neal said with a grin. "Does the lady want another beer?"

"I'd rather have a screwdriver," Dawn said.

"A screwdriver it is then. I'll give you the good stuff on account of you're a friend of Jack's here. You one of his girls from the gym?"

"You make it sound like he has a harem," Dawn said.

"Why d the government take his gyms?" I asked.

"Money laundering," O'Neal said. "There seems to be some kind of law against it. You remember how Vince liked to moonlight. He took a job as a bodyguard for some Russian big shot out in Brighton Beach. The guy had a lot of enemies, a lot of enemies with guns. The way I heard it, Vince saved this guy's life, so the Russian helped set him up in the gym business."

"And they washed money through the gyms? What kind of money we talking about? Drugs?"

"Drugs, whores, cigarettes from North Carolina, Medicare scams, identity theft, you name it this guy was into it. The gyms were Vince's idea. Think about it. You open yourself up a health club and start selling memberships. There's no inventory and no invoices for the IRS to check. You're selling the same product over and over again to different people. You're selling time and space. And where do the new members come from? Anywhere and everywhere. The phone book; the obit column. Mailing lists. Anywhere you can think of. Hell, you can give away memberships just to fill the place up. Who's going to check to see if they really exist? And then there are all the other services like massages and tanning, and don't forget your thing, personal training. And of course there's always the trade in steroids. It's all cash, and it's all good. Vince will do just fine down here. That is, if he doesn't get himself shot first."

"How'd the feds get wise to what Fernandez was up to?"

O'Neal stared at me for a moment, winked, and tossed a dead soldier into the trash can. He opened another bottle of beer and placed it in front of me, but he didn't answer my question. He didn't have to. His silence told me everything I needed to know about who had dropped the dime on Fernandez and the boys from Brighton Beach.

And I recalled, too, the rumors I had heard to the effect that Fernandez and O'Neal's wife Delores had been making the beast with two backs while O'Neal worked the night shift. I try to keep away from gossip, but I knew Fernandez well enough to believe those rumors were probably true. Vince had a sadistic streak when it came to things like that, and he had enough mesomorphic hubris to make him believe he could get away with anything, including screwing his friends' wives and girlfriends and then making sure they found about it just to see how they would react. It was his way of castrating the competition, and he seemed to revel in the conflict, but he had made a mistake with O'Neal. O'Neal never said a word about the affair to Vince, and this despite the fact everyone knew he was aware of it. His friends had watched him for signs of the eruption that they were sure would come eventually. But O'Neal fooled them all. He stuck it out with Delores, all the while sharpening his revenge like it was a home made shiv, waiting for the right moment to shove it in all the way to the bone.

"How's that drink, lady," Denny asked. "I hope I didn't make it too strong for you."

"There's no such thing as a drink that's too strong," Dawn said. "It's perfect."

"Jack was a pretty good cop," O'Neal said. "I bet he didn't tell you that. He was about a year away from making detective when he quit the squad. If you ask me, he should have rode it out. People forget."

"I don't," I said.

"I see you never got that scar taken care of," O'Neal said. "What's the matter, you got no insurance down here?"

"I like his scar," Dawn said. "It gives him character, don't you think?"

"How is it Fernandez managed to stay out of jail?" I asked.

"The way I heard it," Denny said. "Somebody bought themselves a judge."

"Sooner or later," I said. "Fernandez is going to catch up with you. You had better watch your back."

"Fuck him," O'Neal said. He glanced quickly at the door, but no one appeared. The man in the red dress lifted a finger, and O'Neal limped over to where the transvestite sat and made him another drink. When he returned to our end of the bar, I told him about Anton and Stefan, the two weightlifters I had met at the gym that morning. After I described their tattoos, the ex-cop smiled ruefully.

"They're *Vors* all right, "he said. "That means thieves of honor. You would have thought Fernandez would have learned his lesson by now. If I were you, I'd stay away from that Puerto-Rican son of a bitch. Those friends of his, they're the worst of the worst."

"Fernandez offered me a job."

"Stay away from it," O'Neal told me. "You throw in with those guys and you'll end up dead or in jail."

A slashing rain was blowing in off the ocean when we left the Deuce. For all his bluster, it was plain that O'Neal was scared. He had good reason to be. I would not want to have Vince Fernandez looking for me, not even casually. The only thing worse than a bad cop is a bad cop who is looking for you. O'Neal, like Raul Ochoa, had ample reason for a long vacation, but Denny, despite his fear, was too stubborn to run. His last words to me as we left had been another injunction not to tell Vince where he worked or that I had even seen him. He didn't have to tell me why, but Dawn asked me about it on the drive back to her hotel.

"A couple of years ago," I said. "I came into a little money. I wanted to give some of it to Ed Henry's wife and kid. I didn't think about it then, but it was around Yom Kippur, so maybe it was good timing. Anyway, when I was in New York, I met up with a few of the guys I used to work with when I was on the job. O'Neal was there. After he left, a couple of guys got to talking about Fernandez and O'Neal's wife. I had forgotten about it until this morning when Vince asked me if I knew where Denny was. "

"You think O'Neal was the one who told the police about Fernandez and the Russians?" Dawn asked.

"It was O'Neal all right," I said. I doubt he went to Internal Affairs. He probably gave it to the FBI. Of course, he would never admit to it, but it was him. Vince can't prove it for certain, but when he finds out where O'Neal is, the lack of proof really won't matter."

"You think he'll kill him?" Dawn asked.

"You seem to be having a hard time understanding the kind of people we're dealing with. Sure he'll kill him. Unfortunately for Denny though, it won't be a very quick death. The Russians will see to that. He probably cost them a lot of money."

By the time we reached Dawn's hotel, the rain had already ended. Outside the Holiday Inn, a group of kids loose on spring break were gathered around a van from a local radio station equipped with a satellite dish on its roof, a disc jockey and two giant speakers pumping loud music into the parking lot. The crowd of kids was so thick, I decided to help Dawn steer through it. We were half way through the herd of kids when I spotted Anton Zhukov and Stefan the Chechen sitting on the bench outside the hotel. I took Dawn gently by the elbow and made a quick left turn that put the van between us and the hotel.

"What's wrong?" Dawn asked me.

"When you spoke to Fernandez the other day, did you tell him where you were staying?" I asked.

"I'm not sure. I may have; I don't remember. Why?"

I peeked around the rear of the van and saw Vince's Ferrari parked behind a black Hummer near the front entrance to the hotel. As I watched, a portly bellman pushed an overburdened luggage cart through the sliding glass doors. When he had passed, I spotted Fernandez standing by the front desk talking to the clerk. He was wearing a white linen suit and had his slick black hair tied back in a ponytail. He looked like a man trying to make a good impression on a new girlfriend. I pointed him out to Dawn. I also pointed out the tattoo brothers sitting outside on the bench like a pair overgrown wallflowers at the big dance.

"You see those two men sitting on the bench over there? Trust me: they're not nice people. Let's get out of here."

"What about my things? They're still in my room?"

"I'll come back for them later."

We were heading north again on Collins when Dawn asked me where I was taking her.

"Well, you have two choices," I told her. "Neither of them good. You can pay for another hotel room or you can stay with me at my place. It's up to you."

"Do you have room?"

"No, but the price is right and there won't be any Russians there, and considering what I just saw back at your hotel, that's pretty important. But let me warn you. My apartment is not a particularly clean place; it's not bright, and it's not particularly well lit either, but I keep a flashlight on the nightstand and a loaded gun under the mattress and that's a lot when people like Fernandez are looking for you. So make up your mind."

"Aren't you afraid the neighbors will talk?"

"Of course they'll talk, but we won't be able to understand

them. That's the beauty of living in Miami. Nobody knows what the hell anybody is saying down here. That's why there are so many guns in this goddamned town. It's like the Tower of Babel. What'll it be, lady, me or the Russian Mafia? Take your pick; it's getting late."

"When you put it like that, how can I refuse?"

7

Miami has changed a lot since I first moved down here, but there are still a few constants. One is the venality of the politicians and their shills; another is the unbelievable greed of the developers. A third is the broken neon sign on the two-story walk up where I live, the lovely Lancaster Arms. Though I'm told the "N" in Lancaster has been blacked out for the last eight years, I can only vouch personally for the last four. Those of my neighbors who speak Spanish call the place "La Caster Arms, which drives the landlord, old man Sternfeld, crazy, especially when his tenants make out their checks that way. I've done it a few times myself just to get a rise out of him, but never when my rent is late.

Dawn didn't say anything when I pulled up in front of the building, and I couldn't help wondering if she was having second thoughts about being my houseguest. The Lancaster, as the sign might indicate, was not much to look at from the outside. It's a rectangular, two-story walk up built around a courtyard with a faded yellow paint job and a green tiled roof. It was built during the fifties when long road trips with a car full of kids were common. The place had once been popular with French Canadians and retirees grown wearied of the crime and cold up north. But the Canadians had moved on, and the old Jews had died off, so now it was just me, Sternfeld, a chess playing transsexual named Bobby and a bunch of illegal aliens from South America.

We walked past the kids playing tag in the courtyard, past the mailboxes then up the steps to the second floor where I lived in apartment six. It was a cool night. Without the hum of the ac units you could hear the music escaping into the courtyard through the jalousies. The sounds of a samba followed us down the walkway as though we were part of a parade in Rio and the air smelled richly of saffron and the meaty scent of paradilla, courtesy of the homesick Argentine cook in apartment eight.

As I was unlocking the door to my apartment, Dawn spotted the old mezuzah nailed to the doorjamb. The artifact had been painted over so many times, it had become part of the building's architecture. Just about every apartment had one, and no one paid them much attention, including myself. One day, a kid pried one loose, and a few scraps of yellowed paper with Hebraic lettering had floated slowly to the ground, and I had taken the mezuzah and the bits of paper to Sternfeld to ask him what they were. Dawn touched it briefly for a moment before we went in.

"The landlord told me it was for good luck," I said.

"Is it working?"

"If it were, would I be living here?"

Among the messages waiting for me on my answering machine was one from Vince Fernandez. I listened to it twice while Dawn unpacked the Chinese take-out we had picked up on the way back. I watched her from my desk in the still darkened living room as she opened and closed cabinets in her search for forks, knives and plates. Wisely, she rinsed off the utensils in the sink and folded some paper towels into the shape of napkins and laid the forks and knives on top of them. I watched her like a man watching a film alone in a private theatre as I listened to Fernandez tell me things I didn't want to hear in a New York accent that was both familiar and annoying to me.

I thought back to the phone call of the night before. The strange day had started early. Cal Belkin was missing; the car in the canal; Vince Fernandez here in Miami; a woman I had only met a few hours ago looking for forks in my kitchen. None of those elements could have been anticipated based on the quiet evening of the night before, and I wondered what things might look like now if I had pulled the phone jack from the wall, rolled over and gone back to sleep. I thought I knew at least part of the answer. The road cops would have gotten hold of me eventually. I would still have made the stops at the gym and at Cal's house in the Shores. I would still have spoken to Ms. Potsdam, Cal's banker. I would still have met up with my old friend Vince Fernandez.

The logic of everything I had done thus far would not have been altered by a few hours delay, but one thing would have changed. I would not have been at Cal's place in time to bump into his granddaughter. Dawn would have beaten me there by a few hours and that, as they say, would have made all the difference. She would have found the place locked with no red Cadillac in the driveway, and she would have done the same thing I had done only in reverse order. She would have headed straight for her grandfather's gym. Once there, Dawn would have been introduced to Vince Fernandez, and I knew him well enough to imagine how that first and last meeting would have played out.

No doubt, he would have been caught off guard by Dawn's unexpected arrival. Being the consummate bullshit artist that he was, however, Fernandez would have hidden his surprise with flash of his smile. When she told him that her grandfather was missing, he would have softened his eyes until they had glowed with false concern and fake compassion for her, and of course he would mention that he had once been a police officer. That way she would trust him. Not only would she have believed him when he said that he would help her, but because of his experience in law enforcement, she would have also believed that he actually might succeed in helping her find her grandfather. With his charm and his good looks, Vince would have come off as a godsend to a girl in town with no idea who she was dealing with or who his friends were or what they were capable of doing. She would not have suspected a thing.

Probably, they would have killed her right there in the gym. They would not have wanted to take a chance on her leaving and maybe getting in touch with the wrong people or finding out the wrong things. The gym wasn't large, but there were plenty of places where it might have happened, possibly in one of the storerooms. I doubt that Vince would have killed her himself, but neither Anton Zhukov nor Stefan the Chechen would have thought twice about strangling her. Then it would only be a question of getting rid of her body, and that would be easy for men who could each lift the back end of a car off the ground.

It was all hypothetical, and it takes a lot longer to write it down than it did for me to see it there in my head that night as I watched Dawn Belkin standing in my little kitchenette, polishing a spoon and holding it up to the light for inspection, but I couldn't see any other way that it might have played out. A few things might have changed, but I could not think of any way that she could have walked into that gym that morning without being dead a short time later. But if that was truly the case, and Dawn had dodged a bullet without having even been aware of it, why then did I find the sight of her shining knives in my kitchen so inexplicably sad? Surely, there has to be such a thing as luck in this world, and if Cal's granddaughter was alive tonight and standing in my kitchen because of it, then what was the problem with that? Why the feeling of futility, Vaughn? Sometimes the good guys catch a break. Why the long face?

I was too hungry to fish for an answer I was fairly sure I didn't really want to know, so I walked back into the kitchen and sat down across from Dawn Belkin at the table she had set for the two of us. And it occurred to me then that if some third party were watching the two of us just as I had been watching Dawn, they might have thought us just another couple sitting down for a simple Chinese dinner after a day's work. He would be deceived by a scene so common, and they would have found it ordinary in every way, a scene easily cut from the film. But the third party would be wrong. There was nothing ordinary about any of it.

I looked across the table and made myself try to smile, but it was clear that I had been caught trying to think of things beyond the reach of my brain, and there was no sense pretending otherwise, so I wasn't surprised when Dawn asked me the question no man looks forward too. She asked me what I was thinking. It was strange to hear this question from a woman that I barely knew, but the pace of events had accelerated things between us to the point where it didn't bother me that much. Even so, the answer didn't come easy and after few moments, I gave up trying to think of an answer and told her the truth.

"I was watching you from the bedroom," I said. "I hadn't turned the lights on, so you couldn't see me, but I was watching you set the table."

"You don't know how completely creepy that sounds," Dawn said. "You sound like a pervert."

"Well, you asked me, so I told you."

"Maybe I should have asked you this sooner," Dawn said. "But you're not insane by any chance are you?"

"Do I seem insane?"

Dawn examined my face from across the table for a moment before answering. I tried to keep my head still so she could get a good look at me, but her answer was taking a bit longer than expected. She studied my face for a moment, but at last she seemed satisfied with my physiognomy such as it was.

"I think my grandfather would have told me if you were nuts," she said. "He was pretty good at spotting them. By the way, you could use a few more spoons."

"How many do I have?"

"I could only find two."

"That's twice the number I usually need. Didn't that Chinaman give you any plastic?"

"You shouldn't use plastic utensils with hot food. It causes cancer."

"Fernandez left me a message," I said. "His partner wants to meet me."

"When?"

"Tonight. At the Emperor's Club."

"The strip joint?"

"I believe the proper term is cabaret."

Dawn slid a plate of fried rice and spare ribs across the table while I dug around in a bag for a plastic fork and knife. She shook her head in disapproval. I told her I would take my chances, especially since the take-out would probably kill me long before any lurking cancer had a chance to strike.

"So," she said. "Are you going?"

"I have too. Fernandez gets paranoid when he's on the juice. Not going might make him suspicious enough to take a ride over here to see what I'm up to."

"So what?" Dawn said. "He doesn't even know what I look like."

"You forget you're dealing with a cop. The first thing he would do after you called would be to try and find a picture of you. He's still got plenty of friends on the force up in New York. All it would take is a couple of calls and bingo, he's got a fax with your driver's license picture on it. And what about that band you sing with. Does it have a web site by any chance? "

"Yes."

"This is what I'm talking about. I'd start with the Internet, see what I could find. Facebook, Myspace. See what I mean? Once he has a picture, he has the advantage. He knows what you look like, but you've never seen him. Once he finds out where you are, he can approach you directly or follow you, wait until he can get you someplace alone and out of the way."

Dawn frowned across the table at me and tore off bite of sparerib.

"I thought Jews weren't supposed to eat pork," I said.

"I'm not Jewish," Dawn said. "I converted."

"Into what?"

"I study Buddhism. It's not a religion. It's a spiritual path. I belong to a group. We do yoga and meditation. What about you? Are you into anything?"

"Me? I'm into chanting, myself. I got a drum and everything. Once a month when the moon is full, I strip naked and head up to the roof. Then I just bang away until the cops show up."

"Your neighbors must really love that," Dawn said.

"Fernandez showing up at your hotel tonight is not a good sign. He's worried. Those 'roids are making him jumpy, and knowing Vince, he's probably using coke as a chaser. That's a dangerous combination. The desk clerk must have told him that you had already checked in. Now he's wondering why you're not answering his calls or whether somebody told you something. He won't be able to relax until he gets hold of you. That means he'll be hyper alert to the least little thing."

"You make him sound like a psychic," Dawn said.

"That's because you don't understand cops," I said. "They're always looking for something or somebody. It's their job. They're always looking for connections, for how everything fits together even if they don't. For us, the world is one big puzzle and everything in it is a little piece of the mystery. Right now, Fernandez is sitting someplace, wondering when you'll turn up and what it will mean if you don't. I just thought of something. When you're in New York, where do you stay?"

"With a roommate. She has a loft in Tribeca. Why?"

"Whose name is the place in?"

"Michelle's. She's a painter. Why? Do you think…?"

"It's possible. Vince has friends, some of whom happen to be murderers. How about in the phone book? Are you listed?"

"No. The landline is in her name. I just use my cell phone.

Why? You think he would do something up there?"

"Not if there's no easy way to trace you, no. I guess sometimes being homeless has its advantages."

"What would have happened if I had given you a different answer? If I had said the loft and the phone were in my name?"

"Then I'd be on the phone with your friend, Michelle, warning her to be on the lookout for big men with hawk noses and too many tattoos."

I showed Dawn how to open up the sofa and gave her a set of clean, mismatched sheets plus a pillowcase. I left her sitting in the living room with my remote, leafing through the oddly arranged channels of a new city and reading an old magazine at the same time. When I got to the bedroom door, I turned back for a moment to see how well Dawn went with the décor. She looked good. I tried to imagine what it would be like to have her sitting on my sofa on a regular basis. I hadn't had a girlfriend since the vegetarian's ultimatum. That was the night she told me I had to choose between her and meat. It had been a difficult choice, but in the end I had gone with the New York Strip. The sixteen-ounce. Things had been a bit barren since then, and it occurred to me a spare rib eating Jewish Buddhist might be just quirky enough to make things interesting.

I closed the door to the bedroom and took a quick shower. When I was done, I lifted the mattress and liberated my one good suit from where it had lain, entombed and wrinkle free, pressed against the box springs since my last meal with the vegetarian. It was a khaki suit, which, after some radical alterations, fit me pretty well, a gift of the same fugitive client of mine who had sold me the Chariot. I put it on over a black T-shirt, brushed my hair back and sealed my feet up in a pair of sweat socks and loafers. The only thing missing was the one accessory no well-dressed Miamian can be without. For this occasion, I went with the classic ankle holster into which I slipped the smallest gun I had, a sleek looking silver- plated

Beretta that I picked up cheap at a gun show up in Fort Lauderdale, which was also where I first run into Dennis O'Neal. The little Beretta was not exactly a bazooka when it came to firepower, but it was better than nothing, and a lot less conspicuous.

The door man, all six feet seven inches of him, looked slightly bored as he checked for my name on the VIP list at the Emperor's Club, but at last, the velvet rope was unclipped, and I walked past him and into the club's darkened interior. The music that drifted out was unexpectedly subdued, the hatcheck girl unexpectedly conservative in her white surplice of a dress tied off as it was at the waist with a braided golden rope. Her hair was white-blond and curtain straight, her eyes, ice blue but not cold. I found her very European. Her name was Masha. It said so on her name tag.

"Is Vince Fernandez here yet?" I asked.

"You are early," the girl said in a throaty accent. "I have table ready for you very soon. Please join our bar."

We continued down a short hallway, its walls covered in red velvet and pictures of strippers past and present in various stages of nudity. Many of the photos included celebrities and ballplayers, all them with big smiles on their faces and exotic dancers draped over their shoulders. Now the music was louder, Stevie Wonder's "Superstition" filling the space around us as Masha swept aside the curtain of peach colored silk that led to the action on the other side.

The first thing you noticed was the woman on the slowly revolving stage, the strobe lights bouncing off her naked body as she spun clockwise around the pole, her left arm extended as though reaching for something that would always be just out of reach like the gold ring on a merry go round. Surrounding the stage was a ring of blue lights and beyond the lights, a heart-shaped bar that itself was surrounded by a crowd of men and off duty strippers. The men were staring at the dancer on the stage like of a pack of cannibals watching dinner turning slowly on a spit.

I recalled once again why it was that I had never been very fond of strip clubs. The women were not the problem. It was the men. The room was filled with a feral vibe that kept me glancing around at everything and everyone, as though at any moment, someone might go berserk and hurl a Molotov cocktail against the wall, creating an inferno that would incinerate us all. Then I realized that I was staring at the woman too.

You go into places like the Emperor's Club and you pretend that you're some kind or cop or urban anthropologist or something respectable like that. You are undercover. You tell yourself you are better than the leering bastards around you because you're there for a reason that doesn't live and die in your pants. And true, I did have a mission, but watching this woman doing pirouettes around her silver pole, I was having a bit of trouble remembering just what it was, and for a moment there, I felt like I was on the verge of being shanghaied—not so much as by the shiny woman spinning around her axis of fake desire, but rather by something in me, some failure of focus on my part, some deficit of attention that had always been there, a powerful weakness I had almost forgotten about.

It was only when she turned around that I realized that the dancer spinning around the silver pole was Candy, the curly haired young woman I'd met outside Cal's gym that morning. She was down to just her pasties and purple G-string now, flashing back and forth across the stage, working it like a real pro. Someone had oiled her flawless body into a succulent shine, and now her bronzed skin glistened as though it had been basted for hours with a careful bush like Memphis barbecue.

A few feet away from me, a fat man in a white cowboy hat had leaned so far forward onto the stage that his giant belly spilled out under him like an airbag. He wallowed there, waving a fifty-dollar bill at the dancer, his hand now outstretched just as hers had been a moment before. Candy, now down on all fours, arched her back up and down then rose slowly to her feet, moving her body in such a way as to suggest that she was a genie rising out of a magic lamp. She rubbed her breasts and thighs as she came up, as though trying coax from her flesh every last ounce of sex.

Candy cradled her breasts in both hands and licked at her nipples; then she massaged them with her thumbs and forefingers before offering them up to the crowd. When she was through with that part of the act, she pranced across the stage on the balls of her feet before sliding into a 180-degree split directly in front of the cowboy. She swiveled around on her buttocks like a breakdancer and showed him her bikini wax. Then the stripper leaned slowly forward until she came to rest on her elbows as her nipples grazed the stage. Even in the weak, half-hearted light, they looked as hard as buttons.

I stared down at my beer for a slender moment just to break the spell. When I looked up again, Texas was busy sticking his fifty-dollar bill into the belt of Candy's G-string. As she drew back, her thighs still very much apart, he poked his nose forward and swung his jowls from side to side like a bloodhound, while his three companions howled and slapped him on the back.

But then Texas made a mistake, and it was a big one. As Candy rolled over onto her left side, the cowboy lunged forward and grabbed her by the ankle and pulled her toward him across the stage as his friends cheered. She kicked at him with her free leg, but he was too strong to resist. I brushed the man standing beside me out of the way and reached for the cowboy's thick arm, but I needn't have bothered, because at that moment, a hand far larger and stronger than mine shot through the pack of men crowded around the stage and fastened itself around the cowboy's neck. The cowboy, who must have weighed at least three hundred pounds, was yanked backwards and with such force that his hat flew from his head.

The crowd parted and the friends of Texas grew quiet. I

pushed through to the edge of the gap just in time to see Stefan the Chechen lift the cowboy from the floor, spin him halfway around then body slam the man into the carpet with such force that he actually bounced when he hit. The cowboy lay there face down for a moment as the Bee Gees sang "How Deep Is Your Love." The man rose slowly to his hands and knees, grasping at his face with bloody fingers. He had just began to crawl when Stefan the Chechen took one step forward and tried to kick a field goal with his head. The cowboy fell over and didn't move, and I was afraid he might be dead.

The kick was too much for the cowboy's friends to take. They were afraid, and they were drunk, but they were not without pride and besides that, they were many against one. They rushed at the Chechen from three sides, leaping on him like wolves converging on a bear standing over a fresh kill. Then one of the wolves drew a slender fang. The whirling strobe light struck the blade, and my eye caught the glint as the man raised his hand for the downward stab. The knife plummeted into the darkness surrounding the Chechen and disappeared somewhere in the vicinity of the big man's back. Stefan straightened up out of the mass of bodies surrounding him with a loud, animal roar and whirled around to face his attacker. As he did so, another man rushed forward with a beer bottle and smashed it over the Chechen's head.

Who knows why I did it. The Chechen meant nothing to me, and though I had met him only once, it had been enough exposure for me to know that he and I were never going to be friends. But in this fight he was the underdog, and that always calls your attention when it comes to choosing sides, and while he certainly deserved a good beating for kicking the cowboy when he was down, I decided, more or less, that it was time to act, so I said fuck it and jumped in.

After delivering his blow, the man with the bottle stepped backwards with the shattered remnant in his hand while the Chechen staggered forward with two men clinging to him; one of them wrapped his around his leg and the other riding on his back. I grabbed bottle man's wrist and twisted it counterclockwise with enough force to roll his shoulder forward. Then I rode him toward the floor with my other hand until he went down and I was kneeling beside him with his elbow bent the wrong way across my knee. He screamed and the dropped the bottle. I wanted that to be the end it, but he swung at me, so I pulled him off the ground and drove my knee up into his gut then shoved him into one of his friends.

Someone grabbed me fiercely from behind. Suddenly, my arms were pinned as I was lifted from the floor and spun around in the air. The strobe lights, whirling over me like multicolored neon streamers, made me blink, made it hard to get my bearings. I closed my eyes to shut out the light and tilted my head as far forward as it would go then slammed it backwards. There was the sickening crunch of bone against the back of my head as my arms came free and my feet touched the floor again. There was no time to see who I had hit because bottle man was on his feet again and coming my way, staggering like a drunk. But I had had enough. It was time for the peacemaker. I reached down and pulled the gun from my ankle holster and showed it to all concerned parties. Bottle man stopped, skidded, and tripped. I stepped out of his way then to one side, fanning the crowd with the Beretta until I found the man who had grabbed me

It was the cowboy. My head butt had completed the damage to his face, which the Chechen's kick had begun. His white shirt looked like it had been tie-dyed in his own blood, and when he moved his hand away his nose was a nasty pulp. But it was the Beretta that was getting all the attention now. Even the cowboy, who had far greater worries, was staring at the as though charmed by it. Stefan the Chechen took advantage of the lull in festivities to grab the man who was still hugging him around the leg and toss him with one hand over a table. That left the papoose on his back. The Chechen reached back, got himself a handful of the man's hair and pulled him around to the front and pinned him to the ground by the neck.

The man struggled, but the Chechen's arm was as stiff and as straight as a marble column, and all the man of the floor could do was claw at it with all the desperation of a man about to be suffocated. The man turned his head as best he could under the giant's weight as though searching for someone, anyone, to help him, but no one moved. All of them were still staring at the Beretta, wondering what it would do. The Chechen raised his fist. The face of the man on the floor was bright with fear and with good reason. He was looking at his death.

I took two quick steps and grabbed the Chechen's wrist just as the fist it was attached to began its downward descent. I was still holding the gun and could use only one hand, but as his arm started its descent, I flexed my knees and leaned backwards with all my weight. It was like pulling against the bole of a palm tree with very little give in it, but the leverage was mine and the Chechen's arm stalled in mid-strike. He jerked his head around to see who was holding him. I let go of his wrist and stepped back, thinking for sure he'd make a grab for me. His eyes touched mine for only an instant before dropping to the Beretta. When he looked up again, the Chechen was smiling.

"That's enough," I said. "Better let him up."

The Chechen stared at me for a long moment, his dark eyes strangely placid under the circumstances. He looked down at the man still pinned to the floor by his other hand and remained kneeling in that position without moving for a few moments as though he was studying a brand new species he had just wrangled to the floor. The man had released the Chechen's wrist and was now just lying there, breathing hard and looking desperate. The giant stood up, hauling the man to his feet by the throat and giving him a shove that it sent him crashing into a table. The man, clasping at chairs and turning them over as he tried to right himself, rose slowly to his feet. I dropped the Beretta in my pocket. A dancer handed the cowboy a napkin, which he held against his broken face for a moment before he and his three friends left the room in a silent huddle of confused and broken men.

Belatedly, other bouncers appeared, including the one who had checked me in at the door, but there was nothing left to do. A porter with a mop and bucket began cleaning the floor where the cowboy had done his bleeding. The crowd lost its form as the men, one or two at a time, like disappointed pilgrims, turned their backs on the scene of the fight and drifted back to the night's original distractions. In less than a minute they were zombies again, staring up at the stage where three girls in *Phantom of the Opera* masks were putting on a show that involved candles and a king-sized bed equipped with arm and leg shackles. No one paid me any attention. It was as though the gun in my pocket had never existed. There was nothing to worry about; it was just another night at the funhouse. Candy, the exotic dancer, had disappeared like an arsonist, the house in flames behind her.

8

Five minutes later, after a shower show in which two girls took turns lathering one another up with soap and sponges, Masha led me past the rows of mostly empty tables to a private room at the rear of the club she called the Pasha's Dacha. The scene was something out of the Arabian Nights. Its walls were veils of billowing amber silk, and the floor was covered in Persian rugs and satin pillows, low slung couches, a long table complete with a samovar and bowls of fruit, cold cuts and pickled herring. In the center of the floor, a cherub with oriental eyes drooled braided water into a fountain. The only thing missing was a harem and a couple of fat Ethiopian eunuchs wearing fezzes and scimitars in scabbards studded with rubies and emeralds. I made myself a sandwich and helped myself to the herring in cream sauce.

I was sitting at a large table on a raised dais at the rear of the Pasha's Dacha, drinking what was left of my beer when the curtains parted and Anton Zhukov's shaved head appeared followed by his double wide shoulders now encased in a light gray jacket that was struggling mightily with the massive muscles packed beneath it. He was followed a moment by Stefan the Chechen. He was wearing a jacket too, a nicely cut blue blazer that must have been tailor made, it fit him so well. But it didn't matter how the two of them were dressed because even with their tattoos covered up by bespoke threads, they still looked liked a pair of thugs on their way to a shakedown. Zhukov spoke briefly to Masha who then went back through the curtain the way she had come. Unsmiling, the two men took seats on either side of me, close enough so I could smell their cheap cologne.

"I saw what you did," the Chechen said. "You fight good."

Zhukov said something in what might have been Russian or anyone of a half dozen languages I didn't know, and Stefan the Chechen laughed until the scar on his throat pulsed with blood.

"What did he say?" I asked.

"He said you might not make good bitch after all."

"What about his mother? Is she still in the running?"

My question floored the two Vors. They rocked back and forth, holding their bellies and coughing with laughter. Zhukov slapped my shoulder hard enough to put a dent in it, but I made a point of not wincing in pain. Then Masha brought in a silver tray with a bottle of vodka, the brand of which I had never heard of before, and three glasses. She filled each of the glasses to the brim then took a seat on Stefan's knee while we all toasted one another. The Chechen used his free hand to fondle the hostess's breast, but Masha didn't seem to notice. Instead, she took a big gulp of vodka from his glass and banged it down on the table when it was empty. Watching the three of them, I remembered that Russia had once been settled by Vikings.

"I always did like a whore who could drink," Zhukov said to me. "What about you?"

"I'm not whore now," Masha said. "I am free woman."

She's right," Stefan said. "Now she fucks for free just like everyone else in this great country."

"Where are you from?" I asked.

"Riga," she said proudly. "You know where that is? Have you heard of it?"

"Listen to me, my friend," Zhukov said. "She comes from

a shit city in a little shit country," Zhukov said. "The only thing they have there is ugly woman and bears. Take my word for it."

"Be quiet, you fat dog," Masha said. "I am from Latvia, not from shit hole like Zhukov. They sent my mother and father to Siberia for five years. The Russians are animals."

"Maybe so," Zhukov said. "But at least we taught their stupid daughter to speak decent Russian instead of that peasant tongue you were born with. Before we came and tamed you, your country was full of slaves and savages. Ask anybody."

The Chechen looked at me and smiled. "You see how it is?" he said. "All of us hate the Russians, but all of us speak their language. Those two things we have in common. What do you call this kind of thing?"

"In my country," I said. "We call it irony."

"You know," Stefan said thoughtfully. "It's true the Russians are pitiless dogs like Zhukov here, but just the same, you should have been with me in Afghanistan. Now those people were *real* animals, and the women are worse than the men. I fought in the mountains there twenty years ago, in the south near Kandahar where they say Osama is now. Our superiors advised us to shoot ourselves in the head rather than be taken prisoner by the enemy. And do you know something? As it turned out, he was correct. Let me tell you something, American. It takes much patience and skill to skin a man alive without killing him. They did that to a friend of mine. His name was Andre. He wasn't a man anymore when we found him, only a trembling red thing. I knew it was him by his eyes. Of course, it goes without saying they had already cut off his balls and torn out his tongue by the roots, but I knew what he wanted, so I shot him in the forehead, twice, just to make sure he was dead."

"Listen to him," Zhukov said. "Soon he will be telling you stories about how the Chechens are god's little angels, good peaceful Muslims." He spat. "These are the people who rape nuns and burn alive little children in their school while parents stand outside wailing in the snow like widows. Don't listen to this ape when he speaks of savages. He was born in the shit factory that makes them."

I looked across at Stefan the Chechen and didn't much like what I saw in his eyes. He had stopped working on Masha's breast and was staring across the table at Anton Zhukov like a setter on point and his hand had dropped out of sight beneath the table. Zhukov returned the Chechen's bright stare and added a thin, appreciative smile of understanding. Theirs would be a long struggle. Whenever an empire falls, and eventually they all do, there are always plenty of survivors left, each one of them armed with enough grievances to last longer than the empire itself; each one of them a victim armed with long memories, short fuses, and the rich, embellished fantasies of revenge that they would pass on to their children and to their children's children long after their former conquerors had been reabsorbed into time and space.

"Why don't we try changing the subject," I said. "Let's talk about something that won't result in anybody getting killed."

The staring match continued for a few moments. Then Masha whispered something in the Chechen's ear, and Zhukov let out a loud belch that made the three of them laugh. The tension collapsed, and just like that, we were all one big happy family again. The vodka flowed, but I drank slowly. These men were far too volatile to risk getting drunk with.

"So," Zhukov said to me. "You were police officer in New York with Vincent. Is this correct?"

"That's right."

"I lived in Brooklyn for five years when I came here," Zhukov said. "The man I worked for there owned many policemans, but you I don't remember. Why is this?"

"I worked mostly in Manhattan. Midtown North. Then I transferred out to the one twelve in Queens. I never made it out to Brooklyn like Vince."

"Too bad," Stefan said. "You could have made a lot of money if you had gone to Brooklyn."

"Maybe I can make some down here."

"You know, I like Miami," Zhukov said definitely, looking around as though the Pasha's Dacha was the city itself. "Money goes far here, and the policemen are cheap to buy. We will make a lot of money here."

Stefan and Masha were getting a bit too passionate for public display, and the Russian had begun to suckle on her breast like a large, hairy child. Zhukov said something in Russian that caused the Chechen to open one eye and grin. He jumped swiftly to his feet with the laughing hostess in his arms, swept aside the silk curtains with his shoulder and carried the girl away. Through the silken haze, I watched the happy couple disappear behind a door labeled the *Czar's Lair*. When his friend had gone, Zhukov turned to me and with a tear in his eye said:

"You know it's a shame, but one day I really do believe in my heart and my brain both together that Stefan will force me to kill him. When this happens, it will be a terrible day, because you have to believe me when I tell you I love him like a brother."

Before I could offer him my condolences, the curtain was brushed aside and Candy appeared. She was dressed, as I might have expected, like a slave girl complete with a white, beaded veil and a costume made of red dental floss and three well-placed patches of cloth. Zhukov rose from his chair and laid one of his massive hands on my shoulder.

"Enjoy," he said. Then he passed through the waves of golden curtain and was gone.

Candy whirled around on the Persian rug while I sat there playing the role, I suppose, of the wealthy Pasha auditioning his latest acquisition. She was a better dancer than I had expected. Her movements were precise; her hand gestures, the way she held her fingers, suggested both training and talent, and once or twice, almost as a tease, she would sneak in a flash of the ballet, and suddenly her neck and limbs would seem to lengthen as she held a pose that reminded me first of a bell and then of a flamingo.

I was watching a natural born dancer, one of those rare, weightless creatures from a planet without gravity, who ride music as much as hear it, whose bones are three parts helium to one part calcium. And as Candy spun around my chair, it became apparent that she was no longer vamping it up as she had done for the crowd of zombies whose muffled shouts and catcalls I could still hear beyond the walls of the dacha.

Soon, the only part of her costume left was the veil. But as killer perfect as her body was, it wasn't what Candy was trying to show me. It was her moves, her skills, her verve, her joy, she was offering me—the artist's proof of life. The only part of her face I could see were the eyes shining above the bridge of the veil she wore. They were bright brown, pensive and curious, but there was something different in them now, a bright glint that hadn't been there this morning, and I knew then that I was not only looking at a dancer but at an actress as well.

Long ago Candy had learned the trick of using her body as both a way to make money and as a firewall to keep out the idiots that came with the job. The longer and harder you stared at her body the further away you got from really seeing her; the more powerful your lust, the less likely the chance of revelation. That was how she did her job night after night. That was how she kept the zombies at bay, though I'm sure she knew better than I did that it was only a matter of time before the feeding frenzy would find her secret and wolf it down without a thought. One night, maybe soon, it would happen, and when it did, she would have to get out of the business quickly, because without the power of her secret, she'd be defenseless against men like the judge and the other zombies and vampires that feasted on her flesh each night as she danced.

She began to slow down, her hand movements becoming more suggestive, more hypnotic as the dance drew to a close. Then, with a dramatic flash of her hand, Candy ripped her veil from her face, threw it down on the floor, walked over to where I sat and without a word straddled me. She put her arms around my neck while I sat there quietly taking in her scent with each wary breath. After a moment, Candy leaned back and moved her hips around on my lap as though trying break in a new saddle. Slowly, she began rotating her hips, first clockwise, then the other way, all the while never taking her eyes off mine. The friction was effective but something was wrong.

"Why are you doing this?" I asked

"I just wanted to thank you for helping out with the judge," Candy said. "He's been warned before, but the big idiot never listens."

"Are you telling me that the guy whose nose I just help break is a judge?"

"He's from Ocala. His name's Owen Gibson. Judge Gibson. He comes in whenever he's in town. He says he's in love with me, offered me a thousand dollars to spend a night with him. Can you imagine? And he's got a wife and kids too."

"How old are you?"

"I'm nineteen. Why?"

"This is a hard way to make a living, Candy," I said. "The money might be good for now, but it's not the kind of job you want to get old in. Think about going back to school, getting yourself an education. I know I must sound like your father of something, but I know what I'm talking about."

"What's the matter, don't you like it?"

"Yes and no," I said.

"What's the 'no' part?"

"Don't take this personally," I said. "But I feel like you're trying to pick my pocket. You know what I mean?"

Candy stopped the gyration of her hips and sat back. Being naked didn't seem to bother her in the least. She sat there on my lap with as little self-consciousness as she would have displayed sitting on the edge of a bathtub shaving her legs.

"Vince asked me to do it," she said. "He wanted me to check to see if you were wearing a wire. I'm going to rub my hands over your chest now, okay?"

"Vince thinks I'm some kind of informant, is that it?"

"Please," Candy said. "I have to do it. They're watching

me. Look over my shoulder. See that little statue, the blue bull? The eyes have little cameras in them."

"Merrill Lynch? Yea, I see him. All right, go ahead."

"And I have to start moving my hips too. Otherwise, they'll get suspicious."

"Who's watching us?"

"I don't know. Someone upstairs."

"What happens if you find a bug?"

"If I find something I'm supposed to raise my right hand and wave it around above my head like I'm riding a bull in the rodeo."

"Then what happens?"

"They'll wait for you to go outside and sit down with all the big shots like they always do. Then Stefan or maybe Zhukov will excuse themselves and leave the table. Then, when you're not looking, whoever it is will come up behind you with a cord and wrap it around your throat. Or maybe Masha will put something in your drink."

"What about the other customers?"

"They won't say anything. This is a private club. You have to be invited. It costs a lot of money to join, but you get a lot of perks. Drugs, guns, girls, even boys if that's what you're into. But you have to keep you're mouth shut. You have to sign an agreement not talk about anything you see at the club. If you do, things get pretty bad. That's why we don't have to worry about the judge telling the police. The Russians have too many pictures of him with girls, lots of them, some of them younger than me."

"What about the police?"

"What about them? The police chief is a member. So is the mayor. Hallandale is a small city. No one cares. I have to start now, okay?"

Candy began massaging my chest, working her way across the ribs, and around to my upper and lower back, all the while staring directly into my eyes. It was a fairly erotic pat down, but Candy looked a bit embarrassed by the whole thing. Grinding her hips into my groin hadn't bothered her at all, but the pat down she was forced to administer did. When she finished frisking me for electronics, she swung her hips around so that she was now sitting across my lap like I was a Santa Claus at Macy's. I put my arm around her waist just to give it something to do.

"Satisfied?" I said. She put her arms around my neck and whispered in my ear.

"It's not me; it's them. I like you. It's hard to believe you were ever a policeman like Vince. You don't seem to me like a cop at all."

"No? What do I seem like?"

"You seem like a nice guy."

"How do you know they don't have microphones on us?"

"They tried that, but the music is too loud. As long as I speak softly, they can't hear me."

"You're taking a big chance if you're wrong."

She kissed me on the mouth. I couldn't tell whether it was real or part of the act, and I began to doubt my earlier assessment of her. I wondered if she might not be a schizophrenic. Maybe there was no camera in the blue bull after all. Maybe it was all in her head.

"What's your real name?" I asked.

"Melissa. Melissa Decker. Candy's my stage name. I think you need to start acting a little more excited. You're way too serious for a guy with a hot, naked girl on his lap."

"What do you suggest?"

"Give my breast a little kiss, but don't get carried away. You're really not supposed to touch me, but they expect it."

"Which one should I kiss?"

"Just do it. Okay, that's enough. Now listen. There's something else I have to tell you too," she said. "This morning after you left the gym, you had breakfast with Vince at the Cuban place. Somebody called him right before you left. That was me. He asked me to follow you to see where you went after you left the restaurant."

"And did you?"

"Yes."

"You saw where I went?"

"You went to the old man's house."

"What did Fernandez say when you told him I had gone there?"

"Nothing, because I didn't tell him where you went. I told him you ran a red light, and I lost you in the traffic."

"Why didn't you tell him the truth?"

"I told you. Because I like you. I liked you the moment I saw you standing outside the gym this morning. It's funny, because you're not really that good looking. No offense. Maybe it was the way you stood there. You looked lost but at the same time you looked confident, like you had been lost before and found your way back somehow. I know it sounds strange."

"You didn't tell Vince because you thought that if you did, he'd kill me. Is that it?"

"He might. Or maybe since he's your friend, he'd have Anton or Stefan do it. I didn't want to take the chance."

"Tell me something. Who's the boss of this operation? I'm supposed to meet him here tonight."

"It's not a him; it's a her."

"The boss is a woman?"

"Yea. Mrs. Kaminski. She used to be a dancer here. Then she married the boss. When he died, she took over everything. All I can say is that you had better hope she likes you, because she's a real bitch and a half."

"This Mrs. Kaminski," I said. "What's her first name?"

"Marina. Why? Do you know her?"

"Stand up."

Candy—Melissa—got quickly her feet. "What's the matter? Are you mad at me or something?"

"Is there a back way out of here?" I asked. "A fire exit, something like that?"

"Go out the door and make a left. It's at the end of the hallway. Why? What's going on?"

"Nothing, I just need some fresh air that's all." I reached in my coat pocket and handed her a business card. "Take this. Maybe I can return the favor sometime."

"If you open the door, the alarm will go off."

"I'll take my chances."

I kissed Melissa on the forehead and closed the door to the Pasha's Dacha behind me. I made the left and headed for the exit at the end of the hallway. I pushed open the door and found myself in the parking lot behind the club. I spotted the Chariot by fence on the other side of the lot, and made a run for it, congratulating myself for not having turned it over to valet.

As I ran, I admitted to myself that I might be making a mistake in avoiding Marina Gero, that I was exaggerating the danger. Sure, she might be a bit pissed off when she realized that I had lied to her about looking for a house to buy, and that I was obviously trying to find out what had happened to Cal Belkin, but that wasn't necessarily anything to go berserk about. The real estate agent might even laugh the whole thing off while we shared shots of vodka together. Then again, Marina Gero hadn't exactly struck me as someone with a very good sense of humor. There was a better than even chance that she might not find the thought of an ex-cop running around town, asking questions and peeking up skirts very amusing. If, as it turned out, she considered me too much a threat, then what better place than the Emperor's Club to make that threat disappear? No, I thought. If she and I had to meet up again, then better it should be on my turf and on my terms and at a time of my choosing.

I was halfway across the mostly deserted lot, running as best I could in street shoes when I heard the screech of tires behind me. When I glanced back, a pair of headlights was bearing down on me at top speed. I tried to jump clear but the car—it was a black Hummer —swerved, striking me in the hip with its rear end just as my feet left the ground. I hit the ground hard, and tried to get up, but the pain in my leg made me stumble and fall. I rolled over and reached down my leg, but my ankle holster was empty; the Hummer's impact must have knocked the gun free. I looked around and saw the Beretta lying in a puddle about ten feet away. Again, I got up and again I fell. I was certain my hip was broken.

I began to crawl toward the gun, not because I thought I had any chance of reaching it, but because I like to keep active and because it was better than doing nothing at all. A car door slammed behind me. Then another pair of headlights appeared to my left. I continued to crawl. I knew it was stupid, but even the most futile efforts have a certain momentum behind them and the Beretta was only a few more feet away. A gunshot split the air behind me and two small chunks of asphalt jumped up off the ground and flew away in different directions. I stopped my crawling and got to my feet, trying to keep as much of my weight off my left hip as I could, but even so, I yelled all the way up. Wobbling back and forth like an old man who had lost his cane, I turned and faced the headlights.

Through the glare, I saw two pairs of silhouettes, three of them much larger and wider than the one on the far right. A woman's voice barked orders in what might have been Russian. The lights went dark, and I was staring at Vince Fernandez. He was still wearing the white linen suit I had seen him in at Dawn's hotel earlier that evening, but he was holding an accessory that hadn't been there before, the golden trophy in the figure of a man with his gilded muscular arms akimbo.

Next to Vince, stood Marina Gero. One look at those frozen blue eyes of hers told me that I had been right in making a run for it. She wore a form fitting black leather one- piece jumpsuit and a pair of scarlet red stiletto heels that made her almost as tall as Fernandez. The zipper of the jump suit was pulled down just far enough to show off her assets without giving them away, but it was clear that Candy had been telling the truth when she had told me that Marina Gero had once been a stripper herself, though it was hard to imagine her prancing around on stage while a room full of grinning idiots leered at her. The graveyard stare and the tight, impatient mouth might make a man think twice before requesting a lap dance, and I would have pitied any fool stupid enough to try and drag her off the stage.

Stefan the Chechen and Zhukov climbed out of the Hummer and walked slowly toward us with the casual stride of soldiers long in the field and well adjusted to danger. Zhukov, holding a Mac-9 machine gun as though it was an attaché case, approached me smiling brightly, as though seeing me again had filled him with joy. The Chechen wasn't carrying a weapon, and judging from his calm almost bored demeanor, he didn't seem to think he needed one. The two of them regarded me with the arrogant calm of conquerors, who had long ago forgotten what resistance felt like, and, as if to further the point, Stefan yawned, excused himself, and calmly lit a cigarette.

"You couldn't let it go, could you, Jack?" Vince said. "You had to make me look like an idiot, didn't you?"

"I don't know what you're talking about," I said.

"Then why'd you make a run for it?"

"This is what you get for being stupid, you stupid big gorilla!" Marina shouted, glaring at Vince. "Another one of your stupid American friends to betray you with. What did I tell you? No more of your stupid New York cops. But no, you had to bring another snake into my fucking grass. What a fucking stupid idiot you are!"

Zhukov and Stefan laughed. Vince glared at the Russian woman standing beside him with her fists clenched but said nothing. It seemed to me that he was used to the rough treatment. Then Fernandez turned back to me.

"We were up in the office watching the monitor," Vince said. "Marina recognized you right away."

"So what?"

"You were at the old man's house that's what."

"He owed me money. I went to collect it. What's the big deal?"

"Just shut up and kill him, you idiot!" Marina exploded. "Do it before I make Zhukov shoot you too, you stupid fool!"

Vince laughed, his fake, Hollywood grin flashing like neon. "Hey, Anton," he said. "What about that? You going to shoot me too?"

"What about it, Chechen?" Zhukov said. "Should I kill Vince?"

Before Stefan could answer, the revolving red and white lights of a squad car appeared at the lot's rear entrance. I saw it first, but the loud *whoop, whoop, whoop* of its siren made everybody turn and look. The cop car slowed, rippled harshly over a speed bump, and then headed straight for us, slamming to a stop between Vince's Ferrari and the black Hummer. A uniformed cop jumped out from the driver's side, followed a moment later by a man in a well-tailored dark suit who looked like your typical well-groomed, middle aged, salt and pepper executive except for the gum he chewed and the automatic I spotted clipped to his belt as he hitched up his well creased pants.

The cop in the uniform took up a well-practiced, this-is-official position in front of the patrol car and went on chewing his gum just like his boss, who strolled over to and looked down at me where I lay. His polite, disinterested smile told me that this wasn't the first time he had seen a man lying outside the Emperor's Club. He looked away then used his index finger to drill for wax in his ear canal for a moment before stopping to examine the results. When he was done, he looked over at Zhukov and Anton and nodded. They nodded back. Then he looked around the parking lot with the edge of his palm held against his brow as though shielding his eyes from a sun that had set hours before.

It was a nice act, and I had seen it before, though not since New York. Let's say you spot a gang of hoods you've dealt with many times before congregating on corner. You have no reason to arrest anyone, but maybe you've gotten a few calls from the store owners in the neighborhood who don't like what they see loitering outside their plate glass windows, and want you to do something about it, so you decide it's time to make a statement.

It's time to show everybody who's the MMIC, the main motherfucker in charge. You roll up on the thugs like it's the last five minutes of *Hawaii Five-O* and you're Jack Lord and your partner is Danno. You frisk the biggest guy or the one with the biggest mouth and scare the shit out of everybody else, and then you confiscate any crack or loose joints or nickel bags of pot you find in their pockets. And all the time, you're smiling and cracking jokes, because you want them to know that everything is cool and that nobody should do anything stupid like mouth off or run or pull a gun or a knife because it's all cool and everybody knows the drill.

"Hello, everybody," the main man said with the friendly smile of a game show host. "How's it going, Vincent?" Then he nodded at Marina Gero. If he had worn a hat, he might have tipped it. "Mrs. Kaminski, nice to see you again." Then he looked at me, frowned, and turned back to Vince. "So, what do we have here, kids? Trouble?"

"Nothing we can't handle," Vince said.

"Is that right?" the man in the nice suit said. The uniformed cop, chewing gum and looking serious, stood as still as a sarcophagus in a museum. It was clear that they were all old friends. The suit looked down at me again, tossed his gum over his shoulder and frowned.

"What's the problem, Mister?" he said. "You taking a nap or something?"

"My leg's hurt," I said. "I need an ambulance. My hip's dislocated."

"Your hip's dislocated? You a doctor?"

"No, I'm not a doctor."

"Then how do you know your hip's dislocated?"

"Just guessing."

The suit turned and looked at Vince then pointed at the bodybuilding trophy Fernandez still clutched.

"Hey," he said. "I see you won the Mr. Miami. Congratulations."

"Thanks," Fernandez said. "Look, Ray, we can handle this. It's nothing, really."

"In that case," Ray said. "Why don't you ask baldy over there to put that machine gun someplace where fucking half of Hallandale can't see it, okay? Can you do that for me?"

Marina said something in her language. Zhukov nodded and put the Mac-9 under his jacket. Ray, the man in the nice suit, grinned. Then he pointed at me again.

"This guy here says his hip's dislocated," he said. "What do you make of that?"

"Like I said," Fernandez said sternly. "I'll take care of it."

"You guys are getting out of hand," Ray said. "You don't know half the shit that girl's father put me through last month. You got to tell your associates here that this isn't Little Odessa we're in down here. You got to check IDs, okay? At the very least, you guys owe me a bottle of champagne. I deserve at least that much, don't you think?"

"Don't worry," Vince said. "Christmas is right around the corner."

Stefan the Chechen laughed then winked at me and laughed again.

"What about that ambulance?" I said.

"You don't need any ambulance," Ray said. "You're as healthy as a goddamned horse. Isn't that right, Marina darling?"

"Of course," Marina said. "You are always right, Ray. Thank you so much. You're always such a gentleman."

"You know," Ray said. "You look pretty damned smoking hot in that leather get up of yours, sweetheart. I think I know now what it is I want for Christmas. How about a hug for old Ray?"

The Russian and the bagman embraced while Vince looked on with a dour look on his face. When he was done copping his feel, Ray leaned forward and stared down the real estate agent's cleavage, the tab of her zipper pinched between his two fingers. He gave it a slight tug and shook his head. "Amazing," he said. "Why is it that all the best strippers these days are Russians? I don't get it. It must be that globalization bullshit or something. Anyway, do me a favor, kids, and try to get this shit squared away before the mayor shows up, all right? Okay, Harvey, let's roll. We got places to go and people to see."

As soon as the two lawmen had driven off, Vince resumed looking down at me with an expression of profound disappointment. No one had looked at me that way since my father had appeared at the department store in Queens where I had been caught shoplifting when I was fifteen or sixteen years old. That was the day a new kind of silence had begun to grow between us, one that neither of us were ever able to quite find the antidote for, though I do believe we both tried. That was also the day when I had decided that I would become a cop.

I didn't bother trying to get up right away. For one thing, I knew it would only add to the package of pain my left leg had become; plus, I wasn't at all sure I could manage it without assistance. So instead, I just lay there stretched out, propped up my elbow like a fighter who's been knocked down but not out, who is now resting, gathering his strength and his confidence, while the referee finishes the long count to ten and a maybe another chance for more pain. But Fernandez got bored with my act and yanked me off the ground by the collar of my jacket. I needed the ride, so I let him do it, though the sudden rush of pain tore my mouth wide open.

Fernandez dragged me over to the Hummer and threw open the door. Just as he was about to shove me in, I rotated on my one good leg and hit him in him in the face with the bottom of my palm. He staggered backwards then surged forward, swinging at me with the trophy he had won. I ducked, slipped and landed on my back in an oily puddle. Then Fernandez seemed to lose it. His entire body quivered with rage. With a vicious gesture, he yanked an automatic from his belt clip and leveled it at my head. I heard him yelling, but the pain in my leg was the only thing that mattered; everything else was static. Everything else would have to wait.

"Get up!" he yelled. "Or I'll kill you right here!"

Then the Chechen appeared suddenly at my side. "Zhukov," he said calmly. "I need your help with this."

"Get the hell away from him!" Vince yelled.

The Chechen ignored him. He knelt beside me and passed his hand along the side of my leg until he reached the hip socket. I twisted away, biting down on the scream that wanted to escape, but the Chechen's grip was firm. He told his comrade to hold me still. Zhukov settled his bulk onto one knee with great effort, as though his body were a giant boulder he was trying hard not to drop. Then his hands grabbed me by the shoulder, and after that, I could not have moved even if I had wanted to. A cold sweat had soaked through my jacket, and I felt a deep chill pass through my body, as though a fever had just broken. All I wanted was to find someway to get away from the agony in my leg, a dark closet I could lock behind me and hide in until the pain had passed.

The Chechen grabbed hold of the ankle of my damaged leg with one hand and the nearly obscene bulge of my hip socket with the other. Our eyes met. I understood what he was going to do. He grinned widely. It was his way of telling me it was going to hurt like hell. Then, before I could form another thought or feel another fear, he gave my ankle a powerful twist while at the same time shoving down on my hip socket with his left hand. I had been expecting the pain, but when it came, it struck so hard and so fast that, for an instant, my lungs forgot to let go of the scream that had been building in them like a thunderstorm waiting for the lightning to release it.

By the time I had finished my yell, the pain was already receding. It flowed away from me with an almost pleasant slowness, allowing me the luxury of enjoying its gradual departure. I closed my eyes. My heart rate began to slow, and my breathing returned to its usual unhurried pace. All I wanted to do then was just to lie there for as long as I could, in that dirty puddle that reeked of gasoline and creosote and sweat, wallowing in the absence of pain like a rock star sitting in a Jacuzzi. Then I remembered the company I was in, and sure enough, when I opened my eyes, there was Vince Fernandez standing over me with his gun pointed at my forehead. There was a small gash on his cheek where the flesh had spread away from the bone. The damage was minimal but it was enough to make the 'roid rage worse.

"Get the fuck up," he said, touching his cheek.

The Chechen helped me to my feet. The hip still hurt when I tested it with my weight, but the worst of the pain had gone though it would be a long time before running would be any fun again. Vince patted me down while Zhukov retrieved my gun from where it had fallen. When he found them, Fernandez dropped my cell phone, house keys and wallet in his pocket. When he reached the ankle holster, he ripped it free and tossed it over to the Chechen. Marina looked on as Vince secured my wrists with the plasticuffs the cops hand given him. It was the second time that day that my hands had been bound; only this time it was hard to believe that things were going to turn out as well for me as they had back at Raul's slaughterhouse. When he was done, Fernandez turned back to the Russian real estate agent.

"All right," he said. "What now?

Marina flicked the cigarette from her hand and poked her head forward in disbelief at what she had just heard. "'What now?'" Marina looked around as though trying to find someone else to share this feast of idiocy with. She even looked at me. "I can't believe this! What do you mean what now? No, wait, I want you tell me what is now. Tell me, what do you think we should do? You are my enforcer. So you tell me, my steroid fool, what we do with your friend. I want to hear it! Please, tell me. I must know what you brilliant mind thinks about this!"

Vince stared sullenly at the Realtor for a moment then regarded me with equal disdain. It was clear that I was a big disappointment to him. By going to Cal's house, I had thrown the game. I had put him in the position of the noble coach who has no choice but to banish a promising player from the league for life.

"He said the guy owed him money," Fernandez said plaintively. "What do you expect him to do? Just let it go?"

"He is a liar," Marina said. "And you are a fool. Now take him someplace, and don't speak of him again to me. Do what you are paid for to do."

Vince glanced over at his two assistants and flashed them with his grin. Then he looked back at his boss and smiled again. He had been waiting for a moment like this for a long time, and tonight he had at last found the perfect audience.

"I don't understand, babe," he said. "I thought fucking that big Russian cunt of yours was what I was getting paid for, but I guess I must have been wrong about that."

Zhukov and the Chechen turned toward one another with unexpected delight, their huge faces nearly bursting with merriment. They laughed, fell against one another, reeling, grasping at one another's arms and shoulders, both of them nearly collapsing into their laughter like two drunkards outside a dockside bar. Marina watched them for a second then grabbed Vince's trophy from where he had placed it on the hood of the Hummer. Fernandez made a grab for it, but she was too fast, and before he could stop her, she had hurled the trophy against the ground with such force that it broke in half like a cheap toy.

The sight of the broken trophy on the ground drove the Chechen and Anton Zhukov even further into the wilderness of hysteria. Anton actually hopped up and down while Stefan held his sides and tried to get his breath back. Fernandez just stood there, silently staring down at his broken prize. Then the laughter of the two men drew his attention in their direction, and something in his expression made them stop laughing. They coughed into their hands and looked at the ground, and the Chechen patted his pockets in search of his cigarettes. Then Fernandez exploded toward Marina like a man shot from a cannon, but Zhukov and the Chechen, both of whom moved much more quickly than I would have expected, jumped between them. Vince struggled with them for a moment, but by degrees he began to calm down, and they released his arms.

By this time, Marina had already pulled a small silver-plated automatic from her purse and was pointing it at Fernandez. The gun looked like a novelty cigarette lighter, but at close range it would do the trick. The way she held it reminded me of the can of mace she had threatened me with when I had confronted her outside Cal's house earlier that day. Then as now, I had no doubt whatsoever that she was perfectly capable of using her weapon, but now I knew why. Marina Gero possessed one very important trait: the willingness to do harm to others to a degree greater than most people are ever capable of finding within themselves—even when their own lives are in danger.

You can take all the shooting lessons you want; you can fire ten thousand holes into ten thousand paper targets, but without the willingness to do harm to another human being, the chances are good that when the moment of decision comes, you won't fire. Either that or you'll hesitate and lose both your advantage and your firearm. Marina, I could see, would never have that problem. You could see it in her eyes and in the way she stood there with that half smile on her ice cold pretty face. The only question was had she been born with it as some people are, or had it been a question of training. The most lethal combination, of course, occurred when you took a natural and trained him or her to the make the most out of his gift. It seemed to me that Marina Gero fell into the third category.

"I think the drugs must be as bad for your memory as they are for the size of your balls," Marina said. "Perhaps you should retire from taking them. I have to keep reminding you who it is who is in charge here. Now go and do your job."

9

It was past midnight. A storm, one of the first of the spring, was tearing at the scrub pines swaying above us on either side of the road. The lights of the city were well behind us as we drove northwest on the highway. We were headed in the general direction of Tamarac, though, of course, I had no way of knowing if that was to be our final destination, but somehow it made sense that we would be heading for the place where this had all begun so long ago that morning.

The pain in my leg had dulled enough to give fear a chance to take center stage in my brain, and I knew that we were bearing down on the time when I would have do something, but it was getting late, and so far nothing resembling an exit had appeared in my situation. We were in the Hummer doing a soft seventy mph, slashing through the rain on a mostly deserted four-lane highway. The Chechen was driving. Anton Zhukov was trailing us in the Chariot, which they were probably going to ditch somewhere. I was sitting in the backseat with Fernandez, my wrists bound by plasticuffs. The results of my inventory were clear. Everything would depend on how things went when we exited the car.

Fernandez snorted a few hits of coke from a small amber vial, wiped his nose with his sleeve then turned to me. "Tell me the truth," he said. "What made you go over to the old guy's house this morning? And don't give me that shit about him owing you money. I don't buy it."

"What difference does it make now?"

"Hey, Jack, you think I like doing this? I got no choice. You should have minded your own fucking business."

"Where are we going?"

"The Everglades."

"I see."

"It's your own fault."

I just looked at him and smiled. It wasn't a very big smile, but I'm sure he got the message. "Look," Vince said, "I got some Xanax you can take. It'll make things easier when the time comes."

"Tell me something, Vince. What the hell happened to you out in Brighton Beach? I mean, let's face it. You were always an asshole, but at least you weren't a thug and a murderer. You were crazy but you were a good cop. What was it? The money?"

"Like you said, what difference does it make now?"

"I guess you're right."

"It hasn't sunk in yet has it? What's going to happen. Look at it this way: you got up this morning probably thinking it was going to be pretty much like any other day, right? And then you meet me and everything changes, and now here we are at the end of the day."

"So," I said, "what's the big plan?"

"Don't worry; it'll be quick."

"I appreciate that."

"You sure you haven't heard from O'Neal? I mean, he knows you're down here. It's kind of strange he hasn't tried to contact you, wouldn't you say?"

"Why would he call me?"

"I thought you two were buds."

"I thought we were buds too, but here we are."

"Listen to me, you stupid jerk. This thing is run out of New York. It's not my operation. These aren't a bunch of stupid wops running around shaking down restaurants and fag joints, okay? We're talking Wall Street brokers. Ex-KGB CPAs and scams so big they haven't even been invented yet. This is big time shit, Jack. These people don't play around. What happens to you is not up to me."

"Who's it up to then? The red head?"

"For now it is."

"Candy said she was married to some guy named Kaminski. What happened to him?"

"Candy's got a big mouth. I might have to stick something in it when I get back. Kaminski's dead. Somebody put a bullet in him while he was sitting in his car."

"What a surprise that is."

"What's that supposed to mean?"

I don't know. It might not mean anything. I guess it depends on when you started fucking his wife—before or after the funeral."

Fernandez glared at me for a long, drawn out moment in which his ego struggled with his better judgment, but at last he couldn't help himself. He grinned, throwing in a quick wink in case I hadn't gotten the message.

"I thought it might be something like that," I said.

"Anyway, he was on his way out. I did him a favor."

"Just like Cal Belkin, right?"

"Exactly. That's the way it works in the animal kingdom, Jackie, my boy. You get old; you slow down. Sooner or later a young buck comes along and takes your place."

"And your wife."

"Listen to me. Any guy who falls for a girl forty years younger than he is, especially if he's got money, is asking for trouble. Eventually, he's going to get taken for all he's worth and then some. It was bound to happen sooner or later."

There was the muffled trilling of a cell phone, but it wasn't Vince's. It was mine. He looked at the number on the display, frowned across the seat at me then flipped open the phone.

"Well hello there, Miss Belkin, how are you? What happened? You were supposed to call me when you got down here, but it looks to me like you called someone else first instead. No, sorry, can't do that. Mr. Vaughn is busy. He can't come to the phone right now. Where are you? Sorry, honey I can't do that either; I might hurt myself, but I promise I'll do it to you when we finally meet. Is that right? Well, I tell you what, you stupid cunt, if you go to the police, what do you think is going to happen to your hero here? Think about that. All right, fuck you, so long."

Fernandez closed the phone and looked at me in disappointment. I had let the coach down again. Why is it that the biggest liars always have the hardest time accepting other people's deceptions? This was a man who had betrayed his friends, his family, his community, his city and his badge for money, cocaine, and some psychopathic Russian leg, and yet he was unable to understand why a woman he was trying to kill wouldn't tell him the truth about where she was.

"I guess there's not much chance of you telling me where I can find her, is there?" he asked.

"About the same chance as you letting me go."

"You know," Vince said. "It doesn't have to be quick like I said before. Maybe I should ask my buddies to show you the carving skills they learned in jail over in Mother Russia. What do you think about that?"

I turned my head and pretended to look out the window. Not that I needed it, but the thought of being slowly sliced to pieces by a couple of sadists added to my motivation to somehow work my hands free. I had been trying to stretch the plasticuffs apart ever since they'd been put on back in the club's parking lot half an hour earlier, and I was making headway, but it was slow going and I was getting tired. The sustained isometric pressure I was applying to my bonds was making my muscles burn from the steady build up of lactic acid, the result being a gradual reduction in strength just when I needed it the most.

It would have been easier if my hands had been tied behind me; that way, I would have been able to use my shoulders, chest and biceps to better effect. Even then, it wouldn't have been easy to break the cuffs -- though I had seen it done before, usually by drunken cops trying to show off for their pals. But I had found that by contracting the muscles between my shoulder blades and pulling the shoulder blades closer together while at the same time trying to separate my wrists, I was able to use a lot more of my upper body strength than I would have expected, so much so that I was now worried that the plastic would break before I was ready. The trick was to keep Vince from noticing that I was up to anything, and that meant turning away from him from time to so he wouldn't notice that I was straining so hard that the blood vessels in my temples felt like they were about to burst open at any moment. When I looked again, Vince was intently studying the display of my cell phone, scrolling patiently through my contact list, no doubt looking for any acquaintances we might have in common.

"Find anything interesting?" I asked.

"Who's Susan Andrews?"

"A client."

"What about the Sheik?"

"He's another client."

"Why does he call himself the Sheik?"

"Because that's what he is, you fucking moron."

"What is he? An Arab or something?"

"No," I said. "He's a Presbyterian. Jesus, Vince. I never realized you were so goddamned ignorant. Didn't you ever go to school or anything?"

"Yea, but I was absent a lot. What does this CD stand for?"

O'Neal had never given me his home or cell phone number. CD was his work number at Club Deuce. Until now, I had forgotten I had stored it. I thought fast but not fast.

"That must be Cindy Donovan," I said.

"Another client?"

"That's right."

"You sure about that?"

"Why wouldn't I be? It's my phone."

"I don't know," Fernandez said. "Seems to me you hesitated a little. Tell you what. Why don't we just give this Cindy Donavan a call and see what she has to say for herself. What do you say to that?"

"Go ahead. It's your dime."

"I got another idea. I'll put it on speakerphone. That way it'll be fun for the whole family."

Vince tapped the speakerphone, and I turned back to the window. The plasticuffs had lost most their tensile strength. I was fairly certain that it would now be possible for me to pull free of them if I could just get a little more leverage, but having my hands free in the back seat of a car that was moving as fast we were going wouldn't do me very much good. For one thing, Vince was far too strong and crazy for me to overpower, and I doubted I'd be able to get the door open before he could grab me. Even if I did manage to jump free, at the speed we were traveling, I'd surely end up as road kill one way or the other.

"Club Deuce," a familiar voice said. It was Denny O'Neal. That New York Irish accent was hard top miss. Fernandez was having a good night. He smiled and gave me another wink.

"Who's this?" Fernandez asked.

"Who are you looking for, pal?"

Fernandez didn't answer. Instead, he gently closed the phone and showed me his teeth again. "I guess Dennis didn't recognize my voice," he said. "Just as well. That way it'll be more of a surprise when I stop by for an aperitif. "Where is this place anyway, Club Deuce?"

"Look it up."

"Kind of funny when you think about it, isn't it?" Fernandez said. "The three of us get reunited, and I have to end up killing both you and O'Neal on the same day. That's what I call a real tragedy."

We had left the turnpike now and were passing through a small town with no name and a forlorn single story motel whose only light came from the vacancy sign standing guard over a parking lot empty except for an old station wagon with a rusted rear fender torn half way off. Farther on, there was a weather beaten filling station with two ancient fuel pumps and a sign with gas prices from the previous year. Attached to the garage stood a small convenience store with barred windows and empty milk crates in two stacks on either side of the padlocked door. Over the garage, a bleak patch of light filtered through an open window where a thin yellow curtain lifted and fell, lifted and fell, flirting with the warm, westerly breeze. And looming over the motel and the gas station and the garage and the convenience store, a behemoth of a billboard that was thirty-feet wide and as half as much high that assured anyone who cared that there were plenty of alligator wrestling and airboat rides to be had if you could just last another ten deserted miles.

Past the town and onto another road, this one recently and unexpectedly paved in fresh blacktop, as though some contractor had made a mistake and forgotten that no one lived this far out. The Hummer's headlights pushed ahead into the darkness, strumming the rows of pale birch trees running ahead of us. Then a sharp turn onto a service road and dirt again and the grinding of pebbles underneath the Hummer's big wide tires. Even with the air conditioning on, I could smell the fires. The Everglades were burning again. It was that time of year. Tonight, people as far east as Miami Beach would smell the smoke and wonder where it had come from. I saw flames in the distance. The fires must have been burning for a long time, because a large portion of the sky had been blotted by the rising smoke, as though the stars had been erased and God was starting over.

And me sitting there in the back seat thinking to myself that this was almost *it,* the lady or the tiger, the end or the beginning. Somehow and for some reason, I still felt that *it* was still up to me, not so much in terms of what would happen exactly, but more in the line of how *it* would go down. Did Vince really expect me to kneel humbly in the dirt like some poor kidnapped choirboy so that he or one of the others could more conveniently shoot me in the back of my head?

Surely, Fernandez had to at least suspect that when the time came, and I saw that there was no chance that I would use everything, I had to add some final flourish to my own death; that I would leave at least one of them with some long lasting pain or disfigurement to remember me by? Maybe a kneecap shattered by the heel of my shoe; or an eye that would probably need surgery to fix; or at the very least, a couple of testicles that would never again dare to descend into the fine light of day. Surely, he knew me better than to think I was just going to go peacefully to my death. And what about the Xanax offer? Was he serious? What I needed was that little vial of coke in his pocket; that, and maybe three or four tablets of Ritalin as a chaser. I needed speed and focus, not comfort.

For as long as I had known him, I had always played the part of Jekyll to his Hyde, but with someone as borderline as Fernandez, that wasn't a particularly tall order. I had to admit though that he had never gone so far into the dark side that I hadn't been able to understand him. The difference between us, therefore, wasn't one of kind but rather of a question degree, and in certain situations, especially dangerous ones, Fernandez was the one you wanted with you. When the terrorists storm the cockpit of your plane, it's Vince you want standing in the aisle blocking their way. He was mean and he was crazy and nobody liked him, but he was the always the first guy through the door. As for me, I tended to play by my father's rule: if somebody's going to get hurt, he'd told me once, make sure you're not the first one. When in doubt, put somebody in the hospital. Words to live by, those, and words to die by as well. Whatever happens, do not go gently to your executioner. Make them pay. Make the sons of bitches remember you.

The key thing now was to find the gap. In every situation, no matter how bad it looks, no matter how dangerous it appears, there's always a gap. The trick is to see it and take it before it closes, because chances are, if it does, there won't be another chance. It's like meeting a woman in the subway car of a train you rarely take in a part of town you hardly ever go to. The two of you are hitting it off real well and you can really feel it flowing between you, and you know you don't have that much time to make your move. You are like a salesman at the end of his pitch. The only thing left to do now is to close the deal and get her phone number. Because there are a lot of people in this city and a lot of subway cars, and this train is not part of your usual routine, and meeting this woman is part of a beautiful accident that will never again be repeated. Like Elvis said: It's now or never.

The utility road ended in a patch of sand surrounded on three sides by a forest of saw grass as high as my head. I had time for one last try at the plasticuffs before the Hummer ground to a slow stop. One more surge of strength should do it—but not quite yet, though we were getting close to the time. Right away, the tall grass went into the inventory of things I could use when the time came, and it was coming soon. I was focused now on finding the gap, knowing that it could take any form and be anything: a sound, perhaps a whistle; the dark wing of an owl sweeping by you at the edge of sight; the splash of an alligator hitting the water; a cloud masking the moon. It might be Fernandez stopping to take another hit of coke, or the Chechen turning his back to take a piss against a tree. It could be anything at all. The trick was to be ready when the sign came.

Stefan the Chechen opened the door on my side of the Hummer and stepped back as I climbed out. His automatic was pointed at my midsection in a casual way that told me he considered holding the gun on me more of a formality than a necessity. That was something else I could use. I was stiff after the long ride, and my leg still hurt enough to make me wonder just how much it could take if I needed to do any running. If I got the chance. Vince got out on his side of the Hummer hitched up his pants, and looked around and up at the sky like a tourist. Every nerve in my body was part of an alarm system that was ready to go off the moment I saw the gap, and I had better be seeing it soon too, because the realm of possibility was shrinking mighty fast around me.

Then the glow of headlights appeared as the Camaro, the Chariot, came into sight, and the moment I saw my car, I added it to my inventory. It was a good addition, especially with the gun under the seat. I liked it. It was a package deal, a two for the price of one, but there was still something missing, an element to the plot I hadn't yet spotted. But I knew it was out there waiting to be plucked.

"Look at those stars," Vince said triumphantly. "You don't see stars like that in the city. Too many lights."

Zhukov got out of the Camaro and stretched his arms above his head. He flicked his cigarette away and lit another while we waited. Stefan the Chechen never took his eyes off me, not once. He didn't seem to be enjoying himself very much. I wondered how many evenings like this one he had found himself living through, how many poor slobs, complete strangers, former friends and business associates he had been ordered to kill out here in the middle of the swamp. What a life it must be when even murder becomes boring, another day, another dollar.

"Can you walk?" Vince said.

"I think so," I said.

"You sure you don't want that Xanax?" he asked. "Though I guess it's a little late now. You look okay to me though."

Right then, it came to me that Fernandez had given me something else I could use. My hip. It hadn't occurred to me that an injury could be useful, so I hadn't bothered to consider it. Now, however, I realized my mistake and quickly added my hip to my private stock of possibilities, things I could use. The hip hurt, sure, but with the right people chasing me it wouldn't matter, not for a while anyway. Vince and his comrades were not exactly outstanding examples of cross training. They had sacrificed everything in favor of size and strength and power, and were way too heavy to run either very fast or very far. Their combined mass was another weapon in my bag of tricks, and if I could put enough distance between us, I might yet get away. But not yet.

"Let's walk," Vince said.

We pushed on through the saw grass, me in front, with the three of them trailing me. I had invented an exaggerated limp for myself, one that made it seem like I was half dragging my leg with my foot turned outward at a ninety degree angle from my body. I could feel them going for the act. I could feel their patience with me, their confidence in the presence of a man who was obviously lame. They had done this before and were in no hurry. Then I stumbled deliberately and fell down heavily onto my side, grabbing at my hip and twisting my face into a semblance of agony, lifting my chin and crying out in pain that was one third real.

Vince reached down and offered me a hand, but I knocked it away and got slowly to my feet. Fernandez stepped back and frowned. Anton wiped the sweat from his brow and smashed a bug against his forearm. The Chechen kept his flashlight and gun pointed at me. I got slowly to my feet, but stayed bent over, my head down, my hands between my knees, breathing heavily, like an out of breath quarter miler. They didn't rush me, but I didn't push it too far either, and then we were walking again through saw grass that tore at our arms, drawing blood and mosquitoes and curses from Zhukov and the Chechen.

"Be careful of the quicksand," Vince said. "It starts somewhere around here."

That was it. What I had been waiting for. The quicksand. I could smell it now, like the rot of dead bodies just ahead of us. That was where we were going. Where I was going. It made sense. We were almost there, and I could feel them starting to relax like laborers at the end of a long day, who can taste that first cold beer way before they've punched their time cards out. My escorts had already begun to move ahead in time toward what they would do after they had finished with me. Their minds had already pushed ahead, past me and the quicksand and into the future. But not me. I was totally in the now. I was standing on the edge of time like Greg Louganis with his toes curled around the far end of a diving board, ready for one last jump.

They were already thinking about food or sex or sleep, or, as in Vince's case, a little late night killing. He glanced at his watch like a businessman between meetings. It was like I could read his mind. He was thinking of his old friend, Denny O'Neal, and what he was going to do to him. I was sure of it. If everything went smoothly, He might even have time to do it tonight. Make it back to Miami, find out where Club Deuce was, then go and scope the place out and wait for O'Neal's shift to end.

And if not tonight, then tomorrow would be time enough, maybe even better because then he'd have time to plan it perfectly. I was no longer of any concern to him, or to the others. I was no longer a factor in their equations. As far as they were concerned, I was already with the others they had fed to the sinkhole. I was already part of the past. To Fernandez, Zhukov and Stefan the Chechen, I was already dead. But not to me.

We entered a small clearing with saw grass on one side and a few massive banyan trees to the right. The trees rose high above the water, their thick roots spreading out in all directions like tendrils, looping and curling over one above the muck surrounding the trees. The moment my eyes touched their twisted shapes, I knew that they were what I needed, what I had been waiting for—if I could do it. Everything would depend on how much spring I had left in my legs after so many years.

One day, long ago, after I had gotten myself kicked off the football team at Rutgers, the track coach, a big Jamaican named Wedderburns, had come looking for me with a proposition. He told me he needed someone for the decathlon and that he had had his eye on me for a while. I took one look at the butts on the female sprinters and signed right up for the hardest sport in the world. There are ten events in the sport, and the funny thing is you can win without winning a single one of them, though you have to do fairly well across the board. In fact, a guy who comes in third in all ten events will generally win. You have to run and jump and throw. Generally speaking, you will have a few events that you are particularly good at. I was good at the throws, particularly the javelin. When it came to the long jumps, I was only slightly better than mediocre, though, considering my size, better than some might have thought. A good jump for me has been about twenty-one feet give or take, but tonight I was putting in a request for only twelve. I would not have much of a run up, however—at the most three or four steps, but it would have to be enough.

I focused on the root nearest where we stood. I had to land going forward then get around and behind the tree fast before they could get off a decent shot. The good thing was that of the three of them only the Chechen had his gun out. We walked a few more feet. We were getting close to *it.* I was coiled tightly into myself, but none of them knew it. Then Vince gave the order to stop. I turned around to get a better look at how the were standing, how they were positioned. It was almost what I wanted—Fernandez and Zhukov standing between me and the Chechen' s 9 mm. I tested the ground for firmness with my shoe. It was a bit soft, and I wished I was wearing cleats, but it would have to do.

"Okay," Vince said. "Whose turn is it?"

"Not mine," Stefan the Chechen said. "I did the last one."

"You lie, Stefan," Zhukov said. "What about the jeweler? I killed him. With my hands. The fat one. What was his name again?"

"You're talking about that asshole Grimole," Vince said. "Who told you he was a jeweler? He was a stock broker."

"I thought you said he was a jeweler," Zhukov said.

"I said he was a Jew, you fucking moron!" Vince

exploded. “Not a jeweler. Never mind, give me that fucking gun. I’ll do it myself. You fucking guys make me sick. Now I have to shoot my own goddamned friend in the head. No wonder your whole fucking empire fell apart. You people got no fucking morals, for Christ’s sake.”

Vince looked at me and shook his head in frustration. Proper killers, unlike personal trainers, were in short supply, and it was clear he was having trouble finding adequate help. I waited for him to turn his back and take a few steps away from me then pulled my left hand out of the plastic loop still holding it. Then something inside me shifted, and suddenly, everyone was moving in slow motion. The Chechen was handing his gun over to Fernandez, butt first. Zhukov was lighting another cigarette, his head bent forward as he struck a match. Now Vince was reaching out for the gun, his hand drifting away from his body like smoke. The hand-off seemed to take so long that I almost got bored watching it. I waited for the Chechen to drop his eyes as Vince took the gun from his outstretched hand as though it was a baton. And I said to myself: Now.

10

By the time I heard the first of their shouts, I was already in the air, focusing with everything I had on the sturdy looking root I had chosen for my landing. The gunshots begin all at once, snapping branches and tearing off the bark off trees. A sudden stinging sensation in my side. Falling forward now in a haze of movement, grabbing another root and whipping my legs around and behind me. More shots, a shower of mud and splinters of bark hitting me in the cheek just under the eye as I ease my legs down into the muck and pull myself behind the tree and beyond the reach of their bullets.

Now, and always now, and nothing but the now, so help me God who art in heaven, hallowed be thy name. I am still alive. I am hurt but I am breathing. My breathing is so heavy and deep in my chest it feels automatic, like a vacuum cleaner. No time, yet all the time in the world. I smear my face with mud and peek around the bole of the tree, just like they teach you. Fernandez had dropped to one knee and was now taking his time, gripping the Chechen' s gun with both hands and spreading out his bullets in an arc while his two companions just blasted away in my general direction, making much noise but doing little damage—unless you counted the trees and the mud.

After a moment, they stopped shooting and began probing between the tree roots with their flashlights. I watched as Vince rose to his feet, took a few steps forward, and then backed up as though he was actually considering attempting make the same jump I had. For a moment, I thought he might actually do it too, but not even the 'roids would make him crazy enough to risk landing in quicksand with only Zhukov and the Chechen around to pull him out.

"That was a pretty good jump, Vaughn!" Fernandez shouted. "I always knew you were a nigger! But guess what, scumbag? It doesn't matter! The only thing you did is buy yourself a little more time and a lot more pain. So go ahead, run, Jack flash. Run your ass off. Have yourself a good fucking time! You hear me, Vaughn? Enjoy yourself! Because this time when we get you—and trust me, we will fucking get you—it's going to be slow. Very fucking slow! You hear me, motherfucker?"

Vince went on screaming for a while then grew quiet. I put my back against the bole of the tree and stared at the hunter's moon shining high above the vast plains of saw grass ahead of me. Gradually, when my breathing returned to normal, I felt along my right side where I'd been hit. I thought the bullet might have gone all the way through but I could not be sure. Now it was time to move. I grabbed hold of a vine above my head and hauled my legs free out of the muck then fought to keep my balance as I got my feet onto the roots again. Besides a giant Puerto Rican on steroids and a pair of homicidal Russians, I also had water moccasins and other kinds of snakes to worry about, and that meant staying out the mud as much as possible until I could make it to higher ground. But first I had to do something about the khaki suit I was wearing. It made me much too easy a target, especially with a nearly full moon. I took off my jacket and dipped it into the muck a few times, twisting it around until it was as tie died in mud and as dark as my trousers. When I was done, I wrung out the excess gunk and tied the sleeves of the jacket around my waist. Then I went to work on my arms and neck, streaking the skin there with more of the damp, fertile smelling mud until I was covered in the stuff like a commando.

When I was done, I crouched low again and snuck another glance around the tree. There was just enough light now to make out the movements of three bulky silhouettes against the lighter background of the saw grass, but the bugs and frogs and god knows what else were making such a racket that I couldn't hear much of what they were saying, though I could guess. Vince was no doubt hoping that I had been hit by one of their rounds, and that I was either dead or so badly wounded that I would eventually die anyway, in which case he could head back to the Emperor's Club and claim mission accomplished to the former Mrs. Kaminski.

That would be a bit risky, however. There was a chance, not very large, that I might actually make it out of the swamps alive and go to the cops or better yet, the FBI with my story, and if he claimed to have killed me without actually having seen my lovely corpse, he would have to depend on the Chechen and Zhukov to back up his story with Marina. Nothing I had seen had suggested to me that kind of trust existed amongst them. Vince was too hopped up on steroids and coke to trust anyone other than himself, and as for the two former Soviets, I doubted that either man would go out on a limit for someone they might respect but probably didn't like all that much.

Besides, all three of them were afraid of Marina. So was I. It's not every woman who can convince her lover to kill her husband, a Russian gangster, who just happened to be his own boss. She would have to be very good in the sack indeed to make a crazy idea like that seem like the sensible thing to do under any circumstances. I have done some pretty stupid things while under the influence of a particular woman, but killing husbands, especially mobster husbands, would not have been something that would have crossed my mind. Regardless of how seductive its source, the request alone would have been enough to have sent me easing on down the road again. There are worse thing in this life than sleeping alone, and waking up next to Marina Gero was no doubt one of them, and if she ever found out that I was still walking the earth after Fernandez had told her otherwise, she would make Lorena Bobbitt seem like a Barbie doll by comparison.

No matter how long it took, Fernandez would have to make certain I was dead. I was sure of that, knowing him as I did. The question was: how? For sure they weren't going to follow the way I had come. That meant they would have to find another way around the sinkhole, and at night that wouldn't be easy—that is unless they already new an alternate path. They had probably scoped out the terrain a long time ago and knew their way around. That meant I had to proceed on the assumption that if there was way to cut me off before I got to a road or highway then they would know about it.

Crouched over like a hunchback, I waded away from the tree, but the farther I got from the tree the more I worried about the moon. It was very bright, and even without the help of their flashlights, it was still possible they would spot anything moving out here where there was more of a shine on the surface of the water. I snatched a miniature island of dried grass as it floated by me and pulled it against my body. It wasn't nearly sturdy enough to use as a raft, but by holding onto it and keeping the mass of foliage behind me, I took advantage of the cover it gave me as I made my way toward higher ground.

Two facts told me I was heading west. One was the fact that I could easily spot Polaris, the North Star off to my right. The other clue was the direction the mass of reeds had been floating in when I latched onto it. The Everglades empty into the Gulf of Mexico and anything that floats flows along on that slow, almost imperceptible southerly current made west straight ahead, and the farther west I traveled, the less likely I was to run into any alligators or water moccasins and the more likely to find a trail and maybe, if I got lucky, some decent people who wouldn't be interested in killing me, or at least not right away.

It took me half an hour to make it to the field of saw grass, but now that the adrenaline had begun to wear off, I realized just how tired and banged up I really was. My shirt was soaked with blood, and my right hip felt unstable, and I wondered if I had damaged the ligaments that stabilize the joint. What I needed was a week's supply of pain killers, some gauze, a pint or so of some kind of antiseptic like hydrogen peroxide and a cell phone. I was also a prime candidate for an ambulance and a whole team of paramedics, but those were miles away—if I could make it.

I lay down on the damp earth and lay back against a rotted-out log, too tired even begin to worry about any snakes that might be using it for a nest. While I rested, I thought about Dawn. She would know better than to stay at my place, but if she went to O'Neal for help like I had told her to do, it might turn out that I had given Fernandez a two for one. Just as I was about to get up again, I saw lights moving through the foliage. They were about a hundred yards away and very faint. At first I thought they might be fireflies but their glow was too steady, their procession too precise.

I stopped and stared behind me at the way I had come and wondered if I should take the chance of retracing my steps in the hopes of getting hold of a car, possibly even the Chariot. The thought of driving out the swamps with the Camaro's souped-up engine under me held an appeal that, for a moment, was almost overwhelming, but just then a bright red emergency flare flew into the sky high above the tree whose shelter I had just left. It was answered a moment later by the neon red burst of another flare ahead of me in the western sky, in the direction I was going. The second flare had no sooner fizzled out then a third went off to my right very close to where I had seen the lights a moment earlier.

That could mean only one thing. Fernandez and company had called in the reinforcements, and now it appeared that not only was I being flanked but surrounded as well. I waited for a third flare to split the wall of darkness to the south and complete the circle but it didn't come. The question was why not? Was it that they didn't have the manpower or was it a question of the terrain, of too much swamp and no road? Or maybe, just maybe, south was the way they wanted me to go. Maybe they were trying to herd me into some kind of trap. Surely they would know that I had seen the flares they had fired, and if that was the case they would expect me to head away from them in the only direction left open to me. South.

I decided to stick with my original plan and continue on toward the west. That was where I would find higher ground and a way out of the Everglades. No matter what else might be waiting for me when I got there, I would meet it on my own terms. I would not be herded, not by Fernandez, not by Stefan the Chechen or Zhukov. The sooner I got out of the swamps the sooner I could get back to Miami, back to Dawn and O'Shea and to Cal Belkin—if he was still alive.

I had done the Everglades thing when I had first come to Miami back in my tourist phase, but that had been five years ago when a cocktail waitress I knew named Odaylis had talked me into going camping with her. Odaylis was part Miccosukee Indian and knew her way around the swamps as well as she did around the bars in Key West. She had spent her childhood hunting and fishing with her father and older brothers before they all took jobs in the new casinos. She told me about how the army had chased their ancestors into the Everglades from where they had originally lived up near the border with Georgia. The only reason her people had survived, she told me, was because the Americans didn't care for the swamps with all its insects, alligators and humidity.

According to Odaylis, the Everglades had been the American equivalent of the so-called "White Man's Graveyard" that had killed off so many Englishman over in Central Africa around the same time. A lot of soldiers went into the swamp and a good many of them never returned. For Odaylis's people, however, there was no other option available except to adapt to their new environment. For them, it was a choice between freedom and survival, internment and extinction. Once they had made it into the Everglades, the politicians, the soldiers and the land hungry settlers left the Miccosukee alone, if for no other reason that they simply didn't want such difficult territory.

Looking back, I recalled that Odaylis's family hadn't much cared for me. Her father, after warning me not to take it personally, had told me that while I seemed like a nice enough guy, I still was not one of "the people," which was pretty much the same thing my Jewish girlfriend's father had told me when his daughter bought me home for Passover Seder when I was in college. Ami had tried to talk me into converting. After all, she said, you're already circumcised, so what's the big deal? Besides, you're not religious anyway. What difference does it make if you're Jewish or not? Too which my response had been that, in my opinion at least, the Jews had already suffered enough, and even though there was nothing particularly wrong with my self-esteem, it was hard for me to see how I would be doing them much of a favor by signing up with them.

The funny thing about Odaylis is that she had blond hair and green eyes—not exactly traits of the Red Man as I recall. That made it kind of strange to be staring cross a campfire at her lovely face while she talked on and on about all the evil shit the white man had done to her people. But when you're young and in love and trying to get laid, you tend to overlook these kinds of contradictions and instead try and see the good in people rather than the stuff that makes you want to bash yourself in the head with the lid of a garbage pail.

I tried to remember what Odaylis and her two brothers, a couple of pot-selling delinquents, had tried to teach me about surviving out in the wilderness. One thing hey had told me for sure was never to go camping without food, water, a flashlight a good knife and something to make fire with. Another was never to sleep on the ground at night no matter how drunk you were. Now, four years later, here I was back in the swamps, sitting on a rotten log which was probably a condominium for half the snakes in Miami with no knife, no food, no water, and nothing to make fire with. I put my back against the log, closed my eyes, and tried to come up with some kind of plan.

It's been a long hard day, Vaughn, and you're a bit tired. You didn't expect to be out here in the goddamned Everglades with Vince Fernandez and the local chapter of the Russian Mafia trying to make you disappear. You were just a guy who happened to answer his phone at three o'clock in the morning, that's all. Anybody could have made that mistake. Next time, you'll do the smart thing and pull the phone out the wall and throw it in the closet. But it's too late now for regrets. In fact, it's always too late for regrets when you think about it.

And so that's why, Vaughn, we're willing to cut you a bit of slack tonight for forgetting who you are and for losing sight of what we are really dealing with here and accepting instead Fernandez's bullshit version of the current state of affairs. But, like I said, it's no big deal. You got careless. You walked into the Emperor's Club like you owned the place, and now you've paid the price for that little indiscretion. So here you are, wounded and with a bad hip; both just part of a temporary setback.

So don't be too hard on yourself, Vaughn. It's been a while since anyone has shot at you, and that means you're a bit rusty. But you're okay now. It's just that you've been playing Mister Personal Trainer for so long that you actually started to believe that's who you actually were. What a laugh! But we know who you really are Vaughn, and now you remember too, and that, as they say, makes all the difference in the way you now see things, doesn't it? You're the guy who went up that darkened staircase out in Lefrak City. That was you, wasn't it? Or were we mistaken?

No, that was you all right, remember? Calm, almost too calm, excited, glad, too, in a perverted kind of way that you've never admitted to anyone else, your revolver out, taking the steps one at a time, amazed at how well you could see in the dark, how sharp your hearing was. And the focus. You do remember the focus, don't you, Vaughn? Don't lie. We know you too well. Of course you do. It was the focus as much as it was the bullet from your gun that killed Officer Ed Henry that night. Wasn't it? You still had it even after Ed's bullet had ripped off part of your ugly face. That's how keen it was that night, the focus. If anything, the pain made it even sharper. That's how pure and simple it was. It was like cutting through a thick juicy steak and thinking of little else while you were doing it.

But we're not here to talk about Ed Henry tonight, Vaughn, may he rest in peace. That is an affair for another time and place, another venue, as they say in certain courts of earthly law. Suffice it to say, that he too had a high degree of focus, though that night, his was just a bit off, and that is why he is dead, and you are still alive. An affair of millimeters and milliseconds, the impersonal divisions of time and space. Call it fate. Call it what you will. It's not on tonight's agenda, Vaughn. What is important now is that you remember who you are, who you were, who you always will be. You're the man on the darkened staircase, going up, gun drawn, focused. That's all that matters now, not what that clown Fernandez thinks.

That muscle head thinks he understands the situation. He's under the impression that it's he and his Russian friends who are the hunters, and for a moment you thought so to, but now we know the truth, don't we, Vaughn? Sure we do. For a moment, due to fatigue and other factors we have previously discussed, you had already begun to think of how you were going to escape, how you were going to make a run for it, how you are going get away. But now that you have come to your senses, there won't be anymore of that kind of crap. There won't be any more mistakes concerning who it is who is looking for whom. That was the kind of bullshit we won't stand for it. Now just rest here a bit and pull yourself toward yourself, and try and remember what the Indian girl with the blonde hair and green eyes told you. Then take what you need and throw the rest away, and when you are ready, get up and go and do what you have to do.

I rested for a few more minutes then rose stiffly to my feet. I was a bit worn out, but I no felt longer desperate. I didn't bother fighting the feeling that somehow, crazy as it sounded, what happened now was up to me. The first thing I needed to do was pay a visit to whoever it was that had fired that first flare I had seen in the sky off to the west, and thanks to his thoughtfulness, I now knew exactly where he was.

I used mud to blacken up a bit more then continued west until I came to a patch of marshland. There was plenty of water around, and that meant the possibility of snakes and alligators, though I still thought it was a bit too dry here for the latter to be much of a concern. I got my shirt off, dunked it in the murky water and gathered up the corners so that when I lifted it out, I had a sack of rapidly leaking water filled with that looked like some hard core macrobiotic soup. I held the shirt up over my mouth, lifted my chin and prayed I had remembered correctly what Odaylis had told me. The water drained trough the shirt's fabric in a narrow stream and poured over my face and dawn my throat. The idea, according to Odaylis, was that the shirt would act as a filter, getting rid of a lot of the grass and weeds and some of the stuff that could make you sick. That was the theory; if it proved wrong, my guts would soon let me know about it.

I was tired and hungry, but the ground was firmer now and it was easier to walk. I entered a small forest of punk trees that had been ripped apart by some unknown hurricane in the past. There were hundreds of trees stripped bare of their bark and toppled over one another in every direction like pick-up sticks. I remembered Odaylis telling me that back in the day when the government wanted to drain the Everglades, they had imported trees, from Australia because they were good at sucking up water. Now there was no getting rid of them. But they had hard wood, and after a short search, I found a branch sturdy enough to serve as a walking stick and weapon.

Every few minutes, I stopped and listened but the swamp was so noisy I could not have heard anyone coming even if they had been a few feet away. That meant I had to rely mostly on my sight but the foliage was so dense that it was hard to see very far ahead except when I came to a clearing. The good thing was that my eyes had adjusted so well to the dark that with the aid of the moon, I could see much better than I would have thought, especially peripherally.

Just as I was about to cross another small clearing, I spotted lights to my right again, only this time much closer. I got behind a tree and waited for the lights to appear again, and then, there they were: three stalks of light, crisscrossing one another about two hundred feet from where I was. It was time to move, but I knew that if I ran now they were bound to be breaking through the branches. I looked around for a tree I could climb, one with low hanging branches, preferably another banyan tree.

I spotted the outline of what seemed to be just what I was looking for then ran toward it in a crouch just as the first beam of light hit the tree whose cover I had jut quit. I pulled myself up onto a branch and tested its weight for a moment before continuing to climb. Suddenly, there was a high-pitched screech right in front of me and something dark swept across my face nearly knocking backwards.

The men with the flashlights heard the commotion and turned their flashlights on the tree, but the beams struck just below me, giving me just enough time to flatten myself against a branch. I lay very still as they swept their lights back and forth. Then someone tripped and dropped their lamp. A familiar voice cursed, and I watched as a large shadow bent over to retrieve his flashlight. It was Vince Fernandez. The three men stood whispering to one another then walked over to base of the tree and went around it, shining their flashlight beams into and between the branches, but I was too well hidden for them to see me as long as I didn't move.

A moment passed and the trio of lights swung way from the tree again. I remained still, listening. Vince called someone on his cell phone, and his voice rose to where I could easily hear the conversation. How the fuck do I know, he was saying. No, I don't think so, but if he's still alive then he must have seen the flares. He'll try to avoid them for sure. Wouldn't you? That means we got him boxed in. The only way he can go is toward your boy Ivan and his crew. Don't worry we got more guys coming. Personally, if you ask me, I think he's dead. What? First light though, just to be on the safe side, I'll get one of these rednecks they got out here to bring out some of their dogs see if we can pick up his trail or at least find his body. No, don't you fucking dare say anything to her about it. You let me handle that. Anyway, once he's dead it won't make any difference what happened. Yea, you think so? Well, we'll see what you say when we're face to face, scumbag. Yea fuck you too.

Thirty feet below me, a soft click and more whispers. I lay very still, stretched out along the length of the limb. I'm so quiet by now, not even the tree knows I'm resting there. Something crawls over the back of my hand and it doesn't bother me one bit. I'm one with nature like Walt Whitman and Tarzan. Someone lit a cigarette beneath me. The faint smell of tobacco smoke rose toward me for a brief second before it was overwhelmed by the stronger more feral scents jamming in the night air. One last time before the move off, the men below me probed the branches around me with their flashlights, but I could tell their hearts weren't in it, that they didn't really think I was anywhere in the vicinity. Then they went crashing off through the forest.

I waited for their lights to fade away in the distance, and then, very slowly, because my hip had stiffened up on me again, I climbed down out of the tree. I looked back toward the east, back the way I had come. The sky there was getting gradually lighter; it was still, however, a good two hours before sunrise. I wasn't sure how much farther I had to go before I reached the spot where the man in the west had fired the flare, but I knew he had to be near. I went back to the where I had dropped my stick and set off again.

He was close now, very close. I could feel it, but I still couldn't see or hear anything that sounded human. I closed my eyes and concentrated on the darkness ahead of me. After awhile, I managed to get my mind quieted down enough so that I was no longer talking to myself. I waited until the inside of my head was like a small quiet room, and then I tried to extend—if that is the right word—I tried to extend myself beyond where I was, beyond the cypress tree I was crouched beside. Someone was out there all right. Of that, I was certain, and he or maybe they were waiting too, waiting for me. They would be waiting and listening, but since they were already in place and no longer had to move through the undergrowth as I did, the advantage was theirs, because no matter how quiet I was, they would surely hear me coming before I heard them.

The sound of birds and of insects in their multitudes, buzzing; the damp, sweet air; the sharp crack of branches breaking, and the burnt scent of a far off brush fire. Only the moon was silent. Then, a single muffled cough that wasn't repeated. My attention floated toward it like smoke riding on the wind. There you are, I thought. There you are. Glad you coughed when you did, buddy. You did me a favor, because otherwise I was heading right for you. You must have a rifle. What the hell else would you have? And you got to have a night scope or something like it, right? But tell me this: are you alone? I kind of doubt it. Not unless Vince couldn't round up enough guys on such short notice. I did a bit more concentrating. It didn't feel like many, probably not much more than two or three, but that would be more than enough, especially since they would most certainly be armed, probably with automatic weapons.

You guys must be getting bored, I thought. The excitement of the case had surely worn off by now, and they had probably begun to tell themselves that I wasn't coming, that I had seen the flare ahead of me and had turned south just as Fernandez had expected. At first they had all been keyed up, expecting me to come crashing toward them any minute now, fleeing for my life like Richard Kimble and making so much goddamned noise in the process that all they would have to do is wait for me to break into the open then blow me apart before I even knew they were there.

But now a couple of hours had passed, and they were getting tired of waiting. It was inevitable. No one can stay alert forever, and there is nothing more tedious than stakeout that lasts too long. Eventually your concentration wanders off and your mind begins to look for something better to do with its time and energy. You begin to cramp up from the lack of circulation in your arms and legs, and your lower back and neck begin to ache. Soon you're telling yourself that it's all just one colossal waste of time. You can't wait to go home to your bed, to your wife or girlfriend. Then you begin to think about the past and all the things you didn't do or wished you hadn't done and then about the future and about what you're going to do tomorrow and next week and so on down the road. You think about a lot of things, and that's perfectly normal, because this whole thing is just a big waste of time, because Vaughn isn't coming tonight. He went the other way.

Come on, move, I thought to myself. Show me where you are. I'm getting tired of this silent stalemate of not-moving and too much waiting. Maybe I'll be able to go round you all together, though I have my doubts about being able to do it without you hearing me. That's what you're waiting for, isn't it. Even if turns out to be a black bear or deer, what difference will it make? The next time around it might be the Motivator himself. You won't even have to hide the body. Why bother when the swamp hides its secrets so well.

Just give me some kind of sign, gentlemen, so we can finish this thing off once and for all. I need your car, and I need your food, and I need your water, and I need your cell phone. I'm a needy kind of guy tonight, so don't take it personally. I'm just like that crooked detective back at the Emperor's Club. I've got places to be and people to see. Now that I think about it that was a pretty nice suit that bastard was wearing. I'll say that much for him. Tailor made, bespoke. But one day it'll all come crashing down around you, and when it does, we both know that the feds will be the least of his problems. When that happens, it'll be a race to see who can get to him first, the gangsters or the cops. Can anybody here spell Witness Protection Program?

It would be light soon. The sun was a narrow neon bulge

welded to the earth's shadowy arc, but the moon still dominated the sky. Another cough, this time louder. I turned my head and stared at the spot where the sound came from. After a moment, I saw a tiny spark of light so brief that at first I thought I might have dreamed it. A cigarette lighter or a match, something that had sparked and flared and gone out. And I think to myself: that's good; they're starting to relax now. They've begun to give in to the desire to move around and get their blood flowing again, and if there's more than one of them, then they'll be anxious to talk as well. It's only human.

Because it's been a long night and they've been quiet for a long time, and their blood cells are scavenging through their veins, searching for nicotine and other stimulants like coffee and white sugar. Plus, they're all but sure it's almost over now. Any minute now the call will come that releases them from their long vigil; the man thy have been sitting out here getting bug bit for is dead. It's all been a waste of time, but at least they're getting paid to be out here. Now they can go home and get that shower and a few hours of sleep because Vaughn didn't come around last night, and he's not coming this morning either. Yea, that's what you think.

Then as I watched, two shadows rose slowly from the ground about a hundred feet away and the men began brushing themselves off. Both held long slender shapes that I took to be rifles of some sort. At first they were quiet, still on guard. Then one of them said something that made his companion laugh. The long dark ponchos they wore made them look like a pair of friars. They turned to face one another. One of them raised his voice, and at first I thought he was talking on a cell phone, but the harsh cackle of static told me it was more than likely a walkie-talkie that he was using.

As he spoke, the man with radio turned his back on me while his friend walked off by himself into the woods. I circled around as quickly as I could, running bent over like a chimp and staying as low to the ground as possible, until I heard the man who had walked away moving through the underbrush ahead of me. He had only gone about fifty yards away from his companion, but the underbrush hid from view. I came around a tree in time to see him squatting next to a fallen log. At first I wasn't sure what to do, because I had never attacked anybody while they were taking a shit before, but these were strange times, and besides, I couldn't have asked for a better opportunity. He had his pants pulled down and his rifle was leaning against a tree and this was an emergency. Sometimes you just have to be realistic about these things.

He never heard me coming. I just walked up and brought my stick down across the back of his head as hard as I could, though I tell you, I had to force myself to do it. It's never like the movies, never, and even as I hit him again a second time just as hard as the first, I had to block out the fact that what I was doing was wrong, even though I knew for a fact that he would have shot me to pieces if given the chance. There was no satisfaction in what I did, none at all, and I was horrified to realize that I had nothing personal against him. Not a single thing. That made it even worse, because if you're going to bash somebody upside the head with a piece of Australian wood, you should at least be human enough to dislike them while you're doing it.

The man fell forward, away from the log and his own crap as the flies zoomed toward the stench like fighter jets equipped with the best radar in the world. I took his gun and stepped back behind the tree and stood there listening and staring at him lying still on the ground. I knew it was stupid considering what I had just done, but I was none too happy when he didn't move at all. But there was nothing to do about it except o go after the other one and not stand there looking stupid, trying to pretend that all of sudden I had turned into Gandhi or somebody.

I went back the way I had come and found the other man down on one knee shoving his poncho into a knapsack. He had his back to me and that gave me enough time to get close enough so that when he finally heard or sensed my presence it was already too late. He turned around leisurely with no sense of alarm, expecting to see his companion standing there and not Vaughn of the Wilderness. He stared at the barrel of the assault rifle pointed at his midsection. I told him to stand up very slowly. His eyes stayed on mine the entire time he was getting to his feet. He was young, not far out of his teens with dark restless eyes and a hawk nose that someone had bent to one side. He looked worried but there was a flicker of hope in his eyes that I needed extinguish very quickly if he was going to live.

"Don't bother looking for your friend," I said. "I already took care of him." His face dropped and his eyes brightened.

"Did you kill him?"

"I don't know."

His accent took me by surprise. It was Israeli.

"He's my cousin. Can I go and look?"

"What are you doing out here?"

"Waiting for you."

"I know what you're thinking," I said. "But let me set you straight before you do something stupid. If you think you can get to that other gun, all I can say is, go ahead and try. We'll see what happens."

He didn't say anything but his hand drifted away from the knapsack like it was a shy girl's knee at a movie theatre, like he hadn't known what he was doing. I made him toss it and his radio over to me.

"Who were you talking to?" I asked.

"Mr. Fernandez."

"Where is that prick?"

He pointed off toward the south. "Over that way. There's a road. They were waiting for you there."

"What's an Israeli doing out here in the middle of the goddamned Everglades?"

"I want to go and look for my cousin."

"How old are you, kid?"

"Twenty-three."

"We'll go together."

I pointed him in the right direction then followed behind

him at a safe distance. By the time we got to the spot, the cousin had already rolled over onto his side and was trying, unsuccessfully, to get up. I was glad that I hadn't killed him, but now I had two of them to worry about and that meant everybody's longevity was still in question, including mine. The first boy ran over and knelt by his cousin's side while I went through his knapsack. Inside, I found a handy little Mauser 9 mm, which I pocketed. There was also a bottle of water and a Power Bar that I helped myself to while the boy ministered to his cousin.

"How's he doing?" I asked.

"I think he has a concussion."

"What's your name?"

"Ariel."

"Tell me something, Ariel. What were you planning to do to me? I mean if I hadn't got the drop on you that is?"

The young Israeli didn't say anything. He didn't have to. We both knew the answer. Then the radio cackled, and I heard Vince's voice come on. Ariel stared at me. His cousin sat up. He was a bit older, lighter skinned, and stockier. His light eyes stared at me without really seeing me. I tossed the radio to his cousin.

"You have a choice," I said. "Tell him I'm nowhere to be found and we'll all three walk out here like one big happy fucking family. Anything else and it's just going to be me. Capiche?"

I listened as he told Fernandez that neither he nor his cousin David had seen me. Ariel's eyes never left mine for a moment as he spoke. When he was done with the radio, he took a step toward me, as though to hand it back to me, but I stepped back and pointed the rifle at his chest and smiled.

"Have you been in the army yet?" I asked.

"Of course. Everybody goes. In my country it is required."

"I'll tell you what, Ariel. You try and get close to me like that again, and I'm going to shoot you in the knee. You understand?"

Ariel shrugged. "One has to try you know."

I made him place the radio on the ground then backed

him up a bit, so I could pick it up without him jumping me. Then I went and collected his cousin's guns—a Kalashnikov and a .45 Magnum. I stuck the handgun in my knapsack and slung the rifle over my shoulder. Ariel stared at me and smiled.

"You look like Rambo," he said.

"You better pray I don't start acting like him. Where's your car?"

"Back there near the road."

We left his cousin sitting against a tree with enough water and shade to keep him comfortable. Then Ariel led me out into the saw grass until we came to a narrow dirt road, which we followed for a few minutes until I spotted a black Audi sedan. Ariel frowned deeply when I demanded the keys from him, and for a moment I thought he might try to rush me, so again I backed him up a good twenty feet before letting him toss them to me.

"You better get your cousin to a hospital," I said. "Head injuries are nothing to play around with. Use that radio of yours to call for help."

"Why is Mr. Fernandez trying to kill you?"

"Because his girlfriend thinks I'm too dangerous. Come to think of it, she's probably right."

"You mean Marina?"

"You know her?"

"She's my stepmother."

"She's your stepmother?"

"Unfortunately, this is correct. She's a real bitch and a half."

"You're Ed Kaminski's son. Is that what you're telling me?"

"So?"

"How'd you end up with that accent? Kaminski was from Odessa."

"Did you know him, my father?"

"I didn't know him, but I heard about him."

"When my father left Odessa, he went first to Italy, then

to Tel Aviv. Then to New York, to Brooklyn. I went back to Israel with my mother when they got divorced. I was born there."

"And you work for your stepmother now?"

"Why not? She has the money."

"Tell me something: How'd they tell you your father died?"

"Why do you ask?"

"I don't know. I've heard different stories."

"The Italians from Brooklyn shot him. The Mafia." Ariel shrugged. "You know how it is. Drugs or something like that. It was business. My father had many enemies."

"You ever read Shakespeare?"

"Of course."

"How about *Hamlet*?"

"You ask strange questions. Yes I read it. In three languages. So what?"

"Maybe you should read it again."

"I don't understand you."

"You know, Ariel. You seem like a nice enough kid. I'd really hate to have kill you or your cousin. I wouldn't get any satisfaction out of that. I was thinking maybe that the next time your Uncle Vincent asks you to help track me down, you can tell him you're busy or something. What do you think about that?"

"You are a very strange person. I am glad now that I didn't kill you. May I ask your name?"

"Jack Vaughn."

"Why did you mention Hamlet before?"

"Because sometimes not everything is the way it seems. So long, Ariel. I sure hope you and your cousin can get in with a better crowd. No offense, but these fucking Russians you're running with are crazy. Fernandez too."

Ariel studied me for a moment then nodded solemnly. Something stirred in those dark moody eyes of his. He was smart and would eventually figure out that something was rotten in Miami, but I thought it better that he do it on his own schedule. Then he could decide on his own what to do about it.

"Goodbye, Rambo," he said. "I hope you have enough guns."

"I doubt it."

I dug David's .45 out of the knapsack and stuck it in my belt while Ariel Kaminski looked on. I was still not so sure that given the chance he wouldn't try to jump me, so I kept the Audi between us while I loaded the knapsack and two rifles into the car's tiny trunk. It was quite an arsenal I had collected for myself. I had gone from having no guns at all to having too many. Ariel didn't move. He just stood there watching me as I climbed into the Audi and spun quickly away, the brand new tires spewing pebbles and loose dirt in all directions as I headed for the main road.

11

The night's supply of adrenaline had begun to wear off and now the patient vultures of fatigue that had been circling above me for the past twenty-four hours were slowly spiraling in for their due. Everything hurt, especially my side where the bullet had grazed my ribs. I needed to get it cleaned up before any infection set in and that meant a pit stop for supplies. I was just about to pull into a Walgreens parking lot when I happened to glance into the rearview mirror and got a good look at my mud-streaked face. Then I remembered where I had been and what I looked like. If I had sauntered into a drugstore looking like the way I did, I would have attracted too much attention and may have even prompted a call to the local constable by some concerned citizen. Not that I would have blamed them for dropping a dime on me. I looked like hell.

Then again, I thought, maybe the cops showing up wouldn't be the worst thing in the world to happen to me at this point in time. I could tell them my story and hope that they believed enough of it to help me out, but the more I thought about it, the less I liked the idea. Cops are trained to operate by the book, and even if they believed me, confirming all the details, contacting Dawn Belkin and Denny O'Neal would take time. Time I didn't have. In the meantime, someone would eventually get around to reporting the Audi I had borrowed as stolen, though not right away of course. Fernandez would no doubt try and find me on his own and wouldn't want the cops brought into it until he was sure I had gotten him and his crew. The problem was that if I happened to be sitting in a police station when the call came in the police would have to hold me until the whole convoluted crap was unraveled, and that would mean a lawyer, bond and even more time.

So for now at least, the cops were out. O'Neal, I realized, was the key to the situation. With him on my side, I could bypass the local police and proceed directly back to Hackbart and the Feds with my story. All they would have to do then was pull up O'Neal's case file and contact the agent who had handled the case against Fernandez and Kaminski. Once they did that, I reasoned, I'd have a lot better chance of convincing them that Cal's strange disappearance was something they needed to look into. But I knew that I had to be careful with the feds as well. They would most certainly be interested in Vince Fernandez and his new ventures into the wonderful world of fitness. I would, as they say, become a "valuable source," but whether anything that I might tell them would translate into anything that would help Cal while there was still time—well, that was another question entirely.

Hackbart, and especially his superiors, would naturally have their own agendas. They would be interested in building a case, in furthering their careers through a successful prosecution with plenty of publicity, and, of course, they would, like all good underpaid civil servants, be interested in moving on up to a higher pay grade. I had no reason to believe that they would be willing to take time away from going after Vince and his friends in order to go looking for a missing old man. A nice fat money laundering case would be more than enough for them to handle, and if in the process of building said case they were able to get Vince on kidnapping, extortion and unlawful imprisonment charges—so much the better.

On the other hand, it was possible that in exchange for more information from Fernandez, the government might even agree not to pursue any charges at all regarding Cal's disappearance, especially since, for now at least, they still had no body to make a case with. The defense would just use the lack of evidence to call into question the validity of the other charges. If the feds got too greedy and piled on too many charges, there was reasonable chance that, with enough money and the right team of top-shelf lawyers, Fernandez might even walk away completely. That is unless his Russian friends didn't get to him first.

What it came down to finally was that the best way for me help Cal was to find him myself. That way, even if I couldn't get him out of wherever he was on my own, then, at the very least, I would surely be able convince somebody to go and check it out for themselves, and if I couldn't convince anybody, then I would try my best to make enough of a stink one way or another that the cops would have to sit up and take notice. All of this, of course, would depend on what Cal's banker could find out. The banks wouldn't open for another two hours, but if Ms. Potsdam had somehow managed to find out where the government was now sending Cal's Social Security checks, then at least I would have a place to start my search.

But first I needed to get myself cleaned up a bit. About fifty miles north of Miami, I pulled into the parking lot of a campground and used their showers to make myself look a little more presentable, though there was not much I could do about my famous khaki suit, which was soaked through with mud and swamp water. I hated having to squeeze back into my wet clothes after I had washed off, but at least I flushed out the wound with plenty of soap and water. I wet my hair and smoothed it back and used a finger to get some of the over night gunk off my teeth then checked the mirror. I still looked a bit feral and a bit worn, but I no longer looked like a candidate for *America's Most Wanted.*

In the Audi's trunk, along with my collection of stolen guns, I found an emergency kit. The only things missing from it were a few of the flares. I brought the kit with me into a bathroom stall and used antiseptic on the wound then slapped a piece of gauze over it and taped it into place as best I could. The wound seemed fairly superficial, and while a doctor might have opted for stitches or a few staples, I was confident it would close up on its own—that is if I didn't give it too much exercise. But I had to hurry now. Vince and company wouldn't be very far behind me, and they would know that I would be heading south as fast as fast I could on the only road out of that part of the Everglades.

I didn't stop until I reached Sunrise City. It wasn't much of a town, but it was big enough to have roads parallel to the main drag that I could use to avoid Fernandez. I pulled into a Citgo station, grabbed a quick espresso then called my apartment. As expected, Dawn didn't answer, which was either a good sign or a bad omen. Next, I tried to call O'Neal. My hope was that Dawn had gone to him for help like I had told her. I didn't have Denny's cell phone number and the bartender at the Deuce refused to give it to me. He did, however, consent to calling O'Neal and giving him my number at the pay phone I was using.

Five minutes passed. I sat at the counter, sipped my coffee and watched the road for signs of trouble. Then, just as I was about to ask for the key to the men's room, the pay phone rang. It was O'Neal and Dawn Belkin was with him. After her talk with Fernandez, she had taken a cab back to South Beach, arriving just in time for the end of his shift. According to Denny, he hadn't been surprised by what she had told him. Fernandez's anonymous call to the Deuce with my cell phone had made him suspicious enough to check the bar's caller identification service. He guessed what had happened almost immediately and was just on his way out the back door when Dawn showed up. They had spent the night at his girlfriend's apartment up in North Miami Beach. He gave me the address and said he would wait for me to get there and not to worry because he was armed and dangerous. Then he told me that Dawn was awake and wanted to talk to me.

"Where are you?" she demanded.

"Do me a favor," I said. "Remind me to stay away from strip clubs for awhile, all right? Especially the Emperor's Club. They've got a nasty crowd there." "What happened?"

"I'll tell you in person."

"O'Neal said you were probably dead." "O'Neal was almost right. Did the bank call yet?"

"No, not yet. It's too early. Where are you?"

"A few miles outside of the Everglades. Why don't you go back to sleep, and I'll be there in about an hour."

"What were you doing in the Everglades?"

"Mostly, I was trying to get out. Our friend Mr. Miami didn't make that too easy, but I'm all right now."

"You must be tired."

"Go back to sleep. I'll be there as soon as I can."

I finished my coffee, ordered another one for the road then headed south again, only this time I used one of the streets west of the highway. I was taking a risk sticking with the Audi. At first, I considered ditching it as soon as possible. Vince hadn't bothered taking my wallet from me, and once I reached civilization again, I could have rented another ride, but in the end I decided to stick with the Audi for a while longer for a couple of reasons. The first was that it was faster than just about anything else on the road; if I had to run, then this was the car to do it in. The second reason was that it was highly unlikely that Fernandez would want to bring the cops into it by reporting the car stolen as I had originally feared he might. The last thing he would do is send the cops after me himself. Even if they didn't believe my story right away, once I was in their custody there would be little chance he could get to me before someone started asking questions.

Soon enough, of course, Vince would realize that I had gotten away, and then he'd have no choice but to prepare himself for the shit storm that was sure to follow once word of my escape reached Marina Gero's cute little ears. I just wondered how long it would take for him to realize that I had no intention just yet of going to the cops. Judging by the way Fernandez had responded when Marina erupted after recognizing me back at the club, he probably thought she had overreacted. Fernandez, despite anything else he had become, was still enough of a cop to be able to understand why I would have gone to Cal's house. The reason for that was simple. No matter how far Vince had fallen since our days together on the job, he would still be able to appreciate the traits of curiosity and loyalty, because he still possessed and respected those attributes himself.

Unlike Marina Gero, he wouldn't have necessarily seen my actions as a threat to the organization. The Vince I knew would most certainly have been pissed off when he learned that I had done an end run around him, but he wouldn't have interpreted my going to Cal's house as an act of betrayal punishable by death in the Everglades. Hell, given the right circumstances, he would have done the same thing himself, especially if he believed that someone was giving him the run around. It's the nature of cops to look into things, and Fernandez, unlike his Russian girlfriend, would have understood that. He would have dressed me down, cursed me out, and given me fair warning to mind my own goddamned business and that would have been the end of it as long as I agreed to cease and desist. Then he would have slapped me on the back and bought me a beer.

But it was Marina who called the shots here and not Vince. He had been bought and paid for, and killing me was just another business expense he could write off along with everything else he had done in service to his employers. The way I saw it, Fernandez, despite all his bluster and steroid enhanced ego, was little more in the scheme of things than hired muscle with special bedroom privileges. He might not be willing to admit it, but at some level he had to understand that if he got on the boss's nerves one too many times, he would end up just as dead as Ed Kaminski.

There was another possibility to think about as well. The group of people Fernandez had thrown in with were involved in so many rackets and scams that there was a strong possibility that the dumb ass Puerto-Rican didn't even know what had become of Cal Belkin once the gym had been placed in his name. As I recalled, Vince had never been very good at paperwork when he was on the force. He could barely write a complete sentence and had to pay his partner to polish up his reports to avoid getting written up.

Fernandez's name and signature might appear on all the right documents and in all the right places, but he wasn't one for the fine print of contracts. That would be Ms. Gero's department. She would tell him what and where to sign and he would do it without hesitation. As for what had happened to Cal: Vince might have his suspicions but so what? He was down here to run gyms and service the former Mrs. Kaminski, not concern himself with the intricacies of what was clearly a widespread, well run crime syndicate with more departments than Walmart. Keeping Vince on a need to know basis would be to the way to go. The less Fernandez knew about the full scope of the syndicate's other operations, the less he would be able to tell the cops if something went wrong.

What worried me was what Marina would do once she found out I was back on the warpath again. Cal was a gold mine she had obviously intended to suck dry at her leisure without having to worry about anyone showing up to look for him. Then, the next thing she knows, she's got me and Cal's granddaughter running around asking questions and threatening what had started out as the casual bleeding of an old man's finances. With me on the loose again, Marina might decide to cut her losses and hope that if the cops did show up, all her documentation concerning the sale of Cal Belkin's property would pass inspection. If they did, all Dawn and I would have to work with would be our shared suspicions. Maria and her people could bury us in lawyers and long delays and countersuits until we either went away on our own or were by other means made to disappear.

Under the circumstances, getting rid of Cal might be the smart and prudent thing to do. Once he had been disposed of, Marina could take her time tracking down me and Dawn if, through our combined efforts, we made that necessary. It would be the smart thing to do, and Marina Gero was not only smart, she was also cunning, but she was also greedy, and that's why I didn't think she would be able to take a pass on letting the rest of Cal's money languish in Miami Shores Savings and Loan until such time as the bank, as determined by law, would be forced to hand over to the state whatever assets were left once the accounts were deemed dormant.

Somehow, I couldn't see Marina Gero walking away from a half million dollars or more, even though, for all I knew, her ex-husband had left her a hundred times that much, and she was set for life, the poor man's way of defining wealth. But the woman I had encountered outside Cal's house the day before was not the kind of woman to spend her life traveling from one day spa to the next. Such a life would be beyond her comprehension. She struck me as a woman who had once been very hungry, not just once but chronically hungry in a way and to a degree so, that over the course of many years, that hunger had become a permanent part of how she saw both herself and the world.

She had done everything a person can do for food, of that much I was sure. She had searched for, dug for it, lied for, stolen for it, run for it, hid for it, worked for it, slaved for it, smiled for it, sang for it, danced for it and, of course, when the time came, she had fucked for it. Once that body of hers had blossomed and the men appeared, staring up at her as though she was a prophet, she had never had lacked for food again. But by then it was too late. She would never be able to enjoy the feeling of a full belly. She had been rendered immune to that kind of satisfaction. Hunger was what she knew; it was the world she lived in; the fuel she ran on.

There were only two types of people in Marina's world who mattered—herself and those who were trying to keep her from what was rightfully hers—that is to say, whatever she wanted—in this case, what remained of Cal Belkin's fortune. I was one of those people. By showing up at Cal's house that day and at the Emperor's Club that night, I had sparked in her a reaction equivalent to that which occurs when a single hyena tries to force a starving lioness off her kill. It is an affront so profane that it cannot be tolerated, not even for a moment, and the penalty is, without a question, instant death. The thought of Fernandez having to tell his girlfriend that I had gotten away made me smile, and I wondered if it had dawned on him yet that as far Marina went, he was nearly as expendable as I was.

O'Neal's girlfriend lived on a quiet street between the back of a shopping mall and a high school athletic field whose well-trimmed emerald colored grass was being systematically watered by underground sprinklers while a bent-over custodian raked away at the dirt between third base and home. I left the car on the top floor of the mall's parking lot with its rear end against the wall to hide the tag number then walked three long blocks until I reached a small yellow house with red roof tiles and a trellis on the front porch interlaced with ivy and some unruly purple bougainvillea

O'Neal answered the door with a beer in his hand and a grin on his wizened face. He looked me up and down and shook his head and told me to come around by the back door because I was getting mud all over the front steps, and Cynthia was going to kill the both of us. I followed him down a narrow path that ran between the house and the red wooden fence that separated it from the house beside it. The backyard was larger than I had expected with a kidney shaped swimming pool surrounded by terracotta tiles with plenty of grass along the perimeter. Dawn, wearing a red two-piece bathing suit, came rushing toward me. For a second, I was sure she was going to throw her arms around my neck, but at the last possible moment she stopped short and looked down at my mud streaked pants and shoes. O'Neal laughed at our awkward near collision.

"I don't blame you, sweetheart," O'Neal said. "Your boyfriend here reeks to high heaven."

"Are you all right?" Dawn asked

"No," I said. "I'm not all right. I need to sit down for a minute."

I went over and nearly fell back into one of the wrought iron chairs. A plate with the remnants of a breakfast of sausage and eggs beckoned to me from the table. I began scooping up the scraps with my fingers. There was also half a glass of orange juice. I gulped that down too and wiped my mouth with the back of my hand. Dawn and O'Neal were watching me, their faces etched with an odd mixture of concern and fear. Grinning at them didn't seem to ease their fears much either, but the sugar in the orange juice had given my brain a much needed jolt of energy, and I felt a lot better. The two of them exchanged nervous glances. Dawn's soft eyes searched mine for signs of sanity. I couldn't help but laugh. I wanted to tell them that I wasn't insane, but I was too busy using the last bit of rye toast to wipe up the smear of egg yolk on the plate's rim to be bothered. When I was done, I was still hungry; I was still hurt and tired, but I thought that if I could close my eyes for a few hours, I might be ready to go again.

"Look at you," O'Neal said. "What are you, some kind of fucking cannibal or something Where's your goddamned manners?"

Before I could answer, the screen door opened, and I was looking at a petite black haired woman in the pale green scrubs of a hospital worker. She was about thirty-five or forty and way too pretty for a reptile like O'Neal. She was definitely Asian, possibly Thai. Her fair skin was blemish free and the smile on her pert-lipped oval face struck me as a more or less permanent condition. The name tag still clipped to her pocket told me she was registered nurse at Jackson Memorial. O'Neal introduced her as his girlfriend Cynthia. I tried to stand. I made it half way and fell back. When I felt along my side, my hand came away red.

"Are you hurt?" Dawn asked.

I didn't have the strength to talk, so I showed her my hand by way of an answer. Then someone turned the world upside down, and suddenly the ground was on a collision course with my head. I realized that I was falling out of the chair and managed to get my arms out in front of me, but I kept going down and forward until I was stretched out on the ground like I had just slid into home base. Once I was horizontal, all I wanted to do was sleep. It seemed to me that the cold tile of pool deck was the best sleeping spot in the world. I smelled the chlorine from the pool and opened my eye just long enough to catch sight of a wavy line of blue green water sparkling in the sunlight, and then the cool earth pulled me down into its darkness like a lost mother home at last.

I opened my eyes in a darkened room where the sun was trying to force its way in through the window blinds to my right. I lay between cool white sheets. But for my boxers I was naked. I looked around. Above my head, the wooden vanes of the ceiling fan were still, and I could hear the hum of an AC unit somewhere nearby. There was so much medical paraphernalia around that at first I thought I had been taken to a hospital, but there were too many touches of home life for that to be the case, including a small kitchen and bookshelves lined with rows of ragged paperbacks and dotted with knick knacks and figurines. There was even a home entertainment center complete with a geriatric TV set topped by a pair of equally ancient rabbit ears, a VCR and a collection of VHS tapes. There were also framed photographs on the walls and on the some of the shelves. Then I remembered that O'Neal's girlfriend was an RN and the room began to make more sense.

I drew back the top sheet and swung my legs around and put my feet down flat on the cold linoleum tiled floor. Then a short but intense burst of pain along my ribs made me remember. The wound had been re-bandaged, this time professionally, with gauze and two wide bands of adhesive tape circling my torso. I had no idea who had undressed me, but I was hoping it hadn't been O'Neal. My khaki suit and the rest of my clothes had been left washed and crisply folded on a straight backed wooden chair next to a table with thin metal legs and a stained Formica surface. Even my shoes had been shined. I stood up and gingerly tried putting some weight on my bad hip. Like my side, it protested, but it wasn't anything a few painkillers couldn't handle so long as I didn't have to do anymore broad jumping in the next month or so. I wanted very badly to go back to bed, but instead, I began the very slow climb back into my clothes. I was just buckling my belt when the door opened and Dawn appeared in the doorway. She was back in her jeans and black T-shirt again, the same clothes she had worn the first time we met. I remembered then that we had left the rest of her clothes back at the Holiday Inn.

"Was it my imagination," I asked. "Or were you wearing a red bikini this morning?"

"That was Cynthia's. How do you feel? I didn't expect you to be awake so soon?"

"How do I look?"

"Not good."

"Tell me something: who undressed me? I might want to leave them a tip or something."

"You're pretty heavy. It took the three of us to carry you in here. O'Neal didn't want Cynthia to undress you by herself, so she asked me to do it. Then she came in and changed your bandage. Don't worry; I didn't molest you or anything. If that's what you're thinking."

"O'Neal didn't want his girlfriend to see me naked. Is that what you're telling me?"

"Why? You think it's funny?"

"No, but I think it's kind of amusing. How can you be jealous of someone who's unconscious?"

"He does seem a bit possessive."

"Maybe he has reason to be."

"You mean because of what happened with Fernandez and his wife?"

There was a knock at the door, and Cynthia came in. We had our formal introductions, and this time I didn't pass out. She inspected my wound. She had such a sweet way about her that it was only by an act of the utmost discipline on my part that I managed to resist asking her what the hell she was doing with

Dennis. There was nothing about her to indicate that she was out of her mind, but that was the only explanation that made any sense to me. Then again, maybe it was my problem. Maybe O'Neal wasn't quite the asshole that I had always taken him for, though memory made that hard to believe.

"I'm afraid I'm going to have to staple you shut," Cynthia told me. "If I don't, you'll only open up again."

"I appreciate your help."

"How did it happen?"

"Somebody shot at me and almost missed."

"You're lucky," Cynthia said. "If this were a hospital, I'd have to report it."

"This is quite a set up you have here," I said. "Was someone in your family sick or something?"

"My mother lived in this room before she died. I know what to do, so I took care of her. She was comfortable here. Dying in hospitals is no good."

"How long has it been since your mother passed?"

"Five six years maybe."

"And you kept it like this."

"I'll tell you why. In this neighborhood, the people, they don't have the money. Their jobs don't give them insurance. Everybody knows Cynthia works at the hospital. So when they get hurt or sick sometimes they come here, and I help them. No charge."

"Tell me something. How did an angel like you wind up with O'Neal?"

"We met on the computer, online."

"You mean a dating service?"

"Yes. It's a special site for American men who like Asian women. It's called, *Slant Eyes for The American Guy*. Very popular web site."

"Where is Dennis anyway?"

"He went to work," Dawn replied.

"Don't tell me he went back to Club Deuce," I demanded.

"No," Cynthia said. "Not today. Today he drives his friend's taxi. Raise your arm please."

Cynthia sprayed my ribs with something that felt canned ice, but despite the topical anesthetic, I still jumped every time she stamped another metal tie through either side of the wound. When she was through, Dawn helped me on with my shirt.

"I meant to tell you, Mrs. Potsdam called from the bank," Dawn said.

"Did she find out where they're sending your grandfather's checks?"

"I've got it written down. She wants you to call her back."

Cynthia let me use the phone in the kitchen. Dawn sat across the dining room table from me, sipping her coffee while I made the call. She looked a bit drawn, as though the pace of things was getting to her. It was getting to me too, though I've always had a better relationship with chaos than most. You might even say that in some ways it brought out the best in me. On the other hand, I had to admit that having O'Neal and his girlfriend involved in the whole thing took some of the strain off me having to face everything alone, but I was still worried that I would let Dawn down somehow. She must have sensed something of what I was thinking, because for no apparent reason she reached out across the table and placed her hand on top of mine while I waited the secretary to put me through to the bank president.

I looked up at Dawn and gave her a smile and a little wink meant to imply that, despite appearances and the row of fresh staples on my ribcage, everything was proceeding according to plan. Fernandez, the Russians, the Emperor's Club, nearly getting killed in the Everglades, the bullet wound: it was all good. Vaughn the mastermind had it all figured out and was on the case. It was a strategy for dealing with potential disaster that I had learned from my father who was in the Merchant Marines before he became a cop. It consisted of a couple of ploys, one of which was the ability to maintain a poker face under any circumstances, especially bad ones. Another was never to act surprised when things went wrong.

Like the time my mother nearly set the kitchen on fire. My father and I were in the living room watching a ball game when we heard her scream. I looked at my father to see his reaction and his face was exactly the same. In no particular hurry, he stood up and glided over to the kitchen with me right behind him. He took one look at the frying pan full of fire and the flames that were reaching for the ceiling and shook his head the way you do when the other team gets a hit. Then he said excuse me honey to my mother and dumped an entire bag of cat litter on the flames, snuffing them out almost immediately. I had been too mesmerized by fear and fire to recall seeing him grab the bag of litter from somewhere, so to me its sudden appearance had approached the realm of magic. He gave my mother a squeeze and me a smile and a wink then helped clean up the kitchen, all the time laughing and joking and saying nothing at all about the fire, and in ten minutes we were back watching the game again, everything so normal and calm that you would have thought my father had set the fire himself just for the hell of it.

Mrs. Potsdam's secretary put my call through and, after few very brief formalities, the banker and I got right down to business.

"You wanted to know where Mr. Belkin's checks had been rerouted," Mrs. Potsdam said. "I called the Social Security Administration. They are not easy people to deal with and it took considerable time and effort, all of which I explained before. In any case, Mr. Belkin's checks are being sent to an address up in Tamarac. A place called Balmore House. I'm not sure what kind of facility it is, but I suspect it may be a nursing home of some kind. Are you familiar with it?"

"No, but I'm going to be." I jotted down the address she gave me.

"Did Mr. Belkin give you any indication that he was considering moving to a place like that?"

"Cal would never voluntarily sign himself into a nursing home. It wasn't his style."

"I agree," the banker said, with a note of concern that told me I was right about Cal having exerted his charm on her. "And there is one more thing, Mr. Vaughn. You wanted to know if there was anyone with Mr. Belkin when he cashed out his CD the last time he was in. I spoke with the officer who handled the transaction, Mrs. Osorio. According to her, Cal was accompanied by his physician. She also mentioned that Cal appeared to be suffering from something she took to be Alzheimer's or dementia or something of that nature. His doctor had to help him out with signing the documents."

"That was very magnanimous of him. Tell me, Mrs. Potsdam, this doctor, did he have a name?"

"I'm sure he did," Mr. Vaughn. Unfortunately, the officer who handled the transaction failed to make note of it."

"She had no reason to. Anyway, the address should be enough. If Cal's checks are there, then maybe he is, too."

"I suppose I don't think much like a policeman, but maybe it will help if I tell you that according to Madeline, Mrs. Osorio, the doctor had an extremely heavy Russian accent. She also said that he was a very polite, a very charming man. He even kissed her hand before he and Mr. Belkin left together. Madeline's not used to European men so it made quite an impression on her."

"Is that right? He kissed her hand. I like that. It's a nice touch. I doubt it'll work too well with me but you never know. Well, thanks for everything, Mrs. Potsdam. I'll let you know how everything turns out."

"Please do," the banker said. "I'm very concerned about Mr. Belkin, but just the same, perhaps I should be reassured that he's in the hands of professional people. These days it's so hard to find a doctor who really has time for his patients."

"It probably depends on how much the patient is paying, Mrs. Potsdam."

"Excuse me?" she said.

There was no point in worrying her needlessly. "Nothing," I said. "I will let you know."

"Please do," she said.

As I was relaying to Dawn what Mrs. Potsdam had told me, Cynthia stopped by the kitchen to tell us that she was on her way to work and that we should help ourselves to the food she had prepared for us whenever we got hungry. I was right about her smile being permanent. It was exactly the same as the one on her photo ID from the hospital. Before she left she gave me her and O'Neal's cell phone numbers and told us to call either of them if we needed anything. The more I looked at her, the easy it became for me to see her and O'Neal together. She had more joy in her than she knew what to do with while he had less that any man I had ever known, and each must have found in the other a constant source of amazement and surprise at their different temperaments. Like they say, it takes all kinds to make a world.

Then Cynthia realized that she had forgotten something and disappeared back into the house. When she returned, she was carrying a leather pistol case and a set of keys, both of which she set down in front of me. The keys, she told me, were to O'Neal's second car, the one he had driven down from New York, a Ford Taurus. O'Neal had told her that it was too dangerous for me to drive the Audi any longer, and that I could use the Ford for as long as I needed to, but that any damages were mine to pay.

After Cynthia left, I opened the gun case and checked out the little thirty-two O'Neal had left me. It was mostly for show, but it was better than nothing and from the smell of it, had been recently cleaned. I thought about going back to the Audi to choose from the arsenal in the trunk, but what if it had been spotted? Besides, for what I had in mind, I didn't think I needed major firepower.

I loaded five of the chambers while Dawn watched. Then I spun the cylinder and gave Dawn another one of my father's reassuring grins, but she was too smart not see that I was scared.

"We should call the police," Dawn said. "We can't do this alone."

"We can't do what alone?"

"I don't know. Whatever it is you're thinking about doing."

"All right, suppose we call the cops. What do we tell them?"

"That Cal's in this Balmore place. That he's there against his will."

"Okay, Miss Belkin, and just how do you know your grandfather's there against his will? Did he tell you so? So then how do you know he didn't just sign himself in? He's an old man right? Maybe he just couldn't take care of himself anymore. Have you talked to him? So you really don't know for sure if he's even there. Right? Then how do you know he doesn't like the place. Have you been out there? I didn't think so. I tell you what. I'll do you a favor, Miss Belkin, because you seem like a nice person and you're kind of pretty to boot. Let's say we give this Balmore House a call and see what they have to say on this matter. How's that?"

"And you're afraid that if they do that, if they call this place, that whosever there will get scared and do something to Cal. Is that it?"

"The one thing we have going for us at this point is that the people we're dealing with are a very greedy bunch. They'll have a hard time walking away from a half million dollars. The thought of it alone will give them nightmares, but at some point their instinct for survival is going to kick in, and when it does, they'll get rid of Cal. That's why we have to be careful when it comes to which buttons we push."

"What if it's already too late?" Dawn asked. "I mean, they know I'm in town, and what about you? If you ask me, last night changed everything. If they think there's an ex-cop after them, they're bound to get desperate. What if they decide it just isn't worth it?"

"I won't deny it," I said. "You may be right. But keep

this in mind: criminals wouldn't be criminals if they weren't willing to take risks that would scare most people off. And remember, all they really need is a few more days. In the meantime, they're still hoping to get their hands on the two of us, especially you. You're Cal's heir. If anybody has a reason to push this thing it'll be you. That's why we have to keep you out of trouble until we can bring the law into it."

"So what now? Wait till Wednesday and try to get them at the bank?"

"That was my original plan, but now that we know where the government sent Cal's last Social Security check, I don't think we can afford to wait until next week. I think we have to make a move now."

We used Cynthia's computer to check out the Balmore House website. I was very impressed. It was a first class site with plenty of expensive bells and whistles, including high definition and top quality graphics. Our host, a beautiful young woman in a white lab coat guided us on a virtual tour of the home, which, from the looks of it, was first rate. Balmore House was a mental health facility specializing in the care and treatment of the people with a range of conditions including Alzheimer's, depression and schizophrenia. There was also a hospice house on the grounds for those with less than six months to live. The director was a Dr. Nicolas Vronsky, a graduate of the Sorbonne and former resident of Moscow, who had immigrated to the United States ten years ago. Of the ten full-time doctors listed in the staff directory, seven had Eastern European names. Two were of Hispanic origin. One, a Dr. Kim, may have been a Korean.

"The place looks legit," Dawn said. "Of course anybody with enough money can build a fake website, and you can get buy all the pretty scenery you'll ever need online. Just like all those phony online colleges."

"You mean the kind where you can get your PhD in nuclear submarines in just three months," I said. "Could be.

Let's find out."

I called Balmore house and asked the receptionist when I could come out and take a look at the place. It turns out my dear old dad wasn't doing so well, and I was looking for someplace near my home where he would be sure to get the best of care. Where had I heard of Balmore House? Let me see. Oh, yes, now I remember. I asked my secretary to check into the matter. Balmore had been at the top of the list. Could she send me a brochure? Of course. And would I care to schedule an appointment to meet with the director. Nothing could suit me better. Would tomorrow at eleven in the morning be convenient? Unfortunately not. In fact, starting tomorrow, I'll be out of town for the next two weeks on business. How about today? At four-thirty then. May I have your name? Sorry, it's already taken. Try this one instead. Stone. Robert Stone. See you soon.

"I'm coming with you," Dawn said.

"What makes you think so?"

"He's my grandfather, not yours."

"I'm just going to take a look at the place," I said. "That's all."

"And then what?"

"I really don't know. It all depends on what I see when I get there. I want to see what kind of operation they're running. The fact the director is a Russian worries me a great deal. My recent experiences with them haven't gone very well, and I'm not sure how to play it. Cal's check is there, or at least it's in their bank account. That much can be proved, but that would take time and lawyer with a big mouth. The lawyer can be arranged. She's a friend of mine. I'm sure she can get some kind of writ or show-cause order, but if your grandfather's not there, none of that will matter."

"But if they're taking his money, isn't that a crime?"

"Let me explain something to you, Dawn. This is Miami we're talking about, okay? Scam Central. We lead the league in Medicare Fraud. It's pretty simple. All you need is a couple of crooked doctors and someone who knows how to bilk the system, and believe me, if there's any group of people out there who know how to bilk a system, it's the Russians and all their old pals from the Soviet Union. And why not? They had fifty years to master the game. For them, the State is just one big piggy bank. Is it a crime? Sure it's a crime. But it's like drugs. No matter how many kilos you may see on TV, ninety percent of the stuff still gets through. That's just the cold hard facts. The same with this kind of fraud. You shut down one phony clinic and two more take its place, and it's not just the Russians either. Everybody does it."

"All right," Dawn said. "But if all you're going to do is have a look at this Balmore place, then why can't I come along for the ride?"

"For the same reason that you never fly with the whole family on the same goddamned plane, that's why. Because if it crashes there are no survivors. The whole family's extinct. Finished. Try to understand something. When it comes to Cal, you and me are it. There's nobody else, and I'm not talking about his friends or the people from the gym. I don't know why it is some of us end up with no family, but it happens. That's all I know. When you're young it doesn't bother you as much, but you start to think about it as you get older. People die or move someplace else, and they don't ever come back. If you hadn't showed up when you did, it would have just been me. I was prepared for that; I always am. But now there's the two of us. You see what I mean?"

"You're going to do something stupid, aren't you?"

"If I get the chance to, yes."

"And that's why you don't want me along because you're thinking that if anything happens to you then I'll still be around to carry on with this thing."

"Something like that."

I took two business cards from my wallet and slid them across the table. One was from Susan Andrews, my lawyer friend; the other was from Doctor Anwar al Rasuli, known to his friends, including myself, as the Sheik. Susan was the lawyer with the big mouth I had mentioned before. The Sheik was a plastic surgeon with Doctors Without Borders and one of the richest men in Miami, though he was one of the least ostentatious men I had ever met. Aside from Cal, the two of them were as close to family for me as anybody, and I knew that they would help Dawn out if it came to that. Susan would help both because she was a friend and because she would see Dawn as the underdog, which she was. The Sheik would help because he was my best friend and the finest man I had ever met. For Anwar, it would be a question of honor and, potentially, of revenge. I explained all of this to Dawn. She listened quietly, and when I was done, she put the cards in her purse and sat looking at me.

"What's the matter?" I asked.

"Where's your family, Jack? In New York?"

"No, it's just me now. I'm like the last of the Mohicans. We were never a big group to begin with, and my mother and father were both from someplace else when they moved to New York. They met and got married in the big city, but never really got connected to anyone else. So it was just the four of us. My parents, Matt, my older brother and me."

"What happened to all of them?" Dawn asked. "You said it was just you now."

"My brother Matt was already twenty when I was born. I guess you could say they weren't really expecting me to show up, but there I was. Anyway, his plane got shot down over Laos. I must have been three or four at the time. They never found the plane."

"So you don't remember him at all then?"

"No, but I've seen pictures. Here, I'll show you."

"So young," Dawn said.

"And he always will be too. That's the funny part."

"And your parents?"

"I didn't like their looks, so I killed them."

"You say that with such a straight face too."

"Cancer, both of them, a couple of years apart."

"I guess being a cop was like having a family to you," Dawn said.

"Yea, a very large family," I said. "A very large dysfunctional family full of people you didn't really like but still have to deal with everyday. But, hey, at least you know there'll be somebody around at your funeral when you buy the farm."

"You must miss it."

"Not all of it."

"What part then?"

"The danger, the rush, and going through a door with a gun in your hand. Everything else was bullshit and paperwork." I checked my watch. "Which reminds me," I told her. "It's time to go."

12

By the time I reached Tamarac, it was seven o'clock in the evening and the sun was still in charge of the wide empty sky. It was a quiet town with all the personality of someone in a deep coma. There were a lot of subdivisions and strip malls and fast-food joints everywhere you looked. Name a chain store, and they had it. There were enough Walgreens to make me think I was driving around in circles, and the long, blank, empty sidewalks stretched so far into the distance that you needed binoculars to see where they ended. And to top it all off, the city fathers had neglected to plant any trees, so the only shade available to a pedestrian was under the manhole covers.

But the length of the sidewalks didn't matter because no one was using them anyway. Tamarac was a car town where walking was considered a suspicious activity. It was the kind of town where police cars would slow down if they saw you out strolling around like a nomad. Such a thing wasn't considered natural. The cops would cruise slowly by you, tossing you the evil eye just let you know that they were on to you, that they knew that you were up to no good. They might even roll up on you and ask to see your driver's license even though you weren't driving. In a town like that, you were either inside a building, inside your car or dead and buried and inside your coffin. True, there was a bus that came along every year or two like a comet, but few people actually used them. Thus the benches at the bus stops were empty and when the buses finally came they would be empty too. In three miles of driving, I saw only two people walking on the street, and neither of them looked quite right in the head.

I pulled into a gas station with a mini-mart attached to it and filled up O'Neal's Taurus then hit the head for one last whiz before the big show. I was at the register trying to pay for a bottle of water when, just to be on the safe side, I decided to double check the directions to Balmore House with a clerk carefully placing raw hot dogs into a spinning rotisserie. He didn't speak much English, so I showed him the address I had written down. He stared at it for a long time then shook his head slowly from side to side. I didn't know whether that meant he had no idea where the place was or that he didn't believe it existed at all. I was about to walk out when a teenaged girl popped up from behind the counter and asked if she could help me.

"Sure," she said. "I know where this place is. That's where they put my grandma while she was still alive. It's about a mile west of here, that way, past the high school. It's a big old place. You can't hardly miss it."

"What is it?" I asked. "Some kind of nursing home?"

"Mostly," the girl said. "But I think they take in some crazy folks too. I say that because last time I was over there, one of them tried to pull me into a closet. Why? You going to visit somebody out there?"

"I'm going to check it out. It may be that an old friend of mine might be staying there. Tell me something. Your grandmother, how did they treat her?"

"All right I guess. She was pretty much out of it when she got there, poor thing, so there wasn't much they could do for her anyway except to make her comfortable. No disrespect intended, mister, but all I can say is that I sure hope that when I get old my kids don't put me in a place like that. No sir. Just sit me out on the front stoop with a slingshot and bag full of pebbles and let me shoot the wood rats when they come out at night. That's what we did with my grandfather, and he seemed happy enough. Though of course that was in Kentucky and the people there are somewhat less refined. Here's your change, mister. Good luck."

From the outside, Balmore House looked more like a five-star hotel than it did a nursing home or psychiatric facility. It was a long, pale peach colored building with an east and west wing on either side of a tower that dwarfed them both. The tower, which must have been at least eight stories high, came complete with a belfry and a clock below it that told the time with black wrought iron hands. The building, with its tower and two adjoining wings, had the well balanced feel of a pagoda, but the time on the clock was three hours wrong and there was no sign anywhere I could see with the name Balmore house on it, but the address was the one I had been given so I drove up to the gatehouse and waited for the guard to get off the phone. As far as size went, he was right up there with Zhukov and Stefan the Chechen, and I was not surprised when I heard his accent. He hung up the phone and asked me my name and wrote down my tag number. If he had asked to see my driver's license there would have been no use in my staying. I would have backed up fast and gotten out of there in a hurry, but instead raised the bar to let me through.

I followed the sign for visitor's parking past a row of hedges out to the far end of a large lot nearly empty except for the section restricted to employees. The visitor's side was another story. There, I counted only ten cars, but then again, it was getting late. I backed into a spot, killed the headlights and took the gun O'Neal had lent me out from the glove compartment and laid it down next to me on the passenger seat. I looked at it the way you look at someone to whom you are about to broach a rather sensitive subject. If I took it with me and they patted me down I was screwed. On the other hand, the idea of going in there unarmed was far from appealing, especially if the guard at the gatehouse was an example of what their security staff looked like.

In the end I decided to take the gun with me. What I left behind instead was my wallet. The gun I could explain. Concealed weapons permits are easy to come by down here in Miami, and it's not unusual for people to carry a gun. I doubted they would let me take it with me into the facility if only for reasons of liability, but it wouldn't necessarily make them suspicious. As far as identification went, I could always tell them that I had left my wallet in the car or, better yet, back at the office. Playing it that way was risky, but not as risky as letting them know my real name, but a lot would depend on whether or not they had been warned about me and had gotten my description from Fernandez or one of his friends.

The lobby of Balmore House, like the facade, was more in the style of the Ritz Carlton than that of a nuthouse, and it looked even better in person than it had on the web site. There were spiraling, intricate floral arrangements spiked with black orchids and swooning daffodils; there were glass tables, large abstract paintings, and acres of Italian marble tile on the floors. The ceilings were high, and the air was as chilled as Chablis just out of the bucket. The furniture had an unfriendly, showroom feel to it that did not exactly cry out to be sat upon any more than the Persian rugs seemed anxious to make the acquaintance of my plebian feet. In short, the lobby was a painting, an exhibition of some interior designer's good taste. It was meant to be walked through, admired and, most of all, left untouched.

A young woman wearing a black and brown uniform and an ironed on smile greeted me from behind the front desk. Behind her, through an open door that led to a large workspace, I could see the usual array of desktops, fax machines and copiers. At the far end of the back room, three men were watching a basketball game on a small television set. They were hunched forward in their seats like men huddled around a fire. Then one of them groaned and another leaped to his feet, and I caught a glimpse of what it was they were watching. I remembered then that it was March, playoff time in college basketball, a time when work took a backseat to the annual contagion of office and point spreads, and water cooler bragging rights. They called it March Madness.

"Welcome to the Balmore Clinic," the young lady said in a voice that was nowhere close to sounding Russian. In fact, she sounded like she had just stepped off the train from Duluth. Her name tag said Julie.

"How may I help you?" she asked cheerfully.

I leaned slightly forward over the desk and spoke in a whisper. "I've been looking for some place for my father," I said. "He hasn't been well and now, well now I'm afraid he's getting worse. I meant to come earlier, but there was a late day rally in the futures market, and I couldn't leave my people without guidance, you understand."

Julie nodded, her expression softening with empathy. She asked for my name.

"Robert Stone," I said.

"I understand completely, Mr. Stone." she said. "May I ask how you heard about Balmore House?"

"I don't recall exactly. Perhaps I saw an advertisement somewhere."

"Was it the *New York Times* by any chance?" she asked.

"It might have been, though it may have been the *Journal.* I'm not sure. I read quite a bit, you see."

"Would that be the *Wall Street Journal?*"

"Quite possibly," I said. "I can't remember."

Julie smiled and checked a box with her pen. Obviously, it was best to keep a careful eye on those advertising dollars. I imagined one of those black and white ads in the back of the Sunday Supplement right along side the prep schools and the small exclusive colleges sequestered in the countryside of Upstate New York where rich kids in little black hats and jodhpurs ride horses between classes.

Julie handed me a clipboard with a form attached to it. "If you fill this out," she said. "It will help our admission's counselor get a better idea of your family's needs. Tell me: Just how serious is your father's condition?"

"Very serious, I'm afraid." I said. "Physically he's still very strong, but mentally he's hasn't been himself in a long time. Lately, he's developed the tendency of going berserk the moment he gets frustrated. We hired a woman to take care of him, but we're looking for something more permanent, someplace that will take good care of him."

"Well," Julie said. "Just fill out that form, and we'll schedule you for an interview with the director as soon as possible."

"I don't mean to be rude, Miss," I said. "But you see my wife and I are really quite desperate for a solution. We're moving back to New York in about a month and we'd like to have father settled into his new place as quickly as possible."

"Well, we do have quite a long waiting list. Normally, it takes several interviews with Dr. Vronsky and his staff before things are finalized. What kind of work is it that you do, Mr. Stone?"

"I manage my father's hedge fund. That's why I have to get back to New York you see. We have a full-scale office down on Brickell, but the Street is where the action is, and my people tend to get lazy if I'm not in New York to keep an eye on them. So you see, I have to confess to being a tad desperate."

"I understand. You must be under a lot of pressure. I tell you what: you make out that form, and I'll call Dr. Vronsky. He's been known to speed things up in emergency situations when it's necessary for the patient's well being."

"Dr. Vronsky," I said. "Is he the director here?"

"Yes," Julie said. "Director and Head of Psychiatry. Now you just fill out that form, and I'll try to get hold of the doctor. Who knows? He may even be able see you this very evening."

"He's working late tonight then?."

"Dr. Vronsky is very dedicated to his work. That's why he lives on the premises— so he can be close to his patients. I'm sure he's around somewhere. Let's just see if I can get a hold of him."

I went over to a desk and began filling out the form while Julie got on the horn in search of Dr. Vronsky. Someone answered the call on the third ring. She glanced over at me with a hopeful smile on her face. I smiled back, wondering how much she knew about the people she worked for. Not much, I thought, just enough to do her job, but not enough to be a good witness if it should come to that. The people to talk to at Balmore House were the doctors and the accountants. They would be the ones to know where the bodies were buried and where the money was hidden.

Most of the form I filled out was standard issue. I gave them the William's Island address of a rich client of mine who flew in once or twice a year from Dubai for some of the hot young action down on South Beach. I used the names of a few other clients for references, but only those who were safely out of town, and when I got to the part that asked me my estimated yearly income, I made myself a wealthy man with a single stroke of a borrowed pen. I was almost done with the rest of the form when Julie's phone rang. She spoke into it for a moment then gave me the thumbs up. I walked over and handed her back the clipboard with the completed form. She smiled brightly.

"Good news!" she said. "The doctor says he'll see you. He'll be right out."

I thanked her and settled back in my chair to wait for the good doctor. Ten minutes later, as I was sitting there leafing through the pages of *Vanity Fair*, marveling at all the shit I couldn't afford, Vronsky showed up. I stood up. We shook hands. He was a short, dapper man in his early sixties, and very trim in navy blue suit with pinstripes and a white handkerchief in the breast pocket. Everything about him was crisp and wrinkle free, right down to his well-trimmed salt and pepper goatee, and there was a straight- backed elegance about him that made him seem taller than he actually was.

"Mr. Stone," he said. "Sorry to keep you waiting. I was busy with a patient. Please follow me. I'd like to hear more about your father. What is his name, please?"

"Russell," I said. "Russell Stone."

Dr. Vronsky led me down a long corridor toward a dining room filled with elderly men and women, all of them well dressed and prosperous looking. The men wore jackets and ties; the women wore jewelry and too much makeup. This was no nursing home cafeteria with the smell of piss and Lysol intermingled in the depressed atmosphere of the soon to be departed. This was more like the stateroom of a luxury cruise ship, the dining hall of the Titanic before it hit the big party pooper. There was a long buffet table behind which stood men and women in chefs' hats and aprons and at least a dozen waiters and waitresses whirling about the room amidst the chatter and clatter of a room full of people all eating and talking at the same time. I gave the room a quick scan, but as I expected, there was no sign of Cal. He would never have been allowed such freedom of movement. If they were slowly leeching his money out of him, Vronsky and crew would have him somewhere tight, under lock and key and very possibly sedated.

"This is our dining room," Dr. Vronsky said. "You see, it's really more like a hotel here than a nursing home or an assisted living facility."

"It's very nice," I said. "But I don't think my father would fit in here. All these people seem quite healthy."

"Quite right," Vronsky said. "These are our most able-bodied people. They have certain health problems that make it difficult for them to live on their own, but otherwise they are quite healthy, and they have no really severe mental or emotional conditions that can't be treated with the proper medication. Of course, they are free to come and go as they choose. Some of them still drive their own automobiles, though we discourage it. For the rest, we provide shuttle buses to the mall and other places of interest from eight in the morning to seven in the evening. Needless to say, our doctors are on staff twenty-four hours a day should there be an emergency."

"What about someone like my father?" I said. "I don't

see anybody here in his condition."

"I understand. Let me be honest with you, Mr. Stone: we always begin our tours in this part of our facility. It is a much more . . . pleasant introduction to Balmore than, say, our psychiatric wing. That aspect of what we do here can be quite jarring to newcomers. You see, we have a very wealthy clientele here, and we provide the best care money can buy, but there are limitations to what even wealth can do to alleviate some of the more grievous infirmities of advanced old age, especially those that involve the loss of mental faculties, not to mention the question of certain types of behavioral problems and the loss of control of the various bodily functions. As you can guess, these can be very unpleasant things for visitors to see. You say your father suffers from dementia. That is a rather broad term. Can you be more specific?"

"I'm not much of a scientist, Doctor," I said. "I think they mentioned something about plaque in the blood vessels of in his brain. But I'm really not sure."

"Are you sure the diagnosis wasn't Alzheimer's?"

"Maybe, but they seemed reluctant to say so."

"Well," Vronsky said, "It is a rather grim prognosis and there are so many other conditions that can affect our mental faculties that many doctors hesitate to give the entire truth. Let us go to my office now."

Vronsky lived in a cottage a hundred yards from the main building. The office was on the main floor, occupying what would normally have been the living room. The air smelled of cigar smoke and the walls were covered with ceiling high bookshelves complete with a ladder on rollers. Vronsky sat down behind his desk in a high backed leather chair and asked my permission to smoke. He offered me a cigar from a humidor with the copper initials CB stamped into the inlaid black leather cover. I had seen it before and recognized it immediately. It was Cal's. Some old Cuban flame of his from before the days of the Revolution had given it to him as a birthday present. I selected a cigar and nipped off the end with the miniature guillotine Vronsky handed me then puffed away while he lit it for me.

"That's a nice looking cigar case," I said. "It looks handmade."

"The family of one my patients gave it to me. A very lovely piece."

"Is that right?" I said. "Would you mind if I contacted them?"

"And why would you wish to do that?"

"We're talking about my father's health here, Doctor, as well as a lot of money. For all I know, he'll probably live out the rest of his days here. I think you can understand why my wife and I will require references before we commit my father to your facility."

"I understand completely," Dr. Vronsky said. "A full list of references will be provided to you. I'll have my assistant fax it over to you tomorrow. You and your wife should feel free to contact anyone on it, and more names can be provided anytime you like."

The phone rang and the doctor excused himself. He began the conversation in English but quickly switched to another language. It was short call and when it was over Vronsky smiled.

"The problem with living here is that I am never far out of reach."

"Was that Russian you were speaking?" I asked.

"I speak Russian but I am not from that country. I was born in Kiev, in the Ukraine. That distinction may not make much of a difference to you, but it makes a great deal of difference to Ukrainians. You Americans tend to use the word "Russian" somewhat generically. But you are right in the sense that all of us—and when I say all of us I'm referring to the former satellite states of course—we were all strongly encouraged, some might say forced, to learn the Russian language. Perhaps this was the one thing the communists got right, the lingua franca of a dead empire."

"If you don't mind my asking, Doctor where did you

practice before you came to this country?"

"I worked in a mental hospital in Moscow where they specialized in treating a special form of schizophrenia that, coincidentally, seemed especially prevalent among dissidents and political prisoners."

"Meaning that if you disagreed with the government, they had you committed. Is that it?"

"Precisely."

"And you had to sign off on it; is that it?"

"Well, let us just say that in those days one worked for the Soviet state or one did not work at all. That tended to have a great impact the diagnosis a patient received. I was fortunate enough to find someone willing to sponsor me, and I was allowed to immigrate. He was the one who helped me get started in this country. A very great man. Now, sir, your application says you run your father's hedge fund. You have a background in finance then?"

"Yes," I said. "From Wharton. This is a pretty good cigar, doctor. If I didn't know better I'd say it was made it Havana. "

Dr. Vronsky smiled and followed the trail of smoke with his eyes as it swirled upwards toward the open window where it mingled with the white curtain waving in the slight breeze. "Another gift" he said. "I've been blessed with very generous patients."

"You know," I said. "My father worked hard his entire life. We're prepared to do the right thing by him no matter how much it costs."

"Your father," Dr. Vronsky began. "Has he any long-term care insurance?"

"Certainly. I don't know the exact amount he carries, but I understand it's more than enough to protect the bulk of his fortune."

"I should tell you that Balmore offers many alternative therapies not always covered by standard insurance, and certainly not by Medicare. In many cases, though certainly not all, they have been proven to be quite effective. Some of them are showing promising results but they are a bit controversial, especially our use of the latest stem cell technology from Germany. I'm afraid you Americans are losing your edge in that field. Still, if one has the means . . ."

"In other words," I said. "There would be other fees involved?"

"Yes, and some of them quite substantial. That's why we require that every patient have an escrow account to cover the cost of unforeseen expenses. Would this be a problem for you and your family?"

"Not at all," I said.

"The minimum deposit is one million dollars." Vronsky turned in his chair when he said this, the better, I thought, to see my reaction.

"And you say you offer the latest treatments?" I asked.

"Without a doubt."

"Then a million seems more than reasonable," I said. "All things considered."

"Let me ask you something, Mr. Stone. Who controls your father's finances? Is it you?"

"Yes," I said. "That was all taken care of sometime ago. I have full power of attorney."

"Very good. That makes things much easier. In any case, if you decide to bring your father here, and if we accept him, it might be wise for you to arrange a meeting with one of our financial consultants. They can help you determine the most economically sound way to see that your father receives the finest care we can offer. We can help you structure certain annuities and trusts that will reduce your exposure to undue taxation. We can even help you avoid most of the estate taxes the government would require when the unfortunate time comes."

"That's good to hear. I'm all in favor of keeping the government out of my bank account, doctor. I'll have my accountants fax over a financial statement in the morning."

"Excellent," Vronsky said. "The sooner we receive it, the better."

Vronsky agreed to show me the psychiatric section of Balmore House. Based on my description of my father's behavior—most notably the part about his berserker tendencies—the good doctor sadly admitted that it was more than likely that Dad would need more specialized treatment and behavioral modification therapy, not to mention more powerful medication, medication which would no doubt be very expensive and not covered by most drug plans. It seemed to me that Balmore House was turning out be the kind of place with more hidden fees and surcharges than a credit card, and I could tell that Vronsky was carefully gauging my reaction every time he mentioned money. The phrase "not covered by Medicare or most major insurance companies" was something of a mantra for him, and he was particularly attentive to my response each time he used it, but I merely shrugged off any insinuation that money was any object of concern and tried to make it clear to Vronsky that when it came to Big Daddy Stone, money was no problem.

The psycho ward was housed on the other side of the compound in a separate building some distance from the main residence, and while we might have walked, the doctor insisted we use his golf cart. The building was a five-story red brick rectangular box with a cobblestone courtyard and an arched doorway that looked like it belonged on an Ivy League campus. Ahead of us, an old man in a yellow terrycloth bathrobe was slowly making his way toward the front of the building, a female attendant trailing him like a Chinese bride. We passed them by and parked on the grass near the portico and walked up the steps that lead to the front entrance.

I followed Vronsky up the steps and waited while he slid a card through the vertical slit of the security module affixed to the reinforced double glass doors. A pair of jumbo-sized security men watched us from behind the front desk. Both men wore navy blue jackets with the letter "B" embossed on their breast pockets. One of them buzzed us in. Behind them sat a third man, a brown-skinned giant with a shaved head and magazine muscles. He was holding a submarine sandwich in one hand and a TV remote in the other. When he saw Vronsky coming, he quickly clicked off the basketball game he'd been watching and swiveled around to face the entrance. But it was too late. Dr. Cyclops had already spotted the little television set, and he wasn't very happy about it either.

"What did I tell you about watching television when on duty?" Vronsky shouted. "Do you think this is why I pay you?"

The guards said nothing. They just stood there staring silently at the floor like kids huddled in a doorway waiting for a storm to pass.

"One more time," Vronsky said. "And I fine you both one week's pay. Am I understood?"

The men nodded and mumbled their answers, but Vronsky wasn't satisfied.

"Am I understood?" he demanded.

Like members of an unhappy choir, all three men said "yes" at the same time.

"Good," the Doctor said. I wasn't sure whether he was putting on an act for my benefit or whether he was just getting off on dressing down these two men who towered over him. When he was satisfied that the guards had been sufficiently cowed, he turned to me and smiled. I had to admit it; he had the Stalin thing down pat.

"Such a stupid waste of time, this basketball," Vronsky said as we left the desk. "But what can you do? They have no education. Sport is all they know."

Vronsky had to use his card again to summon the elevators. I was beginning to think that if it was half as hard getting out of Balmore as it was getting in, you'd have to be one tricky nutcase to pull off an escape.

"We call this part of the residence Balmore Commons,"

Vronsky said. "We don't like to refer to it as a psychiatric ward. Once they're accepted to our program, new clients are graded according to their degree of functionality. The people you saw in the main building are all level one. Those in level two are less mobile, less aware of their surroundings. Levels three through seven contains our most dependent clients, those whose mental and physical conditions require the most care. They are here in this facility, along with our hospice staff for when the time comes."

"What are the level sevens like?" I asked

"Life support," Dr. Vronsky answered. "This is for those with not much time to live, or perhaps for someone in a permanent vegetative state who will never recover. Most are sedated and on respirators."

We got off at the third floor where once again I found myself facing a reception desk shielded with a thick wall of Plexiglas barricade that ran the width of the floor. There were screens and monitors and a half dozen nurses and orderlies on the other side of it. On either end of the reception desk there were two formidable looking steel doors, each with a tiny window just large enough to frame a face. A nurse behind the partition greeted Vronsky with a smile, but just as she was about to address him through the microphone someone on the other side of the door to my left let out a long, loud howl that sounded like a timber wolf trying out for the Metropolitan Opera.

When the howling had stopped, Vronsky turned to me and started to speak, but before he could get a word out, the insane aria began again. It was not the kind of sound you would want to hear while walking alone at night on a dark street. Even Vronsky, who otherwise had seemed as unperturbed by the howling as Doctor Moreau might have been, was starting to lose his patience. He leaned forward and yelled into the microphone.

"Who is it making this noise?" Vronsky demanded.

"That's Mr. Roth," The nurse said, speaking into the microphone. "His medication is being readjusted."

"But not quickly enough I see," Dr. Vronsky said. "This noise is very disturbing to the other patients. Have Mr. Roth moved to the sixth floor until the Lithium takes effect."

I signed in yet again. Every five feet somebody was asking me for my autograph. Vronsky and I were buzzed through the steel door to our right. There was no howling on this wing. On the contrary, it was as though everyone, including the staff, had sworn an oath of near perfect silence. Rather than speak, Doctors and nurses in and gray and green scrubs merely nodded at us as we passed, and the patients, lingering in the hallway like somnambulists, went by us as though we were invisible. The air was thicker here, harder to stir, like gravy with too much flour, and it seemed to me that we were all moving a bit more slowly now and that the long white corridors were getting longer and the distance farther away. It was as though even the walls of Balmore Commons had been medicated with some powerful soporific.

"I apologize for Mr. Roth." Vronsky said. "I'm afraid that the mad grow old just like the rest of us, Mr. Stone. When that happens, their families send them to us. That is, if they have the means to do so. But please understand that the level of care here is unsurpassed. You won't find a better ratio between patient and staff in the country. I assure you: should you decide this is the proper place for your father, we will take excellent care of him for as long as he lives."

I glanced into some of the rooms as the doctor and I strolled past them. If this place was somebody's idea of a country for old men then they could keep it. The people sat on the edges of their beds and stared at their television sets, or at the ceiling, or at nothing at all. Many of the people I passed seemed sedated. Outside in the hallway, we came upon a man standing with his face to the wall, staring straight up as though he were about to begin climbing like Spider-Man. Behind him crept another man dragging an oxygen tank behind him like a dog on a leash. Farther on, a woman stood in the center of the hallway, running both hands through her white hair over and over again as we passed her. Walking through that place made dying young seem like the easy way out.

"I can't say for certain without examining him of course," Vronsky said as we turned down another corridor, "but based on what you have told me, I would say that it may be here on this floor that your father will be kept. I know it isn't pleasant here, but he'll be comfortable, and if, in time, he shows improvement, he can be moved to a less restrictive ward."

I told Vronsky that I understood, but most of my attention was focused on an old man sitting in wheelchair outside of a room at the far end of the corridor. The closer we got the more positive I became that it was Cal. He had lost a lot of weight and they had shaved his head but it was him. He was wearing a white bathrobe and a pair of disposable paper slippers. His feet were up on the metal footrests and he sat hunched over in the wheelchair with the stooped posture a homeless man on a winter's day trying to pull himself inwards and away from the cold.

I wondered what Cal might do if he recognized me. If he made any sign at all that he knew who I was, I would have to decide fast what to do. I made a point of stopping directly in front of Cal's wheelchair to ask Vronsky a question about visiting hours, even raising my voice a bit in the hopes that I might get his attention, but Cal didn't even look up. He just stared straight ahead at the opposite wall, rocking back and forth or swinging his head from side to side as though in vigorous disagreement with someone.

There was nothing I could do with him in that condition. He had been too heavily drugged. I thought about using Vronsky as a hostage, but that would mean handling Cal and his wheelchair with one hand and Vronsky and my gun with the other. The odds were long, but I was so close now that it was tempting to go for the touchdown, but I knew it was stupid, and that it made no sense to have risked so much and have gotten so far to blow the deal now, so I decided to punt instead. There were too many guards and too many doors and too many checkpoints between me and the outside world for me to make it. Even if I was lucky enough to bluff my way past some of them, once they saw what the deal was they would lock the entire facility down. When that happened, Vronsky would either call my bluff in the belief that I wouldn't shoot him or force me to prove him wrong, and regardless of which way it went down neither Cal nor I would be likely to get away.

I couldn't see any way around it. I would have to come back, only this time I wouldn't be alone. The next time I'd come back like MacArthur came back to the Philippines, talking trash, kicking ass and taking plenty of names. I'd be back with a nasty lawyer and lights and cameras and Geraldo Rivera and megaphones and plenty of bad attitude and of course a gun. I might even ask to borrow that bazooka Raul had mentioned to me the other day at the slaughterhouse. What a difference a night in the Everglades can make in your assessment of what constitutes excessive force. Now, just thinking about blowing Vronsky's little house of horrors to kingdom come made me smile. But not yet, I thought, not yet. So I gave Cal one last look, added to it a silent promise, which I intended to keep, and then, like the old song says, I just walked on by.

Ten minutes later, the tour was over, and Dr. Vronsky and I were in the golf cart speeding again across the sloping lawn. We were halfway back to the main building when his cell phone rang. He apologized and took the call. I looked up at the sky. The farther west you went out here the brighter the stars got, but that didn't help my mood much. Beside me, Vronsky listened in silence to his caller then responded in Russian. His tone of voice struck me as somewhat somber, as though he had just received bad news. I was only vaguely aware of what he was doing. Most of my attention was focused on a pair of headlights heading straight for us on what looked like a collision course.

But the Jeep stopped just in time, and two guards I had never seen before jumped out from either side and ran toward Vronsky's golf cart, one of them already reaching for his sidearm. I didn't wait to see what the problem was because I had the nasty feeling that it was me. Instead, I reached down and yanked the gun out of my ankle holster and jumped out of the cart. Both men stopped when they saw the gun, and the hand of the man who had been reaching for his revolver stopped reaching and hovered uncertainly in the air with nothing to do and nowhere to go. I started to turn back toward the doctor, but suddenly every nerve in my body fired at once and the gun flew out of my hand and my fingers seized up as though stricken with an unexpected palsy. Then my gut muscles convulsed and I doubled over and fell to one knee.

I turned my head in time to see Dr. Vronsky standing about five feet away from me holding a Taser in his hand. I pulled one of the stingers out of my arm but got zapped twice more by the guards. Then the two guards held their guns on me while I lay on the ground bent double like an overgrown fetus in a khaki suit. Dr. Vronsky looked down at me with the bland expression of a mortician at the embalming table and calmly removed a small leather case from inside his jacket. He selected a syringe and filled it with a clear liquid from a small vial from the same case. His movements were very professional, very precise, with nothing wasted. Vronsky spoke quickly in Russian, and one of the guards lifted me up and bent me backwards over the hood of the golf cart while the other man pulled off my jacket. Once my arm was free, I threw a punch that missed everything but the night air, and then I was pinned down and the good doctor was sliding the point of the needle into my forearm. They held me down until my body began to melt out from under me and the light stars went dead.

It was still dark when I awoke, though how much time had passed I couldn't say for certain. I was lying in a bed with my arms and ankles strapped down. Just for the fun of it, I tested the restraints but the leather held. Except for my jacket, I was still in my street clothes, right down to my loafers. I'm was thirsty as I ever had been, but there was no way I could reach the pitcher of water on the nightstand, so I close my eyes and go back to sleep where I dream that I'm drinking down a cold, cold beer from a frosted glass that never empties. I can even feel the foam on my upper lip and the tingle at the back of my throat.

When I come to again Vince Fernandez was staring down at me and beside him stood Dr. Vronsky and Marina Gero. They all wore different expressions on their faces. None of them happy. Vince looked annoyed and disappointed. Marina's was one of extreme rage being held back by some invisible force, possibly a little pill of some kind. It was a rage that was very old and went way back and had nothing to do with me. I was only the latest catalyst in a world full of lit matches. Vronsky was deadpanned. He regarded me only as another specimen, and as such I was valuable only up to a point after which I would be nothing more than medical waste to be smuggled out with regular trash.

"So," Vronsky said. "The hedge fund manager is awake at last. So much for risk management. So tell me, Mr. Vaughn, how are you feeling?"

"Thirsty."

"Marina," the doctor said. "Please give Mr. Vaughn a little water won't you."

The real estate agent glared at Vronsky for a moment in seeming disbelief, and I could feel her vibrating with anger. Then, all at once, the quake subsided. Marina walked calmly over to the nightstand picked up the pitcher, threw me one beautifully malicious smile then dashed the contents of the pitcher, ice and all, full into my face.

"Thank you," I said.

"It didn't have to be like this," Vince said.

"Yes it did," I said.

Dr. Vronsky scooped the ice cubes off my chest and back into the pitcher, which he then held close enough to my face for me to fasten my lips around the cold metal straw and draw what remained of the water. It wasn't much, but under the circumstance I thought it best not to ask for a refill.

"I'm sorry about my niece's behavior," Vronsky said. "You mustn't take it personally. Marina is bi-polar. I've recommended medication on many occasions; however..."

"You should remember better who it was who brought you to this country, my little stupid uncle," Marina Gero said. "And then you should shut your stupid mouth."

"This is my clinic," Vronsky said. "I speak as I please."

"Yes, and bought for with my husband's money," Marina said. "Be grateful you're not back in Moscow driving a taxi cab again with all the other famous psychiatrists."

"All right," Fernandez said. "Let's stop with this family feud crap already. We're late as it is, and Suarez is waiting for us."

"You've got yourself quite a little crew here, Fernandez," I said. "Who's Suarez? Another old man you're going to rip off?"

"For your information, wise guy" Fernandez said with a wide grin. "Suarez is a very rich dealer who wants to buy himself a submarine. You know: the kind that goes under water. I'm his translator. That's the kind of operation you could have been part of. Hardcore global shit and money coming out all pores. But, no, instead, you had to be an asshole, and for what? What did that old man ever do for you? Not a fucking thing I'll bet. And now look at you."

"This is all wrong," Marina said. "This man should have been killed before now."

"Did he tell you where the girl is yet?" Fernandez asked.

"Not yet," Vronsky said. "I have to wait until the sedative I gave him wears off before we can use other drugs. I wish I had some SP-117 available. It's what we used at the clinic in Moscow. It's much better than sodium pentothal or scopolamine for loosening up the tongue, but don't worry, we'll get what we need. And, of course, if all else fails, there's always pain. It's simple, cheap and very effective."

Vince looked at me and shook his head. It was all my fault. The way Fernandez saw it, he and Dr. Mengele were just a couple of honest citizens trying to run a business, and then I come along and start making trouble, leaving no choice but to shoot me full of drugs, and if that didn't work, start pulling out fingernails.

"You could save yourself some trouble," Vince said. "If you tell us where little Ms. Belkin is. It will make things a lot easier."

"She went back to New York," I said.

"You expect us to believe that?" Marina said.

"Not you," I said. "You're too smart. But Fernandez is another story. He believes in all kinds of fairy tales. I bet he even thinks you're in love with him. That's why he killed your husband for you, right?"

For a long moment no one moved while the three of them stood there, staring at me like I was a male gorgon. If not for my restraints, I could have reached out, tipped them over, and strolled out of the room before they had a chance to recover. Vronsky came out of it first.

"What are you saying?" the doctor asked.

"What?" I said. "You mean you didn't know? I'm sorry. I thought you knew all about that. Mr. Miami over there shot Marina's sugar daddy up in Brighton Beach last August. Say, wait a minute, Doc. Now that I'm thinking, wasn't he the sponsor you were telling me about back in your office? A guy named Romanov. The guy who started the Emperor's Club. I guess maybe your niece forgot to tell you about that."

"You're so full of shit it's pathetic," Vince said. "Where did you that get piece of crap from?"

"An old friend told me," I said. "He couldn't help himself." And that is when Vronsky jammed another needle in my arm and everything went blink-blink.

13

The room was white. The walls were white, and the sheets and the pillowcases on the bed were also white. The shades on the windows would have been white, too, except for the yellow glare pushing against them from behind. I was sitting up in bed with my hands folded in my lap, but for some reason that fact didn't concern very much. In fact, nothing concerned me very much except for the game going on inside my head.

I don't know how long the game had been going on or how long I had been playing it before I became aware of the fact that there was a game and that it was something that I could play and actually get better at if I kept trying. The first key to the game was pretty simple: I had to stay in the white room. That was imperative. The white room was the arena where the game was played and beyond it, as far as I could tell, there was nothing.

The white room was the arena but what was the purpose of the game? It was really simple but at the same time very hard to do. The goal was to put words together inside my head so that I could talk like the two black guys and the Puerto Rican girl could talk. Their words were very close together like a long train. You see? A long train. That's something new. A little while ago, I didn't even know what a train was. Now I do. That's it. That's what I want. I want my words to be close together like the boxcars of a long train, so I can talk with them about basketball. I want to talk about March Madness.

Right now, the problem is my words won't stay together. The words. They run away from each other like they're afraid or something. I try to grab them before they can get away, but it isn't easy, because if I chase down one word, the other words get away. Sometimes I'll try and drag one word with me when I try and catch the other one, but that's very tiring, and getting tired is something I have to be careful about. Because when I get tired, I tend to leave the white room. Now when that happens, I get mad. I curse and I yell. The two black guys tell me to shut the fuck up, but they think it's funny too. But it's not. I don't laugh at their game, and they shouldn't laugh at mine either.

That is also something that's new: getting mad. It doesn't happen all the time but when it does I feel good. I feel strong. For some reason, I seem to feel better when the little Puerto Rican girl is not around. Maybe it's her needles I don't like, though it doesn't hurt very much when she does it. Lately, I have begun to notice that I get mad the moment she opens the door with her keys. Sometimes I even start to cry. I don't know why I don't like her. She doesn't seem like a bad person.

But I know who is a bad person. They call him Doctor V. He is definitely a bad person for sure. Everybody is afraid of him, even the two black guys who watch me. When Dr. V comes they hide the little television in the closet. The doctor has more needles than anybody else. He stuck me with one the other day and left and when he came back he asked me some questions. Like where my parents live. When I told him they were both dead he was happy. Why would he be happy about something like that? That's how I know he's not a nice person. He thinks it's just great that both my parents are dead.

He asked for my social security number too. I didn't even know I had one before Dr. V asked for it, but then the numbers just came out of me, all of them close together. He asked me other things too, like if I had a wife or a girlfriend. When I said no, Dr. V. was happy about that too. The only time he got mad was when he asked me if I had any really close friends, and I told him Cal Belkin. I wasn't exactly sure who Cal Belkin was, but Dr. V didn't like that I said it.

When I told Dr. V. what my social security number was he told me it was the key to a gold mine, because even though I didn't have insurance, he could still make money from the government with my number. He said I was a sick man and that I would always be sick and that as long as I was sick the government would pay him to keep giving me needles.

Dr. V likes talking to me, but only when we're alone. He's always quiet when other people are around. I think he likes to talk to me because I don't answer him. He say's I'm one of his best secret patients, and that if I continue to improve, in a year or so he will change my medicine, and I'll be able to go outside and walk around. But he doesn't know about the game, or how good I'm getting at it. He doesn't know what I can do now. For example, today I got two words to stay together for a long time. And guess what? I know what they mean too. My name is Jack Vaughn.

I had no idea how long I was out of it, but suddenly all at once I was myself again. I was solid. It was not at all like waking up from a deep sleep. There was no sense of grogginess, no lingering dream to swim out of, no doubt about who or where I was or what had been done to me. The still life picture had become a movie. I was hyper-alert, almost to the point of panic. I was a fawn hiding in the darkness, surrounded by predators who were very close by. I could sense their presence all around me. Something detached itself from my body and traveled beyond the white room out into the hallway. It seemed to me I could see what it saw, hear it what it heard. It went forward slowly, quietly, its belly fur scraping the white sterile tiles. It came to the end of the hallway and paused at the turn. I listened with it and heard footsteps coming closer.

I propped myself up on my elbows and listened. The footsteps stopped outside my room and a shadow broke the line of light beneath the door. The soft jangle of keys. Then, the sound of keys hitting the floor and someone coughing. It sounded like a man. This is it, Vaughn, your last chance to win the game. If you don't make it out of here tonight, there won't be a next year. Vronsky will make sure you never get a second chance to escape.

The slight scrape of a key sliding into the lock, and me, lying back, peeking through my eyelashes, hoping that whoever comes through the door isn't be too big or too tough or on steroids. The door swings inward, and a medium sized man in a white uniform looks in at me, flicks on the light, and restores his key ring to his belt. He quickly pirouettes and with his back now to me, begins pulling a cart into the room. Once inside, he turns again and pushes the cart up to the edge of my bed. The door clicks shut behind him. Hold it, Vaughn. Not yet. Let him get close.

I see his face. It will not be easy. He is about forty years old, slightly paunchy but beefier than I would have preferred. I had been hoping for a midget with a limp. It will have to be hard and fast and maybe permanent. But I can't think about that now. I can't think about the thin, silver wedding band on his finger or the pictures of his kids in his wallet. This is it.

He doesn't look at me. He doesn't have to. I'm not going anywhere—or so he thinks. By now, I'm just a part of his nightly routine, another nut waiting for his nightly needle. He picks up a clipboard and makes a mark with a pencil, sets it down again. Then he picks up a small vial and upends it into a syringe. The clear liquid rapidly floods the glass cylinder. He steps around to the right side of my bed, points the needle at the ceiling and gives it a squirt. Then he reaches down and begins rolling up my sleeve with his left hand.

I surge out the bed and grab his left arm with one hand and his throat with other. He drops the needle and tries to pull back but I hold him, gauging his strength as I kick free of the sheets. He's no weakling, but whatever they gave me is working overtime, because his face turns red almost immediately, and I hardly feel like I'm squeezing at all. I stand up and shove him back against the wall with a thud I'm sure they can here up at the state capital in Tallahassee.

I bring my knee up into his gut with everything I have. Then twice again, like I'm driving piles into soft dirt. His hand drops from around my wrist, and I feel his weight begin to sag into me, and for the first time I look him in the eyes. They are terrified. A shadow of guilt passes quickly over me. I want to tell him that it wasn't personal; that I was sorry for rupturing his spleen or liver, sorry for the internal bleeding; sorry for the blood that would surely be in his piss by morning.

"I'm going to talk and you're going to listen," I said. "If you yell or try to fight me, I'll kill you. Nod if you understand."

He nodded. As soon as I let go of his throat, he rolled over on his side and vomited then coughed and spit. I waited for him to finish then turned him back around.

"What's in this syringe?" I asked.

"Lithium," he said.

"Is that all they've been giving me?"

"No, you're on Clozapine and some other stuff. Mostly sedatives"

"Clozapine: What's that for?"

"Schizophrenia."

"Tell me the truth, Hopkins: do I seem schizophrenic to you?"

"Don't take this personal, mister, but yea, you do."

"Listen to me: I'm getting out of here," I said. "How do you want to play it?"

"I don't understand."

"I'm leaving. I don't belong here. Now you can either help me or not. If not, then I'm going to pop every one of those needles on that cart back there into your ass and pull the trigger. Then we'll see who's crazy. What do you think about that?"

"Okay, I'll help you."

"Good. Get up."

He got slowly to his feet, holding his ribs and wiping his mouth as he straightened up. I took his keys off of him then walked him over to the bed and told him to start tearing the bed sheets into strips. The only weapon I had was a needle full of Lithium but for now that seemed to be enough to maintain his cooperation. When he was done with the sheets, I bound his hands in front of him then made him sit back on the bed while I tied his ankles together. Then I put a washcloth over his mouth and tied it in place with a length of rubber tubing I took from the cart. I spotted a row of bottles in a wooden rack on the bottom shelf. One of them caught my eye. It was Ritalin.

I got Hopkins straightened out in my bed and propped his head up with pillows. You couldn't ask for a better hostage, and I felt a little sorry for having had to hurt him the way I did. The least I could do was make him comfortable. I pulled the washcloth away from his mouth so I could speak with him.

"Look," I said. "I'm really sorry about this. Is there anything I can do for you before I go?"

"You won't get out of here," Hopkins said. "But since you ask, a couple a Xanax would be nice. They're on the second shelf."

I got the pills and fed them to him one at a time. I even held a cup of water up to his lips while he washed them down.

"How many people on duty tonight?" I asked.

"I don't know. Ten maybe, not including security. Who knows? You might get lucky. They're all busy watching the basketball game."

"You put any money on the game?"

"Yea, and so far I'm doing pretty well too."

"Who do you have?"

"I got the Tar Heels."

"You should have taken the Bruins. They always beat the spread."

"The Bruins! You must be out of your mind."

"Sure I am," I said. "Why else would I be in this trap?"

I tied the washcloth around the nurse's mouth again and flicked off the light. Then I went looking for my clothes. I would not get far in the hospital gown they had given me, and besides that, half my ass was hanging out. I found my suit hanging neatly in the shallow metal armoire near the window. My shirt had been starched and ironed and my khaki suit still smelled from dry cleaning. Of course, Dr. Vronsky had never intended that I would ever wear it again, but the people who did the laundry didn't know that.

I dressed quickly in the weak light but skipped the tie and socks. Whatever they had injected me with instead of the Lithium was beginning to wear off. I was beginning to lose that keen sense of heightened awareness it had given me, and worse than that, the walls were starting to billow and flutter when I looked at them. There was no telling how much worse it would get, so I opened the bottle of Ritalin and swallowed two pills dry, hoping that they would give me the time to get out of Crazyville before the world turned into melted cheese.

I went to the door and listened. Not much on the other side but silence. I turned the door handle, crouched and peeked out into the hallway. My room was roughly in the middle of the corridor. I could see the light from the nurse's station about thirty yards to my right. At the other end of the hallway, an exit sign shone above a door. I scanned the ceiling for surveillance cameras and spotted one at either end by the windows. Security cameras are only as good as the men watching them, and people tend to get complacent over time, but if someone glanced up and saw me strolling down the hallway, it would all be over very quickly.

I pushed Hopkins's drug cart out into the hallway and began walking as calmly as I could toward the exit sign. I was hoping that whoever was at the security desk would be too busy keeping track of their basketball bets to give more than a cursory glance at the cameras. They had no doubt seen the pushcart a thousand times before, and I was counting on them not giving much thought to the man who was following it. I would know soon enough if I was wrong.

Then I made the mistake of glancing down at the floor and letting my gaze linger there to long. All at once the tiny specks in the tile began to whirl around like the stars in some speeded up version of the Milky Way galaxy. I stopped to stare at the show for a moment. The intricate, intelligent patterns, the double helixes, the ballet of a billion separate particles spinning in concert with each other sucked the attention out of my eyes with such force that I felt I was falling forward into the vortex the floor beneath me had become. I touched the wall to steady myself. At this rate, I would never make it. The Ritalin had better kick in soon, I thought, or I'm never going to make it out of here.

I willed the vortex to stop but it only slowed down slightly. Still, it gave me a sense of control that encouraged me to reach out again. This time, though, instead of trying to stop the spinning completely, I tried to reverse its direction. There was a searing pain in the center of my forehead as the vortex of little specks began to slow down like a carrousel at the end of a turn and then the specks stopped whirling and begin to fall gently toward the floor like snowflakes from the sky until just like that they were only tiny black specks on the square faces of the polished white tiles.

I steadied myself and headed for the exit again. It seemed to be receding in the distance. I heard a shout behind me and glanced around in time to see a man in a white lab jump into the air with his arms raised above his head. He turned to look in my direction but only for a moment. I resumed my march toward the end of the corridor. Score one for the home team, I thought. It seemed to me now that I was trying to hold back the urge to panic as though it was some kind of beast on the other side of a flimsy door, a door I was tempted to open if only get it over with.

The irony of trying escape from an insane asylum during

what sport fans called March Madness wasn't completely wasted on me, but it couldn't distract me from the terrible knowledge that everything I was and everything I was ever was going to be depended on what happened not tomorrow or the day after but on right here and right now. Margin of error: zero. I tried to remember a time when I had had time to spare, the luxury of the eternal do-over and the handmade T of the time out. I couldn't do it. Compared to this swollen moment of fear, the moments of the past were irrelevant, vague rumors, a frozen collection of statues shit on by pigeons.

I reached the exit door and peeked out the window and down into the employee's lot where I had left my car how long ago I didn't know. I couldn't be sure, but it seemed to be exactly where I had left it. Mr. Glock was waiting under the front seat. All I had to do was get to him. In the meantime, I needed something to fight with. I checked the cart to see what I could find.

What I needed was a machine gun and a few hand grenades. What I found instead was what we used to call a peacekeeper, a retractable metal baton with a steel ball on the end. It was like meeting an old friend in a bad neighborhood. I also found a bottle of rubbing alcohol and a box of cotton balls. I stuck the baton in my belt and opened the exit door with the keys I had taken from the nurse and found myself in a dimly lit stairwell with only the roof above me. I started down, listening for voices. Meanwhile, I was still having a hard time keeping the floors and walls from flexing and bulging like long pieces of sheet metal. Twice, I had to stop and hold tight to the banister to keep from tipping over. I told myself it was all in my head and that nothing was really moving, but my feet didn't believe me. They belonged to a drunken sailor on a floundering ship, and they kept shifting around beneath me despite everything I could do to make them stop.

I was two floors into my descent when I heard a door below me open followed by the sound of giggling. I pulled myself into the narrow gap between the wall and the coiled firehouse. I had to wait for my heart to slow down before I could hear properly. They were on the floor below me, a man and a woman. I could hear their muffled laughter as they whispered at one another then something that sounded like a struggle of some sorts. When I was sure they weren't in my direction, I risked a peek over the banister.

The doctor, it seemed, was about to make a house call. His scrubs were down below his knees, and a stethoscope still swung from his neck. The woman was bent forward in front of him with her hands braced on the stairs above her and the white skirt of her uniform was pushed way up high over her back. There was just enough light for me to see her white buttocks rise up to meet his advance. He grabbed a handful of her long dark hair, twisted it around his hand and wrist like a braided rope then went to work like Buck Benny at the Denver Rodeo. Some other time, I would have thought it was funny, but not tonight. But there was nothing I could do except settle back into my gap between the wall and the firehouse and hope this was just a short cigarette break and not their dinner hour.

When I checked back a few minutes later, the happy couple had changed positions. They had dropped the cowboy act and were now going at it vertically. They weren't laughing now. In fact, save for a few moans and groans, they hardly made any noise at all. She was standing now with the wall behind her and one of her feet up on the banister like a ballet dancer practicing for the Nutcracker and the man was digging into her with the silent mania of a deranged gravedigger. When it was over, the doctor and nurse dressed quietly, like teammates in a locker room after a game that had left them both too exhausted to talk about it. They didn't even kiss goodbye. The nurse opened the exit door on the landing below, while the doctor continued on down the stairs. Mission accomplished.

I decided to follow the doctor if only because he knew where he was going, and I didn't. He went all the way to the first floor. I stayed a flight above him, making as little noise as possible, but even so, he must have sensed something, because twice he stopped and looked back, both time barely giving me enough time to pull myself into the shadows. He was just about to exit on the ground floor when the door flew inwards and Vince Fernandez came barging through with his gun drawn.

Vince shoved the doctor against the doorjamb and held him there for a moment while he glanced up the stairs in my general direction. It was a quick glance but not quite quick enough. I leaned back away from the railing and listened as he barked questions at the doctor. I couldn't make out what he was saying, but I knew it could only mean one thing; they had found the nurse I had jumped. Then, somewhere on one of the floors above me, I heard another door open and the tumult of someone in a hurry, running rapidly down the stairs. Suddenly they stopped and Mr. Zero's voice echoed through the semi-darkness of the stairwell.

"Vince!" Mr. Zero yelled from above me. "You see him?"

"Not yet!" Fernandez shouted. "He must be between us. What floor are you on?"

"Five. It's all clear, bro."

"Bring him to me if you get him. I'm coming up."

I opened the door that led to the third floor. The hallway was empty, each tile a tiny island of fluorescent light. I broke into a run toward the exit doors at the other end of the hallway. The Ritalin had kicked in and my heart was King Kong banging on the village doors. I was halfway down the hall and glancing behind me every few steps when I passed a supply closet with a mop and bucket wedged between the door and jamb to keep it open. I stepped over the bucket and flicked on the light switch. The shelves were stacked with cleaning supplies and uniforms.

I grabbed handfuls of shirts and pants and coveralls and dumped them into the big aluminum sink under the tiny window. I opened the bottle of rubbing alcohol I had taken from the nurse's cart and poured it over the clothes along with a gallon of furniture polish and whatever else I could find that looked flammable. I doused a roll of paper towels with the rest of the alcohol and tossed it in the sink. The nurse's little red lighter did the rest. The nasty stew of clothing and chemicals exploded into flames so intense I had to cover my nose and mouth in order to breathe. There was more smoke than fire, and the metal sink would keep it from spreading very far beyond the storeroom, but it would be enough to bring the cops and the firemen and the distraction of their noisy arrival, and maybe give me my best chance of getting away in the confusion.

I grabbed a pair of faded blue coveralls as I backed away from the fire. Black and gray smoke followed me out as I stepped over the bucket and back into the hallway. I took a few steps to the right, but as I tried to wave the smoke away from my face, a man wider than he was tall came running through the haze with his head down and rammed me in the chest with his shoulder. Mr. Zero.

There was no way to stop the momentum of his rush, so I just rode with it, falling backwards with Zero on top of me. We grabbed at one another. He tried to pin my arms to the floor. If he did that it would be over. What stopped him from succeeding was that he was still holding his gun with one hand and couldn't quite get a good grip on my left arm without dropping it.

I hit him across the temple with my fist then grabbed his gun and pushed it up and away from me. Zero was strong, stronger than I was, but the smoke was in his eyes now, distracting him from applying his strength. I struggled to my feet, twisting the gun away from me with both hands, and then, before he could regain his balance, I yanked the baton out of my belt and chopped down hard on his wrist.

The gun hit the floor and I swung again, this time sideways, catching him in the side of the head. He staggered to one side and slumped against the wall. We were both coughing violently now and fighting with the smoke as much as with each other. I waited, hoping he was done for but he reached for me again through the smoke. I dropped the baton and grabbed the metal bucket by the handle, twisted my hips and swung around like a hammer thrower. The impact of the galvanized steel against the bodybuilder's head sounded like a gong, and dirty water drenched us both. Mr. Zero staggered away into the smoke. A moment later something that sounded like a human head hit the tiles and then silence.

The ceiling hissed above me. When I looked up my face was sprayed with jets of cold water as the fire alarm sounded. I dropped quickly to my knees in hopes of finding either the baton or Zero's revolver. Far down the corridor, a door open, and I knew it had to be Fernandez. I reluctantly straightened up. I hated to leave without finding a weapon but there was no choice now, so. I headed for the stairs through the smoke.

I fought the urge to head downstairs and instead headed up to the fourth floor. If I had any hope at all of making it out of Vronsky's clinic I would need a crowd to cover me. Evacuating so many patients in such poor condition would take practically the entire staff, and I doubted they would pay much attention to any able bodied person who didn't need help getting to safety. My hope was to be long gone by the time Fernandez realized what was happening.

I stopped at the fourth floor and peeked out into the hallway. About a dozen patients were lined up against the wall like over-aged school kids going on a field trip. They were as quiet and as docile as a troupe of zombies. The nurse I had seen a few minutes before with the doctor in the stairwell was now busily taking a headcount. I stepped back and listened for any sign of Fernandez on the landings below me, but the alarm was making way too much noise to hear anything.

Quickly, I pulled the overalls I had grabbed on over my clothes then stepped out into the hallway and walked as calmly as I could toward the nurse. She saw me coming and hailed me with a look of relief. Her name tag said *Ward* but her accent, her features, the dark luster of her hair made me suspect she was Thai.

"Hey!" the nurse shouted. "Give me a hand over here! I need you to help me get these people downstairs."

I hurried over to her. She didn't give my face a second look; she saw only the coveralls and took the part for the whole. I walked to the end of the line as it began to wander more or less in a straight line for the exit. The nurse led the expedition while I took up the rear. Behind us, further down the corridor, another group was being rounded up by a pair of nurses. Our group began moving forward. The slowness of the procession annoyed me, but there was no way I could speed it up.

Up ahead, the nurse held the exit door open while the patients passed through in single file. A few of them walked with their arms stretched out in front of them like blind men trying to find their way. More patients from the floors above joined us as we made our way down. A bottleneck formed on the second floor landing and the crowd of shuffling sleepwalkers piled up. Suddenly the exit door opened and Fernandez thrust his head into the stairwell and scanned the line of evacuees.

I turned my face to one side and tried to use a man built like an elderly Cro-Magnon as a shield as Fernandez scanned the crowd. His gaze swept over me like a mine detector without pausing for a single moment. He said something to the nurse I couldn't catch then closed the exit door and was gone. A moment later, I managed to get the line moving again. It was like being cowhand on a cattle drive.

My guess was that Fernandez had charged straight down to the first floor exit in the hopes that I would be in a hurry to get out that way, forgetting that the guards would be waiting for me there. Now he would realize that I was above him and no doubt looking for another way out, possibly through a window. It was an idea I had considered then abandoned because someone would surely spot a lone figure shimming down a drainpipe. I wanted to be in the lobby when the fire department showed up then try to get out while they were making their way into the building.

What I couldn't figure out was why Fernandez hadn't recognized me? I noticed then a man standing on the landing above me, his face and hair covered with grime. I gently wiped at my cheek with my fingertips. They came away covered with thick black soot that smelled of creosote and chemicals. I must have been covered with the stuff. That and the coveralls I had boosted had saved me.

The exit door below us opened suddenly and a fireman's helmet appeared, followed by three more firefighters wearing oxygen tanks and carrying axes. I was in the middle of a throng of patients, herding them down the stairs. Some had become frightened and were clinging to the handrails, creating a sense of inertia and bringing the line to a dead stop. The dank air smelled faintly here of smoke, urine and sweat and of fetid breath, but I was more scared than they were, and it took all my remaining nerve not to make a break for it, to head for the fresh air at full speed.

Ten more steps and the group I was with spilled out into a large open space at the rear of the lobby where at least a hundred patients were being funneled by the staff through the open glass doors that led out to the parking lot. Flanking the doors like a pair bouncers in front of a nightclub stood Vince Fernandez and the doublewide Mr. Zero.

They were up on their tiptoes, craning their heads back and forth across the mass of people shuffling toward the door, every now and then grabbing some poor soul by the arm and spinning him around to get a better look. Zero was holding his right arm as though it hung in an invisible cast.

Even with soot covering my face, there was way too much light in the lobby for me to get lucky a second time, so I edged closer to a trio of janitors, one of whom was standing by with an empty wheelchair. I went over and asked him if I could borrow it. He handed it over without hesitation. I let the crowd well up around me until I was pretty much in the middle again then pushed the wheelchair toward the door, crouching as low over the back of the chair as I could and keeping an eye on Vince and Zero.

I could see plenty of cops, firemen, and paramedics out in the lot. The whirling red lights of the cruisers were bouncing off the glass doors and washing over the faces in the crowd like strobe lights at a rave party. I gave some thought to the idea of handing my story to the nearest policeman then thought the better of it. What would I tell them? That I had been kidnapped and drugged? That I didn't belong there? I knew exactly what they would say. Sure, they would say. Let's just get you back to your room, mister. All you need is to take your medication. You'll be well again in no time. Vince and Vronsky would sweet talk them, and no one would ever hear of Jack Vaughn again.

I found the old, long-haired Cro-Magnon again and drafted behind him until I was thirty feet or so from the front door. I glanced around to make sure no one was looking, grabbed the blanket off the seat and hopped into the chair. I put the blanket around my shoulders and spun the wheels forward, my head down like a sprinter leaning for the finishing line.

I stayed behind the big man as much as I could. I was too low for either Vince or his partner to easily see me, but I wanted as much camouflage as I could get. Just as the pack I was in was about to pass through the door, I pulled the thin gray blanket over my head and rolled forward. The surge of the people behind me pushed me out the front door into the cool night air where the rain that struck my face was like redemption.

The staff, some of them holding umbrellas or blankets over the heads of their patients, had gathered about fifty people to one side of the lot. A few yards away, a pair of determined paramedics was unloading gurneys from the back of an ambulance. Moving slowly to avoid attracting attention, I began weaving my way past the slower moving people until I was behind one of the ambulances. I got out of the wheelchair, dropped the blanket and began walking toward the parking lot. I was halfway there when a small crowd of patients and staff parted in front of me, and there, no more than a twenty feet in front of me stood the young doctor I had seen doing the wild thing in the stairwell talking with Dr. Vronsky.

They were directly in my path. I thought of turning around

but it was too late. All I could do was try and walk in such a way that kept people between us. Vronsky was in his bathrobe and slippers and yelling at someone on the other end of his walkie-talkie. I veered off to the right, watching him for any sign of recognition, hoping the soot covering my face would be enough. Vronsky stopped talking and turned and looked in my direction as I walked quickly through the gate into the parking lot.

I got halfway down the row of cars when I looked around to see if I was being followed. Sure enough, Vronsky and his protégé were standing there watching me. Vronsky said something to him and the doctor began trotting toward me. I ran so fast I nearly missed the Taurus. This was it. I reached under the rear fender for the magnetic key case.

My movements had a precision that surprised me, and time seem to have slowed down for me. Maybe it was the Ritalin. I got the door open and had the engine started just as Vronsky's assistant appeared at my window. I reached under the front seat for the Glock and showed it to him. He must not have liked the look of it very much because he backed away with his hands up. Dr. Vronsky appeared at the end of a row of parked cars. He was doing his best to keep up, but he was too busy talking on his cell phone to run very swiftly.

I made a hard right turn out of the row of cars and accelerated. Gravel sprayed out from beneath the Taurus's front wheels and the back of the car swerved to one side, struck a jeep, bounced off and tried to go into a spin. I pulled it straight and headed for glory, peeling down the dirt path between two rows of parked cars. There was a blur of movement to my left, and there was Mr. Zero two rows of cars away, running parallel to the Taurus, his dreadlocks barely visible above the cars as he ran to cut me off at the end of the row.

I punched down on the gas but Zero had already made it to the gap gun in hand, but I knew there were way too many cops around for him to risk taking a shot at me. He was probably hoping to scare me into crashing the car, but the Ritalin kept me as level. When Zero saw I wasn't going to stop; he tried to dive out of the way, but he hadn't been built for flying. I gave the Taurus a slight jerk to the left and hit him while he was still in the air. A dull thud and he went airborne. When I looked back, he was draped over the shattered windshield of an old Cadillac, his arms and legs stretched out like the wings of an unlucky butterfly. It was too hard not to smile.

I was a hundred feet from the front gate now. The guard had left the crossbar up to let the cops and firemen through. I could see him up ahead, standing in his well-lit booth. He looked nice and cozy in his little kiosk, talking on the phone, getting the latest news, no doubt, from Vronsky. I shut my headlights off and prayed I wouldn't have to shoot anybody, but there was no way I was going to let them take me back to that clinic again, and anybody who tried to stop me had be ready to do some hard living.

Without thinking, my right hand reached for the radio. I needed a soundtrack. I laughed out loud when "The Boys Are Back in Town" blasted free of the speakers. It was like hearing the national anthem being played in the middle of a battlefield. I laughed so loud that for a moment I scared myself into silence. My laugh had sounded too much like a howl. I thought about it for a moment then laughed again. I was like a half crazy surfer, riding the crest of the world's highest pipeline and praying that it wouldn't collapse beneath me before I was done with it.

The gate started to come down. It came down in slow motion. It seemed to me that everything was moving in slow motion now, including the guard as he stepped out off his box. He turned toward me with the speed of a man trapped in molten glass, his movements so languid I grew bored watching them. I flashed him with my high beams to let know that I was feeling pretty good about what was coming. A criminal excitement jazzed my brain as I bored down on him. I howled again and turned the radio up full blast.

It was a cool night in late March; all four windows of the Taurus were down. I was doing a hard seventy in a 20 mph zone with the speed bumps rippling under me like frozen waves. There were a lot of people after me, including a very strong midget. I was hopped up on Ritalin and god knows what else, but I had a gun, and I was free, and it was my intention to stay that way all the way to the grave. All I needed was a six-pack of Budweiser and a dozen or so squad cars in my rearview mirror.

It was completely crazy, and I realized I was probably going to die, but in some weird way that I couldn't quite understand, I knew that I was living out part of the American Dream. I was heading for the fugitive highway with the drugs swirling inside of me like a coven of witches, every moment waving a new mood in front of my face. There was a loud cracking sound as the Taurus struck the crossbar in mid-slice, shards of shattered wood flying in every direction as we crashed through. I couldn't help but laugh again, this time louder than before. Vaughn was gone, baby. Vaughn was gone.

But I now I had a problem that sobered me a bit: I had no idea where I was. The road I was on bore absolutely no resemblance to the one I had taken to get to Vronsky's little house of horrors, and there were no lights or signs to speak of. I had been so anxious to get free that I hadn't paid much attention to the question of direction. Ahead of me, as far as I could see, there was nothing but trees and the blank shadows of trees. On either side of me, the dark waters of the canals gleamed with a silvery film of moonlight and gasoline. Above, the stars were bright and optimistic, but what I wanted most was the glow of city lights in the near distance and maybe a diner with hot coffee and a blue plate special.

I wondered if I had somehow strayed as far south and west as the Tamiami Trail, a narrow ribbon of road that cuts through a hundred miles of Everglades and cypress swamp to the West Coast of Florida. If that was the case then I was going to be on foot in a few hours, because there were no rest stops to look forward to until you were damned near to Naples, and I didn't have nearly enough gas to get me that far. But wasn't I too far north for that? Or maybe I had just strayed onto one of the roads cut into the Everglades by one of the quarrying companies or one of the failed developers of yesteryear. If so, I was on a long drive to nowhere. Most of those roads all seemed like they might be going somewhere but dead-ended into nothingness, just like the dreams of the men who built them.

Meantime, a hard rain began without prelude. It was as though a trapdoor had opened in the sky and an entire ocean had fallen through, not in drops but all at once like a natural disaster. I had no choice but to slow down, creep along and follow the taillights ahead of me while the wipers did their best to keep the distance open.

The Ritalin had begun to wear off. I was relieved at first, because I had been concerned about the strain on my heart and I didn't know how much more it could take. But now, with the buzz deserting me, I could feel myself fading, and I thought that with one more tablet I might make it without having a heart attack. I managed to get the bottle out of my pocket without taking my eyes off the road, but as I tried to open it I dropped the bottle, which then rolled under the brake pedal the way it always does when you are desperate. I felt around for it, conscious of the rain and the taillights ahead. It may be that I glanced down, if only for a second, but it was enough. Something flashed in front of me. The fact that it was a deer registered immediately but by then the car was already out of control.

If I had been more alert, more awake, I might have had the presence of mind not to have tried to miss it, to have just hit the animal and kept going with only a few miles of guilt and some front end damage to show for the impact. Instead, my souped-up nerves overreacted, and I swung the wheel way too hard to the left. The Taurus went slip sliding away on the wet road and whirled around like a ride in an amusement park. The back end spun around to my right and I was looking back at the way I had come, headlights coming toward me from a long way off. I turned into the spin but it was no good. The car hydroplaned, skidded and left the road. At the last second I remembered the canals on either side of me, but it was too late for anything except the splash, which was strangely hushed, as though the Taurus and I were being baptized.

I was slantwise and slightly sideways, staring at black water. The front end of the car was in the water, and the rest was settling in fast. At first I panicked and tried to open the door then remembered my training and began cranking on the handle, trying to get at least one window down before we sank. Before I could finish, the front of the car tilted violently forward, slamming my head into the steering wheel as the back end jumped up like the rear end of a horse, and suddenly I was up at a steep angle, looking down at the water rushing toward the car's windshield with a bubbling momentum that could not be stopped or understood.

Too many things happened at once. The car flipped over on its back and the water rushed in through the half open window. Something hard hit me in the head. I grabbed the Glock out of pure instinct. Then I was upside down, the fear ripping away at me. Panic set in like spooked horses running. Calm down, Vaughn. You know what to do. You still have some air left in here. You wait for the water to completely fill the car. It was on the news just the other day, remember? Then you can open the door. It was all very rational, very scientific. It all made perfect sense. You fight the sense that you are about to drown and you wait patiently while the music from the submerged radio mocks you. It was as simple as that.

The water came in faster now and being upside down made it worse. All the air was on the floor of the car, which was now above me. I took a deep breath and pushed across the seat to the passenger side where I twisted myself upright until I my head touched the floor of the car. A floor mat flapped down over my head like a hood. I looked at the gun in my hand. There was no way I could wait any longer. The sooner the water filled the car, the faster I could get out. I reached down into the water, held the nose of the Glock against the Taurus's windshield and fired twice.

There was a muffled cough beneath me and the water rushed in like a home invasion. The bottle of Ritalin floated past my face like a little lifeboat, but I didn't need it now. Then the car shifted again, this time onto its side, and I lost all sense of up and down. Fear sucked the oxygen from my blood, and I began thrashing around. My head was pounding. It felt strange to die in so arbitrary a way after everything that had happened. I wanted it to be over. I was ready for the first chapter of my death.

The car shifted once again, and I was in an air pocket. I took what I could, ducked down. Then, gloriously, magnificently, I was swimming through the smashed space where the windshield had been a moment before, and I was outside, free of the car, surrounded by water, plenty of it, all I would ever need in this life, rising rapidly toward the rippling surface of the moon with the car's demented radio still trailing me, its music dying behind me like the desperate voices of a sinking chorus.

I pulled myself out of the canal, took a few stumbling steps through the stalks of saw grass and dropped to my hands and knees with the rain falling gently over me as I rolled over onto my back. The rain was soft on my face and didn't bother me at all. I took long, considerate, deep breaths until I got my heart quieted down then stretched out on the rough wet grass like it was a mattress and just lay there for a long time until I was feeling comfortably amphibious and at home.

It takes a hard, dangerous night to make the free air seem luxurious, and though the feeling was soon replaced in me by thoughts of alligators and water moccasins for a few minutes there that night, lying on the muddy banks of the canal that had almost killed me, I felt strangely well-heeled and grateful, not needing much else, and wondering why somebody couldn't invent a drug that could reproduce such a feeling then bottle and sell it at Walgreens and by doing so spare me the necessity of almost dying in order to experience it again.

I got up and walked over to the canal. The water was an eerie phosphorescent Halloween green, bundles of algae and dead grass streaking the surface. I couldn't see the Taurus but the headlights were still on. I was about to turn back and head for the road when a beam of light hit me in the side of the face. Without thinking, I turned into the thick forest of saw grass and began to run, but the mud was too deep and I was too tired. I took half a dozen steps and fell down. I lay there breathing heavily for a moment then tried to get to my feet. As I did, something hard and cold pressed against my cheek and a deep baritone voice I recognized told me to get up.

"You almost made it, Jack," Fernandez said softly. "I'm really sorry you didn't. Let's go."

Fernandez helped me to my feet. The Ritalin had worn off and the world was doing funny things again. The bottom of Fernandez's face was melting and his chin was dripping toward the ground like hot cheese sliding off a slice of pizza. Then, like a Slinky, it snapped back up and looked normal again. I looked up at the road where a black truck was parked and for a moment its side panels puffed in and like trumpet player's cheeks. Fernandez threw me a pair of handcuffs and ordered me to put them on. When I was done, he came over and checked their tightness.

"Look at the goddamn spot you put me in," Fernandez said. "You make me look like a fucking idiot in front of Marina and Vronsky both. Go on; walk on up to the truck. You know I got no choice in this."

"I'm not going back to that clinic," I said. "You better shoot me here."

"No can do, Old Bud. We got some other place else in mind."

"Suppose I just take off running? You'll have to shoot me then."

"What's your hurry, Jack? You got all night to die. Take it easy. Who knows? Maybe you'll get a pardon."

I glanced at the saw grass and wondered if I was prepared to get shot in the back, weighed it against the short, unhappy life of a vegetable in a mental hospital, drooling his time away at the government's expense; weighed it against the fear of death and the lack of hope, and while I weighed all that a breeze blew from behind me and made the blades of the saw grass whisper something to me I couldn't understand.

Fernandez must have read my mind because he cocked the trigger of his revolver and spoke softly to me, spoke to me like I was a wild animal he was trying to coax back into its cage. I took one more look at the saw grass and went with what I knew.

"Relax," Fernandez said with a smile. "I'm not taking you back to Vronsky. I've got other plans you. Now hurry up and get up there. That Russian bitch of mine doesn't like to be kept waiting."

Vince trailed behind me as I climbed stiffly up the embankment and onto the main road. Stefan saw us coming and opened the back door of the truck. One of the tinted windows slid quietly down and there was Marina Gero sitting in the front passenger seat, as beautiful as ever, her dark eyes filled with a compressed anger that was as much aimed at Vince as it was at me. I met her stare and her eyes began to expand until I felt like I was walking into them.

A movement on the ground seized my attention. A horde of tiny leaves swirling around in the most amazing patterns seized my attention. The dancing leaves were all consuming, more intricate than any ballet, and I couldn't look away. As I slowed down to watch, something shifted and the leaves became shapes that quivered and bunched like a drawer full of rolled-up socks, and suddenly I was staring at a quivering mass of enormous gray rats. I waited for them break and run as rats would normally have done, but instead they kept whirling about as though they were still tiny green leaves caught in a spiraling breeze. There were hundreds of them. I stopped and looked back at Vince.

"What's the matter?" he demanded. "Keep going."

"The rats," I said. "We have to go around them."

Fernandez stared hard at me for a moment. He looked down at the road and shook his head. It angered me to see his annoyance turn to pity. I felt like a small child being led to his death by a benign executioner, and I hated Fernandez for having to depend on him.

"Pull it together, Vaughn," he said. "Don't bug out on me now."

"What about the rats?"

Fernandez took me gently by the elbow and urged me forward. I looked at the rats and tried to turn them into leaves again. Nothing happened. I focused on the van, bracing my nerves for the feel of their squirming little bodies rubbing themselves against my ankles and shins and wondering if they would bite.

"Don't worry about the rats," Fernandez said. "They're friends of mine."

He gave me a slight shove, and I began walking. It helped that the rats were mercifully silent. I don't think I would have made it if they had begun to squeak. I took very short steps, like a man wearing leg irons, the black van shimmering in front of me like a mirage. It took me hours to reach it, but at least the rats left me alone.

Stefan got out of the van and held the rear door open while Fernandez pushed me across the back seat. I was so relieved to have gotten past the rats that for a moment I almost forgot what was about to happen to me. The feeling only lasted a second and when it was gone the fear rushed back in as though it had never left. There was nothing to do now but look out the window and wait. My mind began going blank as though making room for something new. Marina turned around to smile at me.

"How does it feel to almost get away," she said. "To be in a car and driving fast, thinking you are free of everything, so happy, so alive, and now to be here in this van, going nowhere?"

"Why don't you ask that Russian psycho sitting next to you," I said. "He's the one that's driving."

"Where to?" Stefan asked.

"Danger Road," Marina said. "We'll do it there."

"Why not back to the clinic?" I asked. "What's the matter? Too many cops?"

“Vronsky thinks you’re too much trouble,” Vince said. “If you had any money to speak of, it might be different, but unfortunately for you, pal, you’re not worth shit.”

“Unlike Cal Belkin you mean,” I said. “His house, his money, his business: he must have been a real gold mine for you guys.”

Fernandez yawned. “That’s right,” he said. “And one more little trip to the bank and his account gets closed down too,” he said.

14

We drove a good twenty miles into the Everglades then left the highway for an eastbound road that ended in a dirt path barely wide enough for the truck to pass through. I spent the time looking out the window, trying to get the world to stay straight and not change shape on me again, but something inside me was still missing. The king had gone out for a walk and hadn't returned. The throne room was empty and nobody could find him and the crowd of people inside my head couldn't agree what to do.

I was a committee of madmen. Some of me wanted to laugh; others to cry and beg for mercy. One fellow wanted to reach out and stroke Marina's shiny red hair then mount her furiously from behind like a stallion, while another wanted nothing more than to peacefully suckle at her breast like a baby. One second I felt like the Dalai Lama and was calm and full of love for everyone, including Vince and the two Russians. Part of me was inclined to do a little howling before jumping out the window and disappearing into the dark mass of trees. One man was quite a reasonable fellow, even scholarly. He understood why he was about to be killed and even agreed with the basic premise. But there was no king. Maybe he was up on the roof, leering at Bathsheba.

The saw grass here was six feet high and the truck muscled its way through with great difficulty, the truck bouncing from side to side as the tires crunched down on the rocky dirt beneath us until we came too soon for my taste to a clearing in the grass and Stefan stopped the truck and jumped out, letting in the fresh smell of the swamp surrounding us on all sides. I turned to look at Vince but he turned his head away the moment our eyes met.

Stefan opened my door while Marina and Vince got out on the other side.

"Why don't you stay in the car, babe," Vince said. "Too many mosquitoes out here for that pretty skin of yours."

He stretched his arms above his head, spat on the ground and looked off toward the red sash of light between the horizon and the eastern sky. It was going to be light soon. A violent flutter wings above our heads that made us all look up. An osprey soared out of the branches. He was close enough for me to see the white-bellied fish he held clamped in his talons. The sea eagle flew off toward the west, banked sharply and made a second pass above us, his dark wings dipping toward at a an angle as he flew off with his catch.

Behind me someone cleared the breech of an automatic. Vince and I both turned around.

"Don't worry about my skin, you stupid fool," Marina answered. "Worry about yours. Take his gun, Stefan."

I turned around. The Russian stepped in front of me with his gun drawn. But it wasn't pointed at me but, strangely, at Fernandez. When I looked again, Marina was holding a tiny silver automatic which was also aimed at Fernandez. Vince looked disoriented. He glanced back and forth between Stefan and Marina with an expression of confused amazement. Without thinking, I moved away from him. No one reacted. I was a member of the audience now. Everything seemed focused on Vince, even the trees.

Vincent Fernandez smiled but not very convincingly. It was a vain smile, as tacky as a billboard and didn't play well with such a small intimate group of friends and former friends. It was almost embarrassing to watch him bomb so badly in front of the three of us, to watch him try so hard to make it all into a joke, but it was no more of a joke than the leaves had been rats, and there was nothing ever going to change that for him. I felt a brief flare of pity for him that lasted less time than the space between heartbeats.

Vince threw a glance at me like a sailor hoping for a lifeline, as though I might possibly know what was actually happening here, but all I could do was stand there with my hands cuffed in front of me while the air buzzed around my head. I stood very still and worked hard on becoming invisible. Stefan made Vince hold his hands out from his sides then plucked the gun out of his waistband and tossed it into the high grass.

Vince watched his gun sail away and disappear in the dense roughage of the saw grass. I watched it to. He had given up on making this into something funny. You could see in his eyes that he knew how it was going to go for him now. It seemed to me he had begun to shrink in scale, as though he was being sucked away from the inside by something that had been slowly growing there ever since New York. Once again he turned to look at me, only this time it was me who turned away. I turned away from him like a criminal turning away as his best friend gets busted. I turned away from him as you do from a beggar standing in a doorway with his hand out. I had problems of my own and no spare change in my pockets.

"Come on, babe," Vince said softly, as softly as a man begging for his life. "Cut this shit out. Let's just do what we have to do and get out of here, okay? Stop playing around." The confidence had fled from his voice and had been replaced with a tone of desperation, but he was still working the angle that maybe just maybe he could change the monster back into something he could handle.

"She isn't playing, Vincent," Stefan said deeply, almost

sadly. The line of his jaw was set as he turned to me. "Go and stand with your friend."

I must not have moved fast enough because he gave me a shove from behind that sent me stumbling toward Fernandez. Vince side-stepped, and I fell heavily on my side. I got up slowly. The world was fairly solid again; the dead leaves were just leaves, and I was starting to feel more like myself, but it appeared that the king had returned too late from his walk on the roof to do me any good.

Vince gave it another try. He was like a bad actor struggling to make his character more interesting. He straightened his arms and clenched his fists and puffed out his massive chest like a man getting ready to take on a crowd in a bar fight. It was anger he was trying to use now, but it too was all a fake. He was down to his last match, and all of us knew it, including Vince.

Like any man who keeps two sets of books, Fernandez must have known this day was coming for a long time now. What he hadn't known was the due date or what it would look like. That information hadn't been stamped on either side of Candy's tight, beautiful ass, but that didn't mean such a date didn't exist. It just wasn't marked on the calendar. Vince must have known since the very first time he and Candy were together, known it the first time he had tasted her alien sweetness, just as he must have surely have known that he had lit the fuse that had led inexorably to this very night in the Everglades. .

"What the hell are you two up to?" Vince demanded. "I don't need this crap. Is this supposed to be funny or something?"

Marina smiled thinly with disgust at Fernandez. Her gun was pointed directly at his groin. "Do you think I am fool?" she said. "Did you think I would not find about you and the girl when you fuck me wearing her perfume in your hair? You are too stupid even to take shower! What an idiot!"

The muzzle of her gun exploded in a small blue flash. Vince yelled, stepped back and grabbed at his thigh. I took another small step away from him.

"What the fuck are you doing?" Vince cried. "You crazy Bitch! I don't know what the fuck you're talking about!"

"Cocaine is a great leg opener, my friend," Stefan said. "The best. Too bad it opened Candy's mouth as well. She talks to the girls and they talk to me." The Russian smiled.

Marina looked at me, but the little gun stayed pointed at Vince's crotch. Vince was standing half bent over with his hand clamped around his leg as blood slowly separated his fingers.

"Welcome to Danger Road," Marina said to me with a smile. "At least you won't die alone now."

I didn't answer her. I was a character in play whose last lines had already been spoken.

Vince glared across the matted grass at Stefan. "All right, I get it now," he said. "So go one, tell me. How long have you been fucking Marina, Stef? What? A year? Six months?"

Stefan grinned and looked over at Marina as though for advice with the timeline of their affair. "I don't know," he said. "What has it been now? Five or six months?"

"Something like that," Marina said, still glaring at Vince. Her gun jumped again with the same blue spark. Vince spun half around, recovered then let out a yell and charged her. Marina stepped back, fired again, this time missing, fear lighting her eyes.

Stefan dropped to one knee like the pro he was, lifted his gun with both hands and took a careful bead on Vince's trajectory. There was a sharp crack and Fernandez was knocked off his feet into the saw grass.

Marina walked cautiously over to where Vince lay and stood over him the way you would a water buffalo you have just shot down in the African brush. Stefan rose from where he had knelt, his gun still pointed at Fernandez. Neither of them was paying me any attention. Neither of them had been aware that I had been inching slowly backwards ever since Marina's first shot. I took one more step away from the action and felt the saw grass tearing

at the skin of my forearms before it parted to let me through, and when the curtain of grass closed again in front of me, I turned, ducked low and took off running, waiting for the inevitable bullet in the back, and knowing that I had absolutely nothing to lose.
I pushed maybe a hundred feet forward a dozen or so more to my left before I forced myself to crouch down in the tall grass and listen. There was no way I was going to outrun Stefan with the kind of jewelry I was wearing and I knew if I kept going in a beeline he'd overtake me for sure. All the Russian would have to do was watch the grass to tell which way I was going, but if I could remain still, he and Marina might pass me by, giving me a chance to circle back and look for Vince's gun.

It's not easy to stop and wait in a situation like that when your heart is telling you to run like hell and the adrenaline is wailing inside your blood like a siren and the molecules of fear are bunched and running through your veins like a team of rabid sled dogs on the trails of the Iditarod. But I did it. I crouched there in the saw grass and listened for the two Russians and waited for them to tell me which way to move. They had seen where I was standing, and it made sense they'd enter the grass there and move in fast on the theory that I'd take off at a dead run. They wouldn't be expecting me to be so close. Then it would just be a question of how much time I had before they realized I had doubled back.

Very slowly, careful not to disturb the grass, I began inching my way to the right of where I had left the clearing, hoping the two of them wouldn't run right over me. I heard the sound of dry grass being rapidly brushed roughly aside. They were about thirty feet to my left, maybe closer, whispering loudly to one another in Russian. The whispering stopped. They were listening for the sound of me slashing through the grass. But if they heard nothing at all, they would know I was hiding somewhere nearby. All I could do was wait to see which way the thing broke.

Then Stefan's voice shouted with excitement followed immediately by gunshots. I flinched, thinking I was dead, that they had seen me. But it wasn't me they had been firing at. If we had been closer to water, I would have suspected they had come across an alligator guarding its nest, but it was too dry here for reptiles. It could be they startled a boar or even a black bear. Whatever it was, I took advantage of their mistake and scooted back on my hands and knees to where they had shot Fernandez.

When I got to the edge of the clearing, I stopped again and used my ears on the distance behind me. I was eager to get to Vince's gun—if I could find it—but something held me back. It was too quiet. I should still have been able to hear the Russians behind me somewhere. Of course, there was always the chance they had continued on and were crossing another clearing, but I couldn't quite convince myself to step into the open just yet. Instead, I got down on my belly and circled until I could see Fernandez's body. With my hands cuffed, it was slow going and my eyes burned from the sweat pouring into them as I crawled along, but after a few moments of slithering there was Vince, right where they had dropped him.

I waited five long minutes with the bug bites mounting every second. Just as I was sure I couldn't take it anymore, the saw grass on the other side of clearing parted and a gun barrel appeared followed by Stefan. They had guessed my trick. He walked over and stared down at Vince's body for a moment then turned and looked in my direction. I was so sure he had seen me that I nearly bolted from the spot where I lay hiding. Then something moved through the grass no more than five feet to my left. I turned my head just enough to see the top of Marina's boots and pant legs. If I had been a little further away, she would have seen me over the top of the grass, but I was too close, too quiet, and the grass was too high. She could have looked right over the spot where I was lying and not have seen me.

Marina Gero walked into the clearing and joined her new boyfriend next to Fernandez's body. The happy couple stared down at Vince for a moment then Stefan lit a cigarette for each of them after which they stood there yelling at one another in Russian. It was clear neither of them was too thrilled with the idea of leaving me on the loose. If I made it back and dropped a dime on their little operation, it would mean jail for both them and Dr. Vronsky. Then, all at once, Stefan stopped yelling and just stood there quietly as she hurled buckets of Russian shit in his face. Stefan stood there listening so intently that I expected him to start taking notes like a court reporter.

Marina Gero walked back and forth waving her cigarette around in the air like a demented bandleader. Getting cursed out in Russian is like being thrown down a flight of stairs over and over again, but Stefan took it patiently, his head down, calmly smoking, inhaling and exhaling, every now and then glancing at the tip of his cigarette as though making sure it was still lit, that everything was going according to plan. Other times, he would lift his chin and stare at the sky for a second while Marina raved on. He passed a hand through his long blond hair and yawned.

After a while, Stefan finished his cigarette, dropped it on the ground and stubbed out the butt with the tip of his shoe. Marina was still shouting. There was something obsessive about the way he did it that caught my eye; it was like one of those strange, exaggerated movements crazy people sometimes make when they are sitting across from you on the subway, the savage tick that gives them away.

Then, as I watched, Marina turned her back on the Russian and raised her slender arms above her head like a prophet and cursed the sky, but this time when she turned around again, Stefan, very calmly and with no expression on his face, drew his gun from his belt and shot her squarely in the center of her creamy white Slavic forehead. Blood and brain sprayed the disrupted air, and Marina fell backwards like a tipped over statue.

There was nothing to say and nothing to do. A line of crows in a cypress tree left their branch and scattered across the sky while a white swan lifted out of the tall grass and with solemn wings flew slowly away. That was about it. In an instant, the wounded quiet had completely healed itself and the renewed silence settled quickly over the scene like an ocean temporarily displaced by a tsunami. All that remained of what had happened was the body on the ground and the blood and brain matter splattered across the front of Stefan's blue shirt.

Stefan restored the gun to his belt, yawned again, and lit another cigarette. Then he stood with his hands on his hips and looked around the clearing like General MacArthur after he took back the Philippines. After a few puffs, he stared down at Marina and circled her body as though appraising it with an eye toward purchase. I lay there watching him behind the curtain of grass, my struggling heart pinned down between my chest and the dampness of the earth.

Stefan, still smoking thoughtfully, walked over to Fernandez and began going through his pockets, tossing what he found over his shoulder and onto the ground: a wallet, a cigar in a silver canister, a cell phone, and set of keys that landed on the ground with a merry jangle. When he was done, Stefan grabbed hold of Fernandez's ankles and dragged him backwards into the saw grass until he disappeared from view. I wondered if he knew I was watching him or if he even cared. The Russian returned after a few minutes. Now he was singing softly to himself as he stepped through the tall grass, his shoes and pants legs covered in muck. He wiped them off on the grass then walked over to Marina and dragged her away by the ankles, still singing to himself like a tradesman content with his mastery of the task at hand.

While he was away, I kept busy by taking revenge on the bugs that had been torturing me. I smeared mud on some of the bites, all the while listening for the Russian's return. For all I knew, he would get it into his head to creep around the clearing in the hopes of catching me off guard. My intention was to wait for him to leave before getting up. Then all I would have to do was walk my way out of the Everglades without compass, food or fresh water.

Stefan appeared again; this time he was even muddier than before and sweating like a Haitian roofer in the middle of July. He scooped up the items he had removed from Vince's pockets and examined them. Then he tossed the wallet and keys on the ground and cupped his hand to the side of his mouth and shouted my name out across the clearing.

"Vaughn," he yelled. "Jack! Come out. Don't worry. I won't kill you. Like the Negroes say, you take my back in fight at club. I like you. Promise on my mother and father. I give you ride back to city. Don't stay in jungle. Too dangerous out there. Come with me. We'll have drink together. Beer, whatever you want! Don't worry, I got the money, that's all what is mattering. I'm out of Miami, now. Bygones is bygones, okay?"

It was a nice invitation but a double murder makes for a bad reference, so I lay there hoping he wouldn't change his mind and start shooting into the grass like the maniac he was. He repeated his offer again and again I declined to answer. Stefan waited patiently for my reply. When didn't come he shouted again.

"Listen to me, Vaughn. I am leaving the keys to the handcuffs and also Vince's wallet and cell phone. He isn't needing them anymore. I don't blame you for being scared. I hope you make it out. Well, don't let alligators bite your ass off, you stupid American asshole." He lit another cigarette and again waited for a response. He seemed neither surprised nor very disappointed when I didn't arrive. Instead, he flicked his cigarette away, pushed aside the grass and left the clearing. A few minutes later, I heard the sound of the van's engine.

I waited five more minutes just to be sure, but there are limits to everything, including how long I can hold back a piss. When I was done watering the punk trees, I unlocked my handcuffs with the keys Stefan had left behind. I opened Vince's wallet and removed about a hundred dollars in cash from the billfold. I pushed through the grass out to the dirt road but the van was long gone. I returned to the clearing and went looking for Vince and Marina. I retraced Stefan's path and soon found another open space much smaller than the first. I took a step forward and my foot plunged down into the muck clear up to the knees. I threw my body backwards and grabbed a fistful of grass with both hands. The grass tore apart in my hand as I tried to pull myself out. I took two more handfuls and pulled until my shoes popped free of the muck.

As I got to my feet, I happened to glance to my right, and there, no more than a few feet away, Vince's left hand and forearm waved at me from out of the mud, a silver ring on his hand glinting in the sun like a failed signal. A few seconds more and I would have missed it. At the last moment, just before it went under for good, the forearm was snapped upright by the downward suction of the mud. Vince's hand hung limply to one side for a moment before being drawn down into the black muck of the sinkhole.

I found Marina a few yards away, around a bend in the grass, near a piece of plywood Stefan had probably used for a platform. Judging by how far from the edge of the sinkhole the body was, it appeared he had probably raised her above his head and hurled her out into the muck, not so much out of necessity as from the kind of sheer athletic enthusiasm that keep people like Stefan on perpetual lookout for ways to test both their strength and stupidity.

Marina Gero had landed on her side with her back to me. Only her legs were submerged. If not for that, a passerby might have thought she had just picked a bad spot to take a nap. A small bird landed on her shoulder, bounced around a few times then flew off. I'm not sure why I didn't leave then but I stayed to watch the end. I sat down on the edge of the sinkhole with my arms wrapped around my knees until it was over. A few final bubbles on the mud's surface and then I was alone. Considering the company I had been keeping lately, I should have been happy about that but I wasn't. The great Mr. Miami himself at the bottom of a sinkhole in the Everglades. All the ambition and the vanity and the pettiness were too much to take, and if I had thought about it much longer I would be still be out there now.

I was tempted to head back to try and trace Stefan's route to the main road and from there back to real life, but I didn't want to take the chance on him waiting for me to do exactly that. It's hard to calculate the motives of a mad man. He might be on his way back to Brighton Beach or off to Russia, but maybe he saw me as a loose end.

I hadn't forgotten my Miccosukee girlfriend Odaylis's sage advice about the Glades: when in doubt, head west. The day was still new enough for me to know more or less which way west was, so I turned my back on the blue faced sun and headed for what I hoped would be higher ground and a way out of the swamp. Now that I was fairly sure of where I wanted to go, the big problem became thirst. There was plenty of water around, but without some way to boil it, there was no way I was going to risk getting sick. The good news was that my head was clear, though once or twice the drugs did try and make a comeback.

I was a little worried about the size of the marsh and gave some thought to finding another way around it. If it got too deep toward the middle, alligators would definitely be something worth thinking about. Having Vince's gun made me feel a bit more secure, but you can't shoot what you can't see and those things can stay under water for a long time after you think they can't, and it can take quite a few bullets to stop an alligator, especially if all you've got to shoot with is a handgun. Odaylis once told me about a neighbor of hers who caught one coming up out of a swimming pool, heading straight for the family dog across the back yard and running a hell of a lot faster than you would expect such a short legged bastard to move. Her father had come flying out of the Florida room out with a Dirty Harry forty-five and shot the gator right in the center of the forehead and expected that to be enough, but three more shots proved that particular theory erroneous. They killed the thing eventually, Odaylis said, but the dog needed replacing.

Fortunately, the water didn't get much higher than my shins. I made it to the other side, all the time waiting for that tell tale sudden twisting in the gut that signals the onset of diarrhea, but all I felt was tired and hungry. Here at least the ground was firmer and much less physically draining to walk across, and I made pretty good time. My big worry now was that I had made a mistake and was heading deeper into the Everglades. That would mean the possibility of spending a night out here, and that was definitely not something I wanted to think about, not with all the creatures that slithered around these parts. In a clump of twisted mahogany trees, I found a branch long and thick enough to serve as a weapon. I snapped off the end at an angle to give it a point of sorts, and then I started walking again.

After I'd gone a while, I found some shade and tried getting a dial tone on Vince's cell phone, but I was still too far from the closest tower to get a signal. I was anxious to see if Cal had made it away from the clinic. It had occurred to me that if Stefan bothered to tell Vronksy I was on the loose, Vronsky might be anxious to get Cal back again, only this time I doubted he would take the chance of keeping him alive for very long. All of Cal's records would be destroyed along with every trace of his stay at the clinic. As for Dr. Vronsky, Medicare was far too profitable a cash cow for him to abandon his business. He would simply close down his clinic and open a new one some place else under another name and when that happened, the government checks would begin flowing in again in as though they had never stopped, no questions asked.

Some time about noon, I came across a river that ran from north to south. It was only about sixty yards across and looked, at a glance, shallow enough to wade across. I was sure I could handle the current, but it was also a perfect spot for alligators. I used the stick to push aside the grasses as I went slowly along the bank, looking for a spot narrow enough to attempt a crossing. I went slowly, scanning the water for any signs of movement. There was a row gators on the opposite side of the river lined up like park benches. They were fast asleep and basking in the midday sun, but one splash and they'd be wide awake before I could make it to the other side.

I went south about a quarter of a mile until I found a spot where the river narrowed enough to look promising. There was even a small, reed-covered island in the center which made me feel better. The more land between me and the other side, the better my chances of making it across. I was a good ways from where I had seen the last gator, but the dense grass on either side might hide anything, so I stood there for a good fifteen minutes checking the water in both directions.

When nothing moved, I removed my shirt and wrapped it around Vince's cell phone and gun and wrapped them into a tight bundle then tied the shirt sleeves around my neck like a muffler. It would mean some awkward swimming but neither phone nor gun would be worth much wet, and I intended to keep them both as dry as possible. I waded slowly into the water, the muddy bottom pulling at my legs and the river reaching for my knees. The key now was smoothness and not too much splashing, nothing to make the alligators curious enough to investigate.

I was more than halfway across. The far shore, if you can call it that, was no more than forty or fifty feet away. I had passed the island in the middle of the river. The water was only up to my waist and I was sure by then that I'd be able to walk the whole way across. Swimming would have been faster but it would have meant more splashing and a fair chance my precious bundle would get soaked, so I was feeling pretty glad about the whole thing when there was a blur of gray coming of the little island I had just passed. I turned just in time to see him plunge head first into the river followed by the long armored tail that fishtailed in behind him as he disappeared beneath the surface.

I couldn't out swim it, and I couldn't out run it, and there was no time to unfurl the automatic from behind my neck and try to shoot it. I turned toward the island and lifted the stick above my head. The water so still that for a second I thought I had been wrong. That I was just tired and thirsty or that the drugs they had given me had made a comeback and were making me see things that weren't there.

There was not a single ripple. Dead calm. There was

nothing until the last possible moment when the head shot out of the water, its jaws opening in mid-dive, twisting sideways and reaching for my thigh as though for something on a high, awkward shelf. I let out a yell of fear and defiance, stepped back and brought the stick down across its snout with enough force to crack the stick in half. The water beast twisted, but I saw it too late and the tail swerved around and knocked me sideways and down into the water. I found my feet under me just in time, because there it was now coming again, the open mouth lunging teeth bared. I was backing up, surrounded by splashing, half-turned in the wrong direction away from it, reckless and thrashing, unbalanced on one hand and two feet like a broken tripod planted in the river.

What was left of the stick was now fit only for jabbing. The snout came again out of the water. I jabbed at the wide, white open mouth and got the arm back just in time as the jaws slammed shut a little past the wrist. Then, suddenly, as though a dial had been turned somewhere, the world changed speed, slowed down. I felt a shift in my favor, a strange unwarranted sense of control, as though some previously inalienable right had been revoked from the adversary and given over to me.

The tail came around again, but now I was better and faster and maybe something of the Ritalin had been revived in me or else just the adrenaline because it seemed the tail this time came round more slowly so that I had the time to study its arc and not so much calculate as predict where it would strike and so be slightly elsewhere at the moment of impact. I stumbled backwards, this time not falling and bringing the half-stick down on the head then seeing, in the still bubble of the frozen moment, the tiny dull bright eye as the stick was again some kind of short, lunging spear aimed now at the vicious light it leapt to penetrate.

A few more moments of splashing, then, suddenly, the quiet again, as though nothing had happened. The water didn't move. Nothing moved, especially not me. I watched for ripples, for air bubbles. I waited for him to clamber out of the river and back onto the little island he had launched himself from. I stood crouched, knees slightly flexed, with my weight forward on the balls of my feet. I still held what was left of my stick. I began to back up. Every few feet, I glanced quickly behind me but only for a second. I didn't trust the water, and I trusted the quiet even less.

I was a few feet from shore when I saw the man sitting in the airboat. Beside him sat a medium-sized brown dog. The two of them sat watching me like they were at a movie, perhaps even a private screening. The dog had floppy ears and wore a look of worried nobility on its somber beagle like face. He sat upright next to the man like a king posing for his portrait, careful of his profile and the message he was sending ahead to posterity.

The man sitting next to him was about seventy years old, well fed, with a shock of white hair that grew from his head in every direction like Einstein's at the height of his ecstasy and genius. He wore a filthy sleeveless T-shirt that revealed the vaguely muscular arms of a man who could still strangle you if need be but who no longer trained seriously for such events. He had a tough, weather-beaten, beware-the-dog look about him that had no doubt been tested many times in his long life. His eyes regarded me with the calm steady expression of a man who had outlived his own vanity and who no longer really gave a fuck what anybody thought of him. Across his knees lay a shotgun or perhaps a rifle.

The man turned to the dog as though for comment on the strange, violent tableau they had just witnessed together, but the dog was noncommittal. The man picked up a can of beer from between his feet, took a long draft then poured what was left into his dignified companion's upturned mouth. Their aperitif now concluded, they resumed studying me with profound, even scholarly interest. I could understand why. I was still holding the broken shard of wood in my hand, still breathing like a cape buffalo after a stampede, still standing crouched over like a hominid not far from human but not yet at the stage where you want him getting too close to you.

Man and dog both seemed to be waiting to see just how far I would evolve into somebody they could deal with on a reasonable basis. A telepathic exchange passed between the man and me which when translated came across as something like: Lord, please don't make me have to shoot this crazy motherfucker; he looks like he's got enough trouble as it is.

I knew it was in my best interest to smile, and I made my mouth do it, though it really didn't want to, the memory of the recent alligator attack being still a little too vivid for my fake friendliness to be convincing. Reluctantly, I dropped what was left of my spear and straightened up out of my Neanderthal crouch. The brown dog remained unimpressed and motionless, but his tail lashed back and forth a few times. The man shifted in his seat and threw me a smile of encouragement, as though to say: you are making swift progress toward not getting yourself shot. Keep it up and we will all soon be fast friends, but please do not make any sudden moves or strange sounds, because you still do not look quite right to me.

I waved. The man waved back. The dog looked on impassively then barked once in a deep voice that seemed too big for him. Then the oversized fan behind the airboat began to whir as the man worked the lever from where he sat and the boat bucked forward, swerved and headed slowly toward me, stopping about twenty feet from where I stood. He let go of the lever and took hold of his shotgun, not in a menacing way but rather as you would a small child that had been sleeping on your lap.

"That was pretty good, son," the man said. "You scared that big sucker off all right."

"Why didn't you shoot?" I asked.

"This ain't the first beer I've had this morning, son. Plus, you were moving around too much."

"You wouldn't happen to have an extra beer lying around would you?"

The man reached down, flipped open a cooler and threw me a can of Budweiser. I thanked him and poured it down it down my throat without recess. The man grinned and threw me another can without any prodding. I drank the second Bud with a bit more civilization than the first as the man in the airboat watched me with approval. Every few sips, I'd study the can like it was an artifact. There was nothing better in the world.

"Mind if I ask you a personal question?" the man asked.

"You want to know what I'm doing out here, right?"

"I hope I'm not being too nosey, but it do seem odd."

"I'm lost."

"Lost from what? There ain't nothing out here to be lost from."

"I had an accident. My car went into the canal."

"Canal? How the hell did you get all the way out here? Should have stayed on the road. Ain't nothing out here except Wally Gator."

I was too tired to lie and, besides, something in me wanted to talk. "I came this way because an old friend of mine was trying to kill me."

"What'd you do? Fuck his girlfriend?"

"No," I said. "It was something else. I hadn't seen him for a long time, and when we met up again, he was a different person. Maybe I was too. All the trouble came from that."

"And this friend of yours, where's he at now?"

I took another sip of beer and looked back at the way I had come. It seemed impossibly far. "He's back there," I said. "Not too far from the road. He's dead."

"What's your name, son?"

"Jack."

"So you killed him then. Is that it?"

"No," I said. "His girlfriend shot him."

"His girlfriend shot him? Jesus, Mary and Joseph! And where's she at?"

"She's dead too."

"Well, I'll be goddamned! "Who killed her?"

"Her new boyfriend."

The man studied me carefully for a moment, the gears of reason turning slowly in his head. He was moving things around, trying to make them fit, reassessing the situation along with my possible lack of sanity. I knew how he felt. At last, he nodded.

"Okay, Jack." he said. "This other boyfriend, tell me—is he dead too?"

"Not at all. He's in perfect condition."

"And where'd he go?"

"My guess would be back to Miami to pick up some bags of cash. After that, who knows? He's a Russian mobster."

None of this seemed to faze the old guy. "Seems to me, you about the only one left, fella. How come nobody ain't kilt you?"

"I was hiding."

"A wise decision, considering the pack you've been running with. Well, will we be needing the law on this matter, son, or is this something you would prefer to keep to yourself?"

"How could I do that?" I asked.

"You'd be surprised how many folks I've found floating around down here. Very few of them ever get read about in the papers. It's up to you."

"You didn't tell me your name."

"I'm Bob Clark and you didn't answer my question."

"Any chance of you maybe giving me a lift? I need to get to a phone."

"You ain't thinking about calling in anymore of your friends are you?"

"Tell you the truth, mister," I said. "I'm running a little low on friends. It's the cops I need now."

Bob Clark shifted over in his seat then commanded his dog into the airboat's sizeable bed where he promptly began sniffing around at a large bulge covered by a canvas tarp. I pulled myself up onto the seat next to the driver who handed me another Budweiser. I would have preferred water at that point, but I didn't want to hurt his feelings.

"What do you got back there?" I asked. "Or should I ask?"

"Go ahead and take a look for yourself. I got nothing to hide. It's open season."

I lifted up a corner of the tarp and found myself looking

at the head and snout of the biggest pig I have ever seen. It was the size of a half-grown hippo. The dog barked at me until I lowered the canvas again.

"That's a pretty big pig," I said. "Where'd you get it?"

"That ain't a pig, son. That there is a wild boar. Easter's coming, and I got me a Cuban who'll pay good money for that size pork."

A half-mile down river I began seeing houses. Bob Clark reached under his seat, pulled a cell phone out a duffle bag and handed it to me. I made three quick calls. The first was to Dawn who spent half a minute of airtime cursing me out for going missing for three days. She quieted down when I told her that Cal was alive. I gave her Susan Andrew's number then called Susan myself. She wasn't too pleased with my disappearance, either, but did tell me that Cal had been transferred from Vronsky's clinic to Mount Sinai Hospital, along with a number of other residents who'd been evacuated during the fire alarm. I could tell by her tone that he was still in pretty rough shape.

My third call was to Special Agent Miles Hackbart at the FBI. I gave him a haiku version of recent events and told him that the last bad guy standing appeared to be Stefan, who was probably headed out of the country along with several suitcases full of money. Finally, Hackbart asked me where I was. I turned to Bob Clark. He had been quiet the entire time I had been using his phone and didn't seem to be paying much attention.

"What's the name of this place?" I asked.

"Give me the phone, son. I don't do three ways with the FBI."

Clark took the phone and cleared his throat. "To whom am I speaking?" he asked. Clark listened for a moment. "I see. Well, this is Chief Bob Clark with the Seminole Police Department. That's right. We're about forty miles north and west of you folks down there in Miami. I got your man right here. Found him playing Tarzan out in the bushes with the alligators. Apparently, there's been some killings. Nothing new there. All right, I'll tell him."

Chief Clark closed his phone and grinned at me. "The man says he's sending a helicopter for you. You must be a pretty important fella."

"Not really," I said. "They just want to make sure I don't disappear before they have a chance to depose me."

"I don't blame them. Judging from what little I heard, you got quite a story to tell."

"Why didn't you tell me you were the police chief?" I asked.

"I don't know when the last time you looked in a mirror was, but you don't look that good, and—please don't take this personal—but you're about a month overdue for a shower. For all I knew, you might have been some kind of murderous lunatic. Once you started talking though I knew you were all right, just a little beat up."

"Supposed I had said that I wanted to keep what happened quiet? What would you have done?"

"Well, twenty years ago I would have arrested you, or have at least tried. You're a fair sized man. Now? Hell, I would of just left you out there then come back with three or four officers and a couple more dogs. We would have found you, or what was left of you anyway. No hard feelings, but that's the way I would have played it."

We took the river south until it fed into a canal passed between two rows of decrepit looking houses parked at the at the water's edge. Almost all of them had airboats either in the water or up on the front lawns. Bob Clark killed the engine and drifted in next to a small pier where I hopped out and tied the airboat to a piling made mostly of splinters. Bob and his dog got out the boat just as battered pickup truck carrying a father his two sons and a backhoe with a crane attachment pulled up in a cloud of unnecessary dust. They all three said hello to Bob; then the two boys jumped down into the airboat and pulled the tarp off the boar while their father slowly counted out a roll of bills into the Chief's open hand.

All three beers hit me at once, and I went over to shady spot under a banyan tree and without hesitation passed out. An hour later, Chief Clark, now in uniform, shook me awake and led me to a squad car with a female officer in it who drove me to an open field where a red and black helicopter waited on the fifty-yard line, its vanes still spinning in the bright air.

15

One month later.

I took a slug of my Bloody Mary and smiled—I know it's a drink you're supposed to sip, but I've never been much of a sipper anyway, and today felt like a day for happy slugging. Drinks, I mean. I'd had my fill of slugging bad guys for a while, especially Russian Mafia goons. I was there among friends, and we were all in one piece as well as in one place, lolling under a soft December Miami sun. It was like the five minutes that comes in every soap opera when the heroine has been saved from the burning building, the evil twin exposed, the kidnapped child returned, and everyone gets to sit around with a cup of tea—or a flagon of 100 proof booze—until the telegram arrives announcing the next disaster.

Dennis O'Neal's kidney-shaped swimming pool looked its sparkling best, and better still was the sight of my old friend Cal, relaxing on a metal chaise. He still looked a little on the scraggly side after his ordeal, but his face was no longer gray and his eyes seemed a deeper and even more sparkling blue than before. Some of that sparkle came no doubt from the fact that reclining beside him was his grand-daughter Dawn, who had stayed to help nurse him back to health.

She was not a bad sight either in a new tangerine bikini that was briefer than the red two-piece she wore back when I'd holed up here for my own healing, before the foray out to Vronsky and his madhouse. I figured she'd brought the red job down from New York with her and found it to be a little on the conservative side in Miami. Only in Miami could you think anything from New York was "conservative."

Dawn had changed in other ways as well since I first spotted her ringing the doorbell of Cal's house. Her long brown hair had been cut and styled to shoulder length and the unruly bangs trimmed to a fringe that my mother might have called "fetching." I always thought "fetching" was code for a look that could make a man go fetch for a woman like a bird dog. One thing I know for sure: Dawn could walk into any South Beach club now and they'd raise the velvet rope for her.

I'm not a club guy myself—a velvet rope gives me the urge to wrap it around the neck of the sniffy guy holding it—but a few days back I had taken Dawn to the Upstairs at The Van Dyke, a place where even peasants like me can get in and enjoy some jazz, if they can manage to pay the inflated prices for their drinks, that is. I had a few bucks in my pocket, and being with a woman like Dawn makes you even more welcomed there. I introduced her to Tim Curtis, a drummer I knew from Cal's gym, and pushed her to stand in with a song that turned into a set, and an invitation to return the next weekend. Now, with her South Beach do-over, and Cal among the living again, she was ready to return to New York and the singing career she'd left behind.

Cal shifted on his metal chaise as if he'd just picked up on my thoughts. "Jack, you thick-headed gym rat, I can't believe you're letting her go," he said.

In fact I'd had a dippy dream of trying to settle down with Dawn, maybe even give the marriage gig another shot after two strikeouts. Now that I was managing Cal's gym as well as training my long-time clients and leading a few aerobics classes, I could afford to support a woman, maybe have her try to pop the kid I sometimes dreamed about after a couple Margaritas and tunes from an old time jukebox.

You know the fantasy—All-American Dad in the backyard with a catcher's mitt, telling the teenage wonder to bring one in, while Mom comes out in an apron (in my version of the dream an apron is all she's wearing) calling her boys to come in for some fried chicken and apple pie. Then I came out of my stupor and realized I'd wandered into a Norman Rockwell museum. As Susan Andrews sometimes gently points out, I watch too many black and white movies on Turner Classic.

It is true that Dawn and I had some fine times together in bed—but when showered and sober, I asked myself why anyone would want to try and trap a true canary in domestic life, she likely to wonder always how far she could have gone with her God-given voice and a new band to back her on the big stage in New York. Even Dawn had her domestic fantasies, but I didn't trust my track record, and I cared for her enough to dispel such wispy dreams. She deserved better, and her voice gave her a bright future.

I realized Cal's question was still hanging in the soft, quiet air and I said, "Who am I to hold back a star?"

"Baloney. I heard she was already a star down here," Cal said.

Dawn smiled at him, a little sadly, then shifted in her recliner and said, "An encore on Lincoln Road doesn't get me a record contract, you know. Besides, Jack and I are different signs. I'm a Scorpio—"

"And my sign's the dollar sign," I said.

Dennis O'Neal, whose eyes had been closed, blinked, sat up, and growled accusingly, pointing a gnarly finger at me.

"I know you, Vaughan—you'll always be trying to coax aerobics bimbos back to your middle-aged bachelor's pad. Trouble with you is you got too much time on your hands. How about moonlighting for me? We need another bouncer at Club Deuce."

"Try an ape from the Metro Zoo."

O'Neal just growled. He managed to stay un-tanned beside his pool in the Florida sun, an old Mets cap pulled down to his eyebrows, a towel hung around his shoulders.

"You inspire me, Dennis," I said. "If an old alligator like you can get Cynthia, maybe I'll have a shot someday. What did you say that website was? 'Slant Eyes for Grumpy Old Guys'?"

"*American* Guys," corrected Cynthia, who appeared at the doorway to the house. Damned if she didn't look as good in her nurse's uniform as a model in a designer gown; I suspected, not without an edge of envy, she would look the same for many years to come, while O'Neal rumpled into geezer-hood. She had come to say goodbye, on her way to work the afternoon shift at Mt. Sinai. Cal and I started to wrench ourselves out of our recliners when Cynthia waved us down.

"Please, stay where you are," she said. "There are refills inside and lots of cold chicken and potato salad."

"Love ya, babe," O'Neal called in his gravelly rasp, and she gave him her glistening smile, touched her fingers to her lips, and blew him a kiss, then turned and stepped quickly and softly from the tiles around the pool toward the driveway.

"You're one lucky old bastard," I said, and raised my glass to O'Neal.

"I'm the lucky old bastard, if there ever was one," Cal Belkin said. "I was in the loony bin and headed for the bottom of the bay if it hadn't been for you people."

"Hell, it was Vaughan playing Indiana Jones that did it all," O'Neal growled. "All I did was give Jack a place to crash and heal between battling the bad guys."

"All I know is that I've got my life back," Cal said.

In fact, the closing on Cal's gym never happened. And with Vince gone and all the rest that had taken place, it was doubtful that anyone with a Russian accent would show up to press the matter.

"That's the one favor they did you, Cal," I said. "Putting all that new equipment in, changing it from the near hovel you were always going to spiff up but never got around to."

Cal muttered something that was about as close as he'd get to a curse with his granddaughter within earshot.

"I'd take it right back to what it was, if I could. Change is not all it's cracked up to be."

I couldn't help smiling. Stefan the Chechen might have taken the trouble to clean out Cal's account completely if he'd managed to kill all three of them out in the 'Glades that day. But with me on the loose, he didn't have the time. He'd had to settle for whatever small fortune Marina had already stashed away. Sly old Stefan had surely found the keys to that kingdom—Marina's vault where the spoils were stashed—probably somewhere in the bowels of the Emperor's Club, and what was left in Cal's bank account was small change to what the Russian must have gotten away with.

Hackbart had thrown up a cordon at the ports and the airlines, but for a guy like Stefan, knowing how to turn invisible was second nature. He'd have had another passport ready and could have been halfway to Dubai or Zanzibar by the time the Feds had their computers talking. He and his ex-Russki mob rats were somewhere working a new scam already, I had no doubt.

"I'm not still straight on all the details yet," Cal said "It's going to take a while to get my brain back in its old working order, but at least they nailed Dr. Vronsky—or whatever the hell his real name is."

"Vronsky trusted Marina," I said, "that was his downfall. He never dreamed that Stefan was a lot smarter than he seemed. He thought *she'd* be the only one coming back from the Everglades that day. He was still waiting for her to show when Hackbart came through the door of his office."

"And we even got your humidor back," Dawn said, referring to the grand cigar chest I'd spotted in Vronsky's office. "Not to mention the fact that you're alive, and well."

"I'm getting there," Cal conceded.

"You better hurry up. There's a heartsick lady banker named Potsdam who's aching for you to give her all call," I couldn't help adding.

"What do you know about that?" Cal growled.

"More than you think, old man." I laughed.

"Mind your own damned business," Cal muttered.

"If I had, you'd be dead," I said.

"I'll drink to that," O'Neal cut in. "You two stop your squabbling."

At that, O'Neal drained his glass, cleared his throat with a sound like the dying engine of an old truck, and heaved himself out of his chair.

"We all need a refill," he said, heading for the house.

I shared a wistful glance with Dawn. At least I hoped she was feeling wistful because I certainly was.

"Never mind the mix," I called after O'Neal. "Just come back with the booze."

About the Author

Anthony Gagliano, a promising Miami Beach writer whose first novel, *Straits of Fortune*, drew critical praise, died in 2009 before he could complete its sequel, *The Emperor's Club.*

In a 2007 *Miami Herald* review of *Straits*, Connie Ogle labeled Gagliano's book "fast-paced, down-and-dirty escapist grit lit. . . [He] stuffs *Straits* with action, and his tough-guy narration never wavers."

New York Times critic Janet Maslin recommended the book for her summer reading list, declaring it "a memorably crisp debut—a plausibly noir narrative rich with the requisite heat and duplicity."

Gagliano graduated from Queens College, where he edited the campus literary magazine, wrote poetry and was nominated for a Rhodes scholarship. Before coming to South Florida, he worked as a New York City cab driver, a hotel detective, including a stint at the swanky St. Moritz Hotel, as well as a bouncer for several New York clubs. When he arrived in Miami Beach he became a personal trainer and aerobics teacher not unlike his main character, disgraced ex-NYPD cop Jack Vaughn.

In 1996 he enrolled in Florida International University's creative writing master's program. It was at FIU that he would meet and be mentored by professors and authors Dan Wakefield and Les Standiford, program director.

Gagliano's mentors were impressed with his graduate thesis, completed in 2002, and helped him circulate it to agents, one of whom signed the writer to a contract and sold the book to Harper Collins, who published it in 2007.

Wakefield and Standiford continued to encourage Gagliano, with whom they had become friends, and when he died while at work on *The Emperor's Club*, the two determined to finish the book. They completed the work in 2014. We are proud to publish it.

CPSIA information can be obtained at www.ICGtesting.com
Printed in the USA
LVOW08s0603090814

398250LV00004B/16/P